DAY OF INDEPENDENCE

DAY OF INDEPENDENCE

WILLIAM W. JOHNSTONE
with J. A. Johnstone

PINNACLE BOOKS
Kensington Publishing Corp.
www.kensingtonbooks.com

PINNACLE BOOKS are published by

Kensington Publishing Corp.
119 West 40th Street
New York, NY 10018

All Kensington titles, imprints, and distributed lines are available at special
quantity discounts for bulk purchases for sales promotions, premiums,
fund-raising, educational, or institutional use. Special book excerpts or
customized printings can also be created to fit specific needs. For details,
write or phone the office of the Kensington sales manager: Kensington
Publishing Corp., 119 West 40th Street, New York, NY 10018, attn: Sales
Department; phone 1-800-221-2647.

PINNACLE BOOKS, the Pinnacle logo, and the WWJ steer head logo are
Reg. U.S. Pat. & TM Off.

ISBN-13: 978-0-7860-4686-7
ISBN-10: 0-7860-4686-4

First printing: June 2014

10 9 8 7 6 5 4

Printed in the United States of America

Electronic edition:

ISBN-13: 978-0-7860-3455-0 (e-book)
ISBN-10: 0-7860-3455-6 (e-book)

CHAPTER ONE

Texas Ranger Hank Cannan was in one hell of a fix. In fact, he told himself that very thing.

"Hank," he said, "you're in one hell of a fix."

He uttered that statement aloud, as is the way of men who often ride long and lonely trails.

About ten minutes earlier—Cannan couldn't pin down the exact time—a bullet had slammed into him just above his gun belt on his left side, and another had hit his right thigh.

In addition, after his horse threw him, he'd slammed his head into a wagon wheel and now, for at least part of the time, he was seeing double.

With so many miseries, Cannan reckoned that his future career prospects had taken a distinct downhill turn, especially since the bushwhacker somewhere out there in the hills was seeing single and was a pretty good marksman to boot.

The rifleman had earlier stated his intentions clearly enough, but Cannan could not bring himself to agree to his terms.

Yelling across a hundred yards of open ground, the

man had demanded Cannan's horse, saddle, guns, boots and spurs, his wallet, watch and wedding ring, and whatever miscellaneous items of value he may have about his person.

"And if I don't?" Cannan called back.

"Then I'll kill you as dead as a rotten stump."

"You go to hell!" Cannan said.

"Ladies first," the bushwhacker yelled.

Then he laughed.

That exchange had happened a good five minutes ago, and since then . . . nothing.

Between Cannan and the hidden rifleman lay flat, sandy ground, thick with cactus and mesquite, but here and there desert shrubs like tarbrush and ocotillo prospered mightily.

The Texas sun scorched hot and drowsy insects made their small music in the bunchgrass. There was no other sound, just a vast silence that had been scarred by rifle shots.

Cannan, long past his first flush of youth, gingerly explored the wound on his side with the flat of his hand. It came away bloody.

One glimpse at his gory thigh convinced him that he had to end this standoff real quick or bleed to death.

But the drawbacks to that plan were twofold: his rifle was in the saddle boot and the horse under that saddle could be anywhere by now, as was his pack mule.

The second, and much more pressing given his present circumstances, was that the only weapon he had available to him was his old Colt .45.

Now there were many Rangers who were skilled with the revolver, fast and accurate on the draw and shoot.

Cannan wasn't one of them.

His colleagues rated his prowess with a Colt as fair to middling, but only on a good day, a "nekkid on the back porch" kind of good day.

Hank Cannan could never recall having one of those.

But most gun-savvy men allowed that he had at least the potential to be a widow-maker with a rifle—except now he had no rifle.

After his horse tossed him, he'd landed in a creosote bush and his forehead had crashed into an ancient wagon wheel half buried in sand. It had been the wheel's iron rim, still intact, that had done the damage and made Cannan see stars and, later, two of everything.

He'd hunkered down in the creosote bush and had propped up the wheel in front of him, where it provided at least an illusion of cover. But he knew he had to move soon before he grew any weaker.

His only hope was to outflank the bushwhacker and Injun close enough to get his work in with the Colt at spitting distance.

Cannan stared out at the brush flat, sweat running through the crusted, scarlet stain on his forehead.

He didn't like what he saw.

The ground was too open. Even crouched, he would present a big target. Two or three steps, and he'd be a dead duck.

Cannan sighed. Jane a widow after just six months of marriage, imagine that. It just didn't seem right somehow. He'd—

"Hey you over there!" the bushwhacker yelled. "You dead yet?"

"Yeah, I'm dead," Cannan called out. "Damn you, I'm shot through and through. What do you think?"

"I'm a man gets bored real easy, and this here stand-off is getting mighty tiresome. When do you reckon you'll pass away, if it's not asking an impertinent question?"

"By nightfall, I reckon. Depending on how I bleed, maybe a little sooner."

"Hell, that's way too long. I got places to go, things to do."

"Sorry for the inconvenience," Cannan said.

"Tell you what," the rifleman said.

Cannan said nothing.

"I'll take your hoss and leave you to die at your leisure. I can't say fairer than that. What do you reckon, huh? State your intentions."

"All I can say is that you're a good Christian," Cannan said. "Straight up an' true blue and a credit to your profession."

"Well me, I learned that Christian stuff from a real nice feller I shared a cabin with one winter over to Black Mesa way in the Arizona Territory. He'd been a preacher until he took up the bank-robbing vocation. We were both on the scout at the time, you understand."

"Yeah, I can see that," Cannan said. "Being on the scout an' all."

"Well, anyhoo, come spring I split his skull open with a wood axe, on account of he had a gold watch chain I wanted. I'm wearing it right now, in fact."

"Well, wear it in good health," Cannan said.

There was moment's pause, then the bushwhacker said, "You're a right personable feller, a white man through and through, and it's been a pleasure doing business with you."

"You too," Cannan said.

He wiped away sweat and blood from his forehead with the back of his gun hand, then gripped the blue Colt tighter.

He needed a break. He needed the drop. And right then neither of those things seemed likely.

But there was one option open to Hank Cannan, stark though it was.

He could die like a Texas Ranger.

Better one moment of hellfire glory, bucking Colt in hand, than to slowly bleed to death in the brush like a wounded rabbit.

But first . . .

Cannan reached into his shirt pocket and found the tally book and a stub of pencil that every Ranger carried.

He held the little notebook against his bent left knee and wrote laboriously in large print:

DEAR JANE, I THOUGHT OF YOU TO THE
LAST. I DIED GAME, AS A RANGER SHOULD.
             YOUR LOVING HUSBAND,
             Henry Cannan, Esq.

Cannan read the letter, read it again, and smiled, deciding it was crackerjack.

He tore the page out of the tally book, folded it carefully, and shoved it into his pocket where an undertaker was sure to find it.

Then he rose painfully to his feet, and, his bloody

face set and determined, staggered toward the hidden gunman.

He planned to keep on shooting until the sheer weight of the bushwhacker's lead finally put him down.

They say fortune favors the brave, and if that is so, Cannan caught his first lucky break.

His ambusher, a big, bearded man wearing a black coat and pants, was in the act of mounting his horse and didn't see Cannan coming at him.

He'd also slid his rifle into his boot. A fatal mistake.

The Ranger tottered forward, then the bearded man turned his head and saw him.

He grabbed for the Winchester under his knee as Cannan two-handed his Colt to eye level and fired.

It was a "nekkid on the back porch" kind of day for Ranger Hank Cannan.

He scored a hit, then as the big man tried to bring the rifle to bear, scored another.

The bushwhacker's horse did not behave well.

A tall, rangy, American stud, it reared up, and white, fearful arcs showed in its eyes. The horse attempted to shy away from Cannan's fire, and its rider cursed and battled to get his mount under control.

It was now or never for the Ranger.

A plunging, moving target is difficult to hit, and he missed with his third shot, scored again with his fourth.

Cannan had no time to shoot a fifth because the bearded man toppled out of the saddle and thudded onto the ground, puffs of dust rising around him.

Aware that he'd only one round left, Cannan, bent over from the pain in his side, advanced on the downed man. But the bushwhacker, whoever he was, was out of it.

Blood stained the front of the white shirt he wore under his coat, and the left side of his neck looked as though it had been splashed with red paint.

The man stared at Cannan with rapidly fading blue eyes that held no anger or accusation.

Cannan understood that, because he recognized his assailant as Black John Merritt, bank robber, sometime cow town lawman, and lately, hired gun.

Professional gunmen like Merritt held no grudges.

"I recollect you from your wanted dodger," Cannan said. "The likeness didn't do you justice."

"You've killed me," Merritt said.

"Seems like."

"My luck had to run out sometime, I guess."

"Happens to us all."

"I got lead into you."

"You surely did."

"I hope your luck doesn't run out."

Merritt licked his lips.

"Hell, got blood all over my damned mouth."

"You're lung shot," Cannan said. "Saw that right off."

"Figured I was."

Merritt had been leaning on one elbow. Now he lay flat and stared at the sky, scorched almost white by the merciless sun. He gritted his teeth against pain, but made no sound.

Then he said, gasping a little, "Who are you, mister?"

"Name's Hank Cannan. I'm a Texas Ranger."

Merritt smiled, his scarlet teeth glistening. "I should have suspicioned that. You boys don't know when you're beat."

"Goes with the job, I reckon."

Cannan lowered the hammer of his Colt and shoved it into the holster.

He felt light-headed, and the pain in his side was a living thing with fangs.

"Why did you decide to bushwhack me, Merritt?" he said.

"I was bored. It gave me something to do."

"You tried to kill me because you were bored?"

"Why not? I'm a man-killer by profession. Another killing more or less don't make much of a difference. I've already gunned more than my share."

"Merritt, I don't much like talking harsh words to a dying man, but you're a real son-of-a-bitch and low down."

"Truer words were never spoke, Ranger."

The gunman was barely hanging on, and gray death shadows gathered in his cheeks and temples. His gaze was still fixed on the sun-scorched sky, as though he wished to carry that sight with him into hell.

Merritt's words came slow, labored, like a man biting pieces off a tough steak. "Where you headed?" he said.

"I'm hunting a man. I go where he goes."

"What manner of man?"

"A man like you."

"Then he'll head for Last Chance."

"Where's that?"

"A town on the Big Bend, down by the Rio Grande."

"There are no towns in this part of Texas. Nothing for miles around but sand, cactus, and rock."

"Last Chance is there . . . due south . . . ten, twelve miles . . . hiring guns . . . gold . . ."

Cannan tensed as Merritt reached into his coat, but the man brought out only a gold double eagle.

"Ranger, take this," he said. "Make sure they bury me decent."

The coin slipped from Merritt's fingers and dropped into the sand.

"Promise me . . ." he whispered.

"I'll send you to your reward in a good Christian manner, Merritt," Cannan said.

But he was talking to a dead man.

CHAPTER TWO

Black John Merritt was a big man, and heavy, and Hank Cannan had a hard time getting the gunman draped across his horse.

Cannon's own bay wandered back with the pack mule, but the Ranger was all used up and it was a while before he mustered strength enough to climb into the saddle.

After the gnawing pain in his side subsided a little, Cannan sat his horse and thought things through.

He'd lost Dave Randall's trail two days before in the deep ravine country up by Dagger Mountain. Figuring the outlaw might head for Mexico, Cannan had scouted as far south as the Chisos Mountains when Merritt decided to take a pot at him.

Now, at least one bullet in him, he was in need of urgent medical care. But around him stretched miles of hostile brush desert and raw, limestone mountain peaks that held themselves aloof and didn't give a damn.

As Cannan had told himself before, he was in a hell of a fix.

Unless . . .

Cannan stared at a sky slowly fading into turquoise blue at the end of the burned-out day, as if to seek the answer to the question he hadn't yet asked.

Could there really be a settlement due south of here on the big bend of the Rio Grande?

Cannan told himself that it was a ridiculous notion.

All this land would grow was a fair crop of rocks and cactus, and starving cattle would soon leave their bones on the desert sands, as would those who owned them.

If there really was a Last Chance, by now it was a ghost town inhabited by owls, pack rats, and the quick shadows of people long gone.

Cannan decided to take the gamble.

Last Chance was the only card he had left to play.

At best, he'd find a town. At the worst, a ruined roof to sleep under.

Or die under.

Hank Cannan would remember little of his ride south.

He'd later recall that the mule and the dead man's sorrel stud ponied well and didn't try to pull his arm out of its socket.

The yipping coyotes challenging the rising moon—he remembered that, and the far-off howls of a hunting wolf pack.

Cannan didn't remember trying to build a cigarette and cursing as both tobacco sack and papers fell from his weakening hands.

Nor would he recall staring at Black John's face in the moonlight, bone-white, the wide-open eyes glinting behind slate shadows.

And perhaps it's best that he'd never bring to mind Merritt's ghostly, hollow voice whispering to him that hell is not hot, but cold . . . colder than mortal man can imagine.

"You're a damned liar!" Cannan yelled. "You're burning in fire. I can feel your heat! You're making me burn with you."

Black John whispered that hell is a gray, soulless place, covered in ice, and it has a constant north wind that cuts and slashes like a knife edge, and leaves deep, scarlet scars all over a man's naked body.

Then Black John said, his voice like a death knell, "Feel them, Ranger . . . feel the winds of Hades . . ."

And Cannan did.

He was hot before, but now he shivered as an icy blast hit him, and it cut like a saber and stank of sulfur from the lowest pits of hell.

"Hell is a wind!" Black John screamed. "A wind that blows bitter from Satan's mouth!"

"Liar!" Cannan yelled. "Liar, liar, your pants are on fire . . . in hell!"

Then suddenly he felt burning hot again.

Then cold.

Then hot.

And when he rode into the moon-splashed town of Last Chance, windows stared at him with blank, emotionless eyes . . . and all at once the ground cartwheeled up to meet him . . .

And then Hank Cannan felt nothing . . . nothing at all.

CHAPTER THREE

"Ah, the sleeping beauty awakes."

Hank Cannan thought he recognized the man's voice, but he lay still amid the soft comfort that surrounded him, unwilling to move.

"This may come as news to you, huh? But you're alive, Ranger Cannan. I saw your eyelids flutter."

Cannan opened his eyes and groaned.

"Baptiste Dupoix," he said. "Then I must be in hell."

"Close," the Creole gambler said. "You've been raving about Black John Merritt and a ghost town. But to set your mind at ease, you're in a burg called Last Chance, and you're a current resident of the Big Bend Hotel."

"What are you doing here, Dupoix?" Cannan said. "I thought I hung you years ago."

"No, you haven't yet had that pleasure," Dupoix said. "Though God knows you tried."

Cannan lifted his head off the blue-and-white-striped pillow and tried to rise to a sitting position.

"Here, let me fluff that for you," Dupoix said.

The gambler reached behind Cannan, pounded the

pillow into shape, then propped it against the brass headboard.

He helped Cannan sit up and smiled, his teeth very white against his dark skin. "There now. Comfy?"

Two oil lamps, lit against the darkness outside, cast shadows in the room, especially in the corners where the spinning spiders lived.

"What the hell time is it?" Cannan said.

"Early. It's just gone six."

"Morning or night?"

"Dawn soon. When a sporting gent like me should already be in bed."

"But you postponed slumber to visit me, huh?" Cannan said. "Out of the goodness of your heart."

"Bad enemies are like good friends, Cannan. They're to be cherished."

"I've got a dozen questions," Cannan said, ignoring that last.

He lifted the sheets and saw that he was naked, but for the bandages around his waist and thigh.

"How I got here will be one of them," the Ranger said. "But first tell me what happened to the dead man I brought in."

"You mean Black John?"

"How many dead men did I have?"

"Only him, and he'll be sorely missed."

"I promised him I'd bury him decent."

"The nice folks of this fair town buried him, with all due pomp and ceremony, I assure you."

"When?"

"Why, two weeks ago."

Cannan was shocked.

"I've been lying in this bed for two weeks?"

"Uh-huh, that's what I said. The doctor told me you

were at death's door." Dupoix grinned. "It was a mighty uncertain thing. Touch and go, you might say."

Cannan waved a hand around the hotel room. "Who did all this?"

"Not me, I assure you. My hypocrisy goes only so far. No, the town fathers put you up here. There are some really nice people in Last Chance."

Dupoix, a tall, elegant man who moved like a cougar, thumped a bottle of Old Crow and a couple of glasses onto the table beside Cannan's bed.

"I did do something for you, though," he said. "A couple young ladies of my acquaintance took care of you. You were out of it, but you did take nourishment now and again. Chicken gumbo mostly, made to a recipe handed down by my swamp witch grandmother back in Louisiana."

Dupoix poured whiskey into the glasses.

"It's a bit early, isn't it?" Cannan said.

"Early or late. It doesn't make any difference to a man confined to his bed. Oh, and remind me to tell you about my grandmother sometime. She's a very interesting woman."

"How did you know that I was the Ranger who brought in Black John?" Cannan said.

"From the description I got from the men who picked you up off the street. Big man, they said, maybe four inches over six feet with shoulders an axe handle wide and the face of a dyspeptic walrus. Who else fits that description?"

Cannan accepted a whiskey, then said, "Do you have the makings?"

"No, I've never succumbed to the Texas habit, but I can offer you a cigar."

"That will do just fine," Cannan said.

"I thought it might."

After Dupoix lit Cannan's cheroot, the Ranger said from behind a cloud of blue smoke, "Now tell me why you and I are breathing the same air in a town a hundred miles from anywhere."

"You first, Ranger Cannan, since you're feeling so poorly."

"I was tracking a feller—"

"Dave Randall. Yes, I know." Dupoix read the question on Cannan's face and said, "He's here in Last Chance." The gambler smiled. "And so is Mickey Pauleen."

That hit Cannan like a fist to the belly. "What's a killer like Pauleen doing here?" he said.

"Him, and Dave Randall. And Shotgun Hugh Gray. And a half-a-dozen other Texas draw fighters. But Mickey is the worst of them, or the best of them, depending on your point of view. The day after he arrived he shot the town marshal."

"And where do you come in, Dupoix?" Cannan said.

"I'm here for the same reason Mickey and them are here. For gun wages. Two hundred dollars a day until the job is done."

"What job? And who's paying you?"

Dupoix, elegant in a black frockcoat, boiled white shirt, and string tie, stepped to the window, then turned and said, "You've never forgiven me for that time in . . . what the hell was the name of the place?"

"Horse Neck," Cannan said.

"Yeah, Horse Neck. A benighted burg at the end of a railroad spur, as I recall."

"It was a hell-on-wheels tent town and I was sent there to keep the peace, Dupoix," Cannan said. "You ruined it for me and nearly got me kicked out of the Rangers."

"Cannan, those three gentlemen playing poker with a marked deck were asking for trouble. They took me for a rube."

"That's why you shot them, Dupoix, because your pride was hurt."

"They were notified."

"You left three dead men in the saloon, then lit a shuck on a stolen horse."

"The buckskin I left at the livery was a superior animal in every way to the one I . . . borrowed. Its owner got the best of that bargain."

Cannan held up his cigar, showing an inch of gray ash at the tip.

Dupoix picked up an ashtray from the table and laid it on the bed.

"You did take a pot at me, you know," he said. "My right ear felt the wind of your bullet. Now why did you do that?"

"I was aiming for the hoss," Cannan said. "My shooting was off that day."

"Ah, yes, as I recall you're no great shakes with a revolver."

"I wish I'd brought my rifle along. Then I would have hung you for sure."

"Suppose I tell you that those three Irish gents drew down on me first?"

"Wouldn't have made any difference, Dupoix. You took me for a rube and my pride was hurt."

The gambler smiled. "Touché, Ranger Cannan."

Dupoix refilled Cannan's glass then his own. He stepped to the window again and lit a cigar.

"You never answered my questions, Dupoix," Cannan said. "Why—"

"Am I here and who's paying my wages?" Dupoix said.

"Well?" Cannan said.

The gambler pulled back the lace curtain. "Look out there," he said. "A fair town with a schoolhouse and a church with a bell in its tower. It's got a city hall where the flag flies every single day of the year and the people dress in their best of a Sunday and go to worship."

Dupoix turned his head to Cannan and spoke over his shoulder.

"Last Chance was started by tin pans," he said. "They came here looking for gold, found none, and most of them left. But a few decided to stay and set down roots. In the early years they went through hell, but in the end they built something worthwhile."

"You still haven't answered my questions," Cannan said.

"Patience, Ranger, I'm answering them. Unless you're planning on going somewhere?"

"Funny, Dupoix. Go ahead."

"All right. Now, where was I?"

"You were talking about folks trying to build a town in a wilderness where there shouldn't be any town," Cannan said.

He suddenly felt irritable, from the whiskey or the pain of his still-healing wounds, he didn't know.

"The people of Last Chance worked together to irrigate the fertile bottomland with canals that carry water from the river. Despite droughts and floods and all the other things that plague farmers, they grew wheat, corn, oats, and now there's talk of planting cotton."

"They built their prosperity on farming?" Cannan said.

"Not entirely. They act as middlemen for Mexican trappers who supply them with fox, beaver, wolf, and bobcat fur. Last Chance also trades hogs, turkeys, and bees with Mexico for hard cash, and a few raise cattle on the floodplain farther along the river." Dupoix smiled. "You could say the hardy folks out there have turned this part of the desert into a Garden of Eden."

"Then why are you and the other gun hands here, Dupoix?" Cannan said.

"Because, Ranger Cannan, we're going to take it all away from them," Dupoix said.

CHAPTER FOUR

Abraham Hacker heaved his great, naked bulk out of bed and used his foot to slide out the chamber pot.

"What are you doing, honey?" The blond woman who'd been lying beside him sat up on her pillows and regarded Hacker with blue, startled eyes.

"Taking a piss. Go back to sleep, Nora."

"What time is it?"

"How the hell should I know?"

Years of using and abusing her body, flaunting it, selling it, had chiseled the woman's face into hard, tough planes, and her complexion was pale, seldom exposed to the light of day. Last night's makeup smeared her face and gave her a bruised look, yet she retained some of her youthful beauty, like a faded portrait in oils.

"Too early," Nora Anderson said. She flopped onto her left side and was asleep within moments.

Hacker held the chamber pot at crotch level and his piss rattled as he waddled to the window, pulled back the curtain and looked outside.

A red and jade sky heralded the dawn and tinted the

panes of the windows of the stores along the street dull scarlet.

There was no one about this early, and the hotel opposite showed only a single light.

It was the wounded Texas Ranger's room, Hacker knew, a fact he'd earlier filed away for future reference.

The lawman's presence was an unexpected inconvenience, but nothing Mickey Pauleen couldn't handle. The gunman specialized in getting rid of such bothersome details.

Hacker laid the foaming chamber pot on the floor, then stowed it under the bed again. When he bent over, the fretwork of bullwhip scars on his back, thirty of the best, stood out in stark relief in the cruel morning light.

On March 5th, 1863, at the Battle of Thompson's Station, Major Abe Hacker deserted his infantry brigade and fled the field. He should have been shot for cowardice in the face of the enemy, but powerful friends in Washington intervened and the court-martial ordered that he be stripped of rank, whipped, then drummed out of the Army of the Cumberland.

Hacker felt no remorse, no dishonor, and no sense of shame whatsoever.

Better a live coward with urgent, exciting things to do than a dead hero.

Now, twenty-five years later, he was a rich man who wanted to be richer, and he had plans, big plans.

And one of them involved the town of Last Chance.

Hacker sat by the window in a wicker chair that creaked under his weight, and his massive belly hung between his legs like a sack of grain.

His great size made breathing difficult, and the man wheezed through his thick-lipped mouth, but his small, blue eyes were never still, calculating, incisive as scalpels, as though making up for the weakness of his heart and lungs.

Abe Hacker was not a well man, but his ambitions kept him alive.

He reckoned he was big and powerful enough to do whatever he wanted, no matter how many people he trampled into the dirt to reach his goals.

Force, ruthlessness, and a readiness to kill were things he understood, never applied in anger, but with a cool head and a complete lack of conscience.

The woman in the bed stirred, sat up, and said, her voice slurred from sleep, "What are you doing, Abe?"

"Trying to think, Nora. So shut your trap."

"Come back to bed, honey," Nora Anderson said.

Hacker rose to his feet and rubbed his huge, sagging hips.

"Damned chair marked me," he said. "My ass feels like the bottom of a shopping basket."

"Come to bed, Abe, and I'll rub it smooth for you," the woman said.

"God, I hate this town," Hacker said. "It smells. Damned place stinks like a farmyard."

"Then let's go back to Washington," Nora said. "I hate it here, too. It's so damned hot."

As though he hadn't been listening, Hacker said, "But you know what I don't smell? I don't smell gold, in the ground or out of it."

"But Senator Huxley said he was sure there was a gold mine, Abe," Nora said.

"Yeah, and he sold me a bill of goods." Hacker

rubbed a hand across his completely bald head. "The only gold around here is fool's gold, and I'm the fool."

"Then why are the folks around here prospering in this wilderness?" Nora said.

"Dung. They're prospering because of dung. Damn their eyes."

"Maybe they found the mine, Abe, and the gold is hidden," Nora said.

"I told you there is no gold," Hacker said. "Pauleen and Shotgun Hugh Gray questioned just about everybody in this town, and those two boys have a way of getting straight answers. But the response was always the same—no gold mine and no gold."

Hacker peered through the shadowed bedroom and said, "One rube said, 'Sure there's gold, white gold. We're planting cotton.'" He swore, then, "Damned idiot."

"But Senator Huxley—"

"Heard rumors spread by the Díaz government that an Americano desert settlement on the Rio Grande was prospering mightily. Huxley jumped to the conclusion that it was gold."

"He wanted his share," Nora said.

"Of course he wanted his share, so did president-for-life Porfirio Díaz and half-a-dozen crooked U.S. senators. And I was supposed to supply the gold for them."

Nora's teeth gleamed in the gloom as she smiled.

"Plant cotton, Abe," she said. "It's white gold, remember?"

Hacker's wide, cruel mouth curled into a snarl.

"Nora, you are one stupid b . . ."

Like a man mesmerized, Hacker stood perfectly still, a grotesque marble statue in the gloom. Then, after a long moment, he grinned, clapped his hands, and did a little jig, his four hundred pounds shaking the hotel room floor.

"Nora, maybe you're not as stupid as I thought you were," he said.

"Abe, lie down now," Nora said, her voice alarmed. "Remember your poor heart."

"The hell with my heart," Hacker said. "I can salvage this. Gold or no, I can turn Last Chance into a nice little earner."

Daylight touched the side of his face and picked out the gray hairs on his blue chin. His cheeks were veined with red from the harsh downstroke of the razor, and his wide nose looked as though a child had modeled it out of putty.

Hacker's pouched, pale blue eyes were scheming, bright with malice.

"But how?" Nora said. Disappointment hollowed her words. "I thought we were going home."

"Thought wrong, didn't you?" Hacker said. "We'll go back to Washington when I add this place to my holdings. As to how I plan to do it, I could tell you but you wouldn't understand."

Abe Hacker's holdings were already vast.

He had shares in railroads in the United States and Asia, Japanese and German shipping lines, diamond mines in Africa, Russia, and India, cattle interests in Montana and Kansas, and he owned fifty-one percent of a British manufacturer of heavy field guns, most of which were exported to the Far East and South America.

Hacker also owned a brothel in the Storyville red-light district of New Orleans, a ten-dollar-a-screw, brass-and-red-velvet mansion on Basin Street. Elsewhere in the city, in the Third Ward, he'd acquired a Chinatown opium den and had recently broken the knees of its Creole overseer, who had kept more than his fair share of the profits.

Hacker's empire also included three grogshops along San Francisco's Barbary Coast, a fruit stand in New York, a sawmill in Georgia, a mom-and-pop toy store in London, and nearby a small boating concern that rented skiffs and boxed lunches on the Thames.

In Hacker's avaricious world no business was too large or too small for his greed, and his pudgy fingers squeezed every last penny of profit from everything he touched.

He was a millionaire many times over, but, like an addict craving opium, he wanted more . . . more . . . more . . .

Money meant power, and it gave Hacker dominion over many lesser mortals.

But what he craved was the ultimate power . . . the presidency of the United States. Should Hacker make a bid, there were some influential politicians in Washington who'd guaranteed him their support, including a few army generals with loyal troops at their backs.

That his faltering heart might betray him before he could seize the White House was a concern. But he was determined, by the sheer force of his will, to live long. Men as rich and influential as he was could not allow themselves to die.

Last Chance meant little to Hacker. It would be a very small, backward province in his colossal empire. But the town prospered, made money, and, by divine right, Hacker considered that those dollars should be his.

That he must destroy the town in the process was none of his concern.

Hacker lit a cigar, then crawled into the protesting bed like a massive, albino hippo, his fat hips as wide across as the butt end of a wine barrel.

After he settled his back against the pillows, he kicked Nora awake again. "Go bring Mickey Pauleen here," he said. "I need to talk with him."

"It's too early, Abe," the woman whined. "He'll still be asleep."

"Then wake him."

Nora looked distressed.

She had wide experience with men, most of them paying clients, and she could read them like a book. What she read in Pauleen's snake-green eyes she didn't like.

Every time they met, the gunman visually stripped her naked, and his thin lips flecked with white spittle as though his mouth watered in anticipation of the feast.

Despite years of male tugging, Nora's breasts were still high and firm, and a few days back Pauleen had palmed one as he accosted her in the hotel hallway. She'd just stood there, staring at him, until he dropped his hand, laughed, and walked away.

To visit his room in her night attire was inviting trouble. And she told this to Hacker, without mentioning the hallway incident.

"Hell, what have you got to lose? Your maidenhood?" Hacker said. "Now do as you're told or I'll take the back of my hand to you."

From past experience, Nora knew Hacker did not make such threats idly.

She rose from the bed, donned a flame-red dressing gown, and went in search of Pauleen. Behind her, Nora heard Hacker laugh, but at what, or at whom, she did not know.

CHAPTER FIVE

The morning sun turned the swamp the color of molten iron and touched with a blush of pink the pale lilac blossoms of the hyacinths that grew in islands among the cypress trees.

Alligators floated like pine logs and made scarcely a ripple in the still water. Everywhere insects chattered and swamp birds made wild whoops among the trees, like the ghosts of the long-gone Choctaws on a war trail.

Henriette Valcour's cabin sat on a spit of land that thrust a hundred feet into the swamp. It was a small, unpainted, timber structure, narrow as a shoebox, with a tin roof, a porch and rocker in front, a privy out back.

Despite the summer heat, a trail of smoke rose from the cabin's cast-iron chimney and tied misty gray bows in the still air.

Henriette stirred a blackened pot on the stove that smelled of crawling things, and the fish crow perched on a shelf nearby studied the swamp witch with glittering amber eyes. Its sleek head darted from side to side as it followed her every move.

"Soon, *mon chéri*," she said to the bird. "The death potion is not to be hurried."

The crow croaked and hopped back and forth on the shelf and Henriette smiled. "You are impatient, *n'êtes-vous pas?* Well, not long now and then we will see what we see."

The woman could have been any age, but she claimed to be ninety-eight. She was actually twenty years younger than that.

Henriette wore a white woman's cast-off cotton dress, but her hair was covered with the traditional Creole turban, the yellow *tête calendé* made from checked madras cloth.

Her skin was the color of old mahogany and deeply scarred by wrinkles, but her eyes were a match for those of the fish crow, bright, intent, the translucent golden hue of Baltic amber.

When Henriette decided the potion had simmered enough, she took a square piece of white linen the size of a woman's handkerchief and dipped it into the pot.

After a while she removed the cloth, now the color of pond scum, and stepped outside, where she draped it over the porch railing to dry.

The crow fluttered out of the cabin and perched on the back of the rocking chair, waiting.

Henriette picked up some twigs and Spanish moss from a wicker table, then sat in the rocker. The fish crow croaked a welcome, and the old woman smiled and stroked his breast feathers with the back of her forefinger.

The rippling water of the bayou was no longer blood red. The rising sun had drawn in storm clouds and to the north thunder rumbled.

A rising wind shook the garlands of moss in the

dead cypress and near the cabin lime green frogs splashed into the water and redfish jumped at gnats.

On the wall behind Henriette's chair, the chained pendulum of a Bavarian cuckoo clock ticked with slow, Teutonic solemnity. The clock had not kept time in fifty years, but in the swamp time was not measured by minutes and hours but by the changing of the light.

But the little bird still popped out twenty-four times a day and proclaimed the hour, the irritated fish crow regarding it with a baleful eye.

Thunder roared closer and vivid lighting seared through a hundred miles of storm cloud in an instant. Rain kicked up startled Vs on the surface of the water and ticked from the roof.

Henriette, busily fashioning a stick man from the twigs, kept two items on the floor by her chair at all times.

On her left, a quart bottle of Dr. Dribble's Peptonic Bitters that said right on the label that not only was it a sovereign remedy for dyspepsia but also an effective cure for female urinary problems.

On the old woman's right stood a jug of moonshine.

Throughout the day, Henriette imbibed liberal doses of both.

The stick man was finished and the old woman rose and got the linen from the railing. The cloth was still damp and had gotten rained on, but she could work with it.

For a few moments Henriette stood and watched the downpour fall on the bayou and the sudden flare of lightning that for an instant transformed the cypress into columns of white marble.

She returned to the chair and her nimble brown fingers packed moss around the stick man. She paid particular attention to the doll's belly, making it big and round, for was that not how she'd seen the fat man in her dream when he'd frightened her so badly?

When the stick man was covered to her satisfaction with moss, Henrietta wrapped the linen around him and tied it in place.

From the pocket of her dress she brought out the head she'd carved from a piece of wild oak. The face was crude, the eyes shadowed with black dye, and the top of the skull was round and bald. Carefully, Henriette positioned the head in place and then nodded her satisfaction.

The voodoo doll was finished.

Urged on by the thunder, black clouds rolled across the bayou, their flanks branded by white-hot scrawls of lightning.

Across the water, Henriette watched old Jacques St. Romain paddle his canoe among the buttressed bases of the bald cypress, the fishing lines dropped fore and aft glinting in the gray light.

A man with blue-black skin and white, curly hair cropped close to his scalp, Jacques feared neither lightning nor alligators, and he always carried a .45 in his pants pocket.

But he studiously avoided looking in Henriette's direction.

A swamp witch could put a hex on a man with a single glance, and Jacques trembled all over until he paddled deeper into the cypress, out of sight.

Henriette watched the empty, rain-lashed space where the old black man had been, then turned her attention back to the doll.

She recalled her dream again and the fat man who had threatened her grandson Baptiste. Although she did not know from whence the danger to Baptiste would come, or when it would happen, she woke, cried out, and felt very afraid.

The fish crow, who possessed the soul of a man who'd blasphemed Bondye, the one true God, had been alarmed and flapped his wings and croaked in a most pitiful fashion.

Henriette had quieted the bird and then told him she would protect her grandson from all harm, especially the dangers posed by the fat white man, who must be very powerful and evil indeed to have taken over her dream the way he did.

As thunder racked the bayou, Henriette took a swig from the jug to steady her nerves, and then removed the needle pinned to the front of her dress.

She did not wish to harm the fat man too much, at least not yet.

If danger threatened her dear Baptiste, other dreams would tell her what she must do.

Henriette took her needle and barely pricked the doll's chest.

She removed the needle and smiled. There, that was enough.

For now . . .

CHAPTER SIX

A niggling chest pain troubled Abe Hacker as he sat higher in bed, waiting for Mickey Pauleen to show. He was a little short of breath but felt only a slight discomfort, so there was nothing to worry about.

His ticker was holding up quite well, and that pleased him.

All he needed was time.

The door opened and Nora stepped inside. She seemed a little disheveled.

Hacker grinned.

"Ol' Mickey nail you?" he said.

"He tried," Nora said.

"I'll kill him for you one day," Hacker said. "But right now I need him."

"He's a snake. He needs killing."

"I know. But he's fast with a gun, maybe the fastest ever. Look what he did to the town marshal."

"An old man. He must've been eighty if he was a day."

Hacker shrugged his fat shoulders. In the dead light of the hotel room he was fish-belly white, like an enormous slug.

"The old coot got his chance to draw. Everybody saw it."

Nora poured her morning glass of bourbon and without looking at Hacker said, "He was a retired type-setter, for God's sake."

"Then he should've stuck to his trade," Hacker said. "Anyways, it doesn't matter much. Mickey doesn't like lawmen, so he would have killed him eventually. Better sooner than later."

Three sharp raps on the door sounded like gunshots in the room.

The door flung open and Mickey Pauleen stepped inside.

His carrion-eater eyes flicked to Nora and a faint smile tugged at the corners of his mouth.

He shifted his attention to Hacker. "You wanted to see me, boss?"

Pauleen was a small, narrow man, who could be as quick and sudden as the crack of a bullwhip. He affected the dress of a small-town parson, sober gray suit, collarless white shirt, and flat crowned hat.

His somber garb was modeled on that of his late foster father, a fire-and-brimstone preacher named Esau Stern who'd tried to whip the fear of God into young Mickey every single day of his life.

When he was fourteen, Mickey bashed in Esau's skull with a posthole auger. When Mrs. Stern saw her husband weltering in his blood, the gory auger in her foster child's hands, she screamed, "Murder!" and Mickey promptly did for her.

Since then Mickey Pauleen had never looked back, and his reputation as a man-killer was well established, as a dozen hard cases buried in Boot Hills across Texas could testify.

"There's no gold, Mickey," Hacker said. "There's no gold mine."

"You woke me up this early to tell me something I already know?" Pauleen said.

"I want to make Last Chance pay," Hacker said.

Pauleen's smile never reached his eyes. "For what? For having no gold or for being run by a bunch of dung-smelling rubes?"

"I don't mean it that way," Hacker said. "There's money to be made here, Mickey, and I want it."

"You planning to be a sodbuster?"

"Something like that. The rubes are growing wheat, corn, oats, and soon, cotton. On top of that, cattle ranches are prospering up and down the river, and the cows are fat."

Pauleen shook his head. His yellow hair was thin and lank, growing over his narrow shoulders. "I'm not catching your drift," he said. "I ain't a damned farmer."

"You don't have to be," Hacker said. "I'm taking this place over, all legal and aboveboard, like. I'll get title to this land and my associates in government will call in favors and get the Katy to lay a railroad spur right to our doorstep."

The morning brightened and sunlight angled into the room and Hacker's bald head glistened with sweat. Released by heat, the musky odor of the cologne that doused his body hung heavy in the air.

"Now do you see, Mickey?" he said. "Tell me you share in my vision."

Pauleen smiled. "Boss, you won't get these people to work for you. They're an independent bunch."

"I don't want them to work for me, Mickey," Hacker said. "That's the beauty of my plan, see?"

"No, I don't see," Pauleen said. His high, narrow

shoulders and small, sharp-featured head gave him the look of a bird of prey.

"Mexicans!" Hacker said. "I'm going to make a lot of money out of this place, and I'll do it off the sweat of Mexicans."

Pauleen said nothing, and Nora looked baffled. She poured herself another bourbon.

"I'll bring Mexicans across the river and put them to work in the fields," Hacker said. "Hell, a Mex will work all day for a couple of pesos and a bowl of corn mush."

He slapped a beefy fist into the palm of the other.

"Damn it, the profits will be enormous," he said. "By Christ—"

"Don't take the Lord's name in vain, boss," Pauleen said. "I don't like it."

Hacker smiled. "Mickey, you don't smoke, you don't drink, and you don't cuss. But I know what you like, huh?"

Pauleen's pinched face was like stone.

"You like women, don't you?" Hacker said. He stared hard into the little gunman's eyes. "Yeah, that's it, you like women."

He waved in Nora's direction.

"Stick with me until this thing is done, and I'll give you that as a bonus. I'll conclude my business here real quick, because Nora isn't getting any younger." Hacker grinned at the woman. "More than a shade past your prime, ain't you, gal?"

The woman looked at Hacker with wounded eyes.

"Sometimes you say cruel things, Abe," she said.

"Well, maybe that's my right," Hacker said. "I pay you plenty to take what I dish out. And lay off the booze. It's turning you into a hag." He was smiling when he turned his attention to Pauleen again. "I'm joking, Mickey. She's got a couple of good years left in her."

"What about the Mexicans?" Pauleen said.

"You want the woman?"

"Yeah."

"All right, here's what I want you to do. Ride into Mexico and find Sancho Perez. He's usually around Chihuahua or—"

"He'll find me," Pauleen said. "I'll be riding a five-hundred-dollar horse."

Hacker smiled at that.

"Tell him to round up Mexican peons, men, woman, and children, and drive them across the Rio Grande," he said.

"How many?" Pauleen said.

"As many as Perez can get. A thousand, two thousand, more, I want them to descend on Last Chance like a plague of locusts."

"And drive the whites out, huh?" Pauleen said.

"That's the idea. The people around here have been at peace for too long. By now they've forgotten how to fight, and they'll cut and run."

"I reckon the ranchers haven't forgotten. They could give us trouble."

"Well, that's where you and the other guns come in."

"We can handle it," Pauleen said.

Hacker smiled. "I know you can, Mickey. By Independence Day I want the Mexicans working in my fields and my own boys in the bunkhouses."

"That's a month from now," Pauleen said. "You're not giving us much time."

"Tell that to Perez. Tell him I need the peons here in a hurry."

"What do I offer him?"

"A dollar a head. Man, woman, or child. The more he brings in, the more money he gets."

Pauleen thought for a moment, then said:

"*And the locusts went up all over the land of Egypt and settled in all the territory of Egypt. Very grievous were they. Before them there were no such locusts as they, neither after them shall be such.*"

"Damn right," Hacker said. "That's good Bible talk. Only this isn't Egypt, it's the Texas Big Bend country."

"I think the result will be the same," Nora said. "The Garden of Eden will become a wasteland."

Hacker was suddenly angry and a vein pulsed on his forehead.

"Maybe it will," he said. "But, by God, I'll squeeze a fortune out of it before it does." To Pauleen he said, "There's no time to waste, Mickey. Find Sancho Perez and tell him what I want."

The gunman nodded and stepped to the door, but Hacker's voice stopped him.

"Mickey, get a couple of boys to take care of the Texas Ranger over to the hotel."

"He's sick in bed, boss."

"Yeah, I know, but he could become a problem later."

Pauleen nodded. "I'll see that he gets out of bed and into a pine box," he said.

CHAPTER SEVEN

"No, Ranger Cannan, you can't get out of bed, not for another three weeks at least," the woman said.

Her name was Roxie Miller, and she was a stern disciplinarian, one of Baptiste Dupoix's lady friends who'd agreed to look after the ailing lawman.

The other, called Nancy Scott, a pert, pretty blonde with huge, baby blue eyes and pink, kissable lips, was more sympathetic.

"Maybe less than that," she said, smiling, a steaming spoon poised at Cannan's mouth. "If you eat more chicken broth."

"But don't count on it," Roxie said. "You're shot through and through, Ranger, and you've got no call to go gallivanting around."

Both women worked as hostesses at the Black Bull saloon and were only as good as they had to be.

Roxie, tall and slender with a glossy mane of auburn hair she left unbound most of the time, had worked a dozen of the rougher cow towns in both Texas and New Mexico, and she had acquired a hard veneer along the way.

Nancy, younger, was new to the profession, and it showed.

There was a wholesomeness and innocence about her that Cannan liked. She reminded him of his wife, but only in small ways, like the way she frowned and how easily she moved around the room, her skirt rustling.

Cannan swallowed a spoonful of soup, and Nancy nodded and gave him a bright, that's-a-good-boy smile.

He was propped up on the pillows and naked under the sheet as a concession to the hot summer weather. Outside he heard the town come to life, the rumble of farm wagons and the thud of pedestrian heels on the boardwalk.

For some reason Cannan felt uneasy, not because of his wounds, though God knows they were reason enough, but something else that he couldn't put a finger on. He felt like a rider lost in the midst of a prairie thunderstorm . . . a man waiting for something bad to happen.

He'd been warned when he'd first signed on that to stay aboveground a Ranger must develop the instincts of a lobo wolf.

"You take ol' Bardolph now, he's out there in the woods howlin' an' fussin' because he reckons hard times are comin' down," an old-time Ranger once told him. "He's only a wolf, so he can't rightly tell what they are, but he sure as hell knows they're comin'."

The old Ranger took time to light his pipe, then said, "If he wants to go on living, a Ranger must mind his instincts just like Bardolph does and know when hard times are sneakin' up on him." He nodded. "Yup, them's true words of wisdom as ever was spoke."

Recalling that advice, Cannan minded his instincts now.

He said, "Roxie, please bring my gun over here."

"You planning to shoot your nurses, Ranger?" the woman said.

Cannan smiled. "No, I don't want to do that. I'd just like it closer, is all."

"You'll get spooked in the night and shoot your toes off," Roxie said.

"I've been spooked in the night plenty of times before and I've still got all ten," Cannan said.

"It might make Hank feel better," Nancy said. "Lawmen like their guns close at hand."

"Well, don't blame me if you shoot your fool head off," Roxie said.

She picked up Cannan's holstered Colt from the corner and buckled the cartridge belt before looping it over the bedpost.

"There," she said. "Does that make you feel better now?"

"Safer," Cannan said.

Roxie smiled. "Now who's going to harm a man in his sickbed?"

"I don't know," Cannan said.

"Me neither," Roxie said. "But if it makes you more at ease . . ."

"It does," Cannan said. "It surely does."

Mickey Pauleen stood beside his saddled horse in the livery stable, the reins in his hand, and said, "You boys got it? A fast in, kill him, and a fast out. Then light a shuck for the hills and lie low for a couple of days before you head back to town."

"We got it, Mickey," Jess Gable said, grinning. "It's gonna be easy."

"Maybe," Dave Randall said. "The Ranger killed Merritt and nobody figured Black John a bargain."

"I can get somebody else, Dave," Pauleen said, his voice iced.

"I was only saying, Mickey," Randall said.

"He's sick. How much can a sick man bring to a gun-fight?" Pauleen said.

"I'll get the job done," Randall said. "I was only saying."

Dave Randall had run with Jesse Evans and that hard crowd in the Lincoln County War, and he'd been at Presidio del Norte in Mexico when Evans was out-gunned and captured by Texas Rangers.

Randall had escaped, turned to bank robbery for a couple of years, then became a deputy marshal for Judge Parker up Fort Smith way.

He'd quit after only a couple of months and had since sold his gun to the highest bidder. By his own count, he'd killed eight white men.

Abe Hacker thought highly of him.

Pauleen, still dressed like a country parson, pointed to a pile of empty burlap sacks in a vacant stall.

"Make a couple of masks out of those, Jess," he said. "It's probably best your faces aren't seen. And wear slickers you can get rid of afterward."

Gable was genuinely puzzled. "What difference does it make, Mickey?" he said. "There ain't no law in this town."

"I know, but until I get back here with the Mexicans we'll play it Hacker's way. He says if you cover your faces and wear slickers over your clothes, the rubes will have some doubt about who actually pulled the triggers."

Pauleen swung into the saddle and adjusted the angle of the Winchester booted under his right knee. "Just get it done, boys," he said, straightening. "Get it done tonight."

Making up for his lapse, Randall said, "We'll do it, Mickey. It's no big thing."

"Killing a Ranger is always a big thing," Pauleen said. "But by the time they find out about it, we'll be long gone from here."

"What about Hacker?" Gable said.

"What about him?" Pauleen said.

"Does he plan to stay on in Last Chance?"

"Hell, no. When his business is done, he'll head back to Washington."

Randall smiled. "The Rangers can't touch him there."

"Nobody can touch him there," Pauleen said. "With his money, he has half the damned government in his pocket." He kneed his flashy sorrel forward. "So long, boys. I'll see you when I get back with the plague of locusts."

After he was gone, Randall said, "What the hell is a plague of locusts?"

"I don't know," Gable said. "Mickey talks strange sometimes. He believes in ghosts and ha'ants and sich and he reads the Bible every single day."

"Why are so many of the boys scared of him, Jess? Even Shotgun Hugh Gray steps around him."

"Because Mickey is a born killer, that's why."

"He don't even carry a gun, for God's sake."

"He does, but only when he needs it."

Gable's hand made a rasping sound as he ran it over his stubbly chin. "Dave," he said, "you ever see Mickey Pauleen strap on a gun and come in your direction, know that you're already a dead man and make peace with your Maker."

"You think he's that fast, huh?" Randall said, his lip curling a little.

"I know he's that fast," Gable said. "Faster than you've ever seen or can imagine."

CHAPTER EIGHT

Moonlight lay on the town of Last Chance like a winter frost. A slight breeze rippled through the acres of winter wheat that surrounded the settlement and stirred the fruit trees, making little sound.

The hour by the town hall clock was fifteen minutes past midnight and the street was deserted, false-fronted buildings casting rectangular shadows the color of blue steel.

Even the sporting crowd was already abed, saving their money and energy for Friday night, when the cowboys came in and the saloon girls were at their prettiest.

Only two men moved.

Their heads covered in burlap sacks, holes cut out for their eyes and mouths, they stood on the boardwalk and studied the blank window of the Ranger's room.

"You reckon he's asleep, Jess?" Dave Randall said.

"Of course he's asleep," Gable said. "He's all shot up, ain't he?"

"How do we play it?" Randall said.

Gable sighed. "How many times do I have to tell you?"

"Once more," Randall said. "I want to get it right."

"Dave, you ain't the smartest puncher in the bunkhouse, are you?" Gable said.

"One more time, Jess."

"And you ain't a listener."

"One more time, Jess."

"All right," Gable said, sighing again, "here's how it will go down. After I kick in the Ranger's door, I'll start shooting. You'll stay back and cover the room, just in case he's got somebody in there with him. You savvy that?"

Randall nodded.

"Man, woman, or child, you kill anybody that's in there," Gable said.

"I got it, Jess."

"I'll make sure the Ranger is dead, then we run downstairs, mount up, and light a shuck," Gable said. "It ain't real complicated, Dave."

"He killed Black John," Randall said. "That was something."

"You told me that already," Gable said.

He pulled his Colt and slid a round into the empty chamber that had been under the hammer.

"The Ranger lying in bed up there ain't the same man as done for Black John," Gable said. "He's at death's door, or so they say."

"He was a rum one was Black John," Randall said.

"Save the conversation for later," Gable said. "Let's go kill ourselves a lawman."

Hank Cannan woke with a start and, his eyes wide, listened into the darkness.

Nothing.

Not a sound.

Yet his heart hammered in his chest and the night seemed oppressive, as though the walls of the hotel room were closing in on him.

His instinct for danger clamored, even as he told himself that he was acting like a scared old lady who hears a rustle in every bush.

There!

A faint creak . . . just a whisper in the silence.

It could be the protest of a stair step recently repaired with green timber or the wooden floor in the hallway reacting to a man's weight.

It was time to move.

Cannan grabbed his Colt from the holster and rolled out of bed. His head swam, and his weak, wounded body shrieked in pain.

The danger was very close now. He could sense it. Smell it.

Still fevered, Cannan sweated as he kneeled behind the bed and pulled the pillows down to form the vague outline of a sleeping man.

His hands were wet, slippery, too sweaty to hold the Colt steady.

He dragged the sheet off the bed and wrapped a corner of it around the gun handle. He grasped the revolver again, his hold firmer now.

Cannan eased back the hammer, its triple click loud in the room.

He fought for breath, fear spiking at him. He grabbed the sheet with his left hand and wiped sweat from his face.

God, he was sick, much weaker than he'd thought.

He was in no shape for a gunfight, or any other kind of fight, come to that.

Slow seconds slid past, then . . .

A booted foot crashed into the door. The door splintered on its hinges but held firm.

A second kick, harder this time. The door crashed inward and scattered shards of wood buzzed around the room like stinging insects.

A man, his bulk huge in the darkness, thumbed two shots into the bed.

An explosion of pillow feathers erupted into the air and then lazily drifted downward like fat flakes of snow.

Cannan fired into the dark, hulking silhouette of his would-be assassin.

Hit, the man cried out and staggered back against the doorframe.

A gun blasted from Cannan's left.

There was another man in the room!

The gunman's bullet tore through the Ranger's left bicep and into his ribs, just below his armpit. Cannan swung his Colt to cover the second assailant, but the sheet had tangled in the trigger guard and the Ranger's shot was delayed.

But it didn't matter.

The gunman, his head covered with a hood, bolted for the door, jumped over the sprawled, groaning form of his companion, and Cannan heard the thud of his boots on the stairs.

The Ranger pushed on the bed for support as he climbed unsteadily to his feet.

He was done, all used up, finished.

His gun dropped from his hand, thudded to the floor . . . and a second later Hank Cannan followed it.

* * *

Cannan woke to the concerned brown eyes of Dr. Hans Krueger.

"How are you feeling, Ranger?" the young physician asked.

"I don't know," Cannan said.

Krueger sat on the bed and Roxie Miller peered over his shoulder. "You got shot again," she said.

"The bullet went through your arm and into your rib cage," the doctor said. "Luckily it didn't penetrate far and I was able to extract it."

"You have to stop getting shot," Roxie said.

Without lifting his head from the pillow, Cannan said, "I didn't have much choice in the matter." He was surprised at how weak his voice sounded.

Krueger smiled slightly.

"I'm afraid Miz Roxie is right, Ranger Cannan," he said. "I keep patching you up, but I'm not a miracle worker. Next time you might not be so lucky."

"Doc, I'm all shot to pieces," Cannan said. "How lucky can a man get?"

"As you can tell, Mr. Cannan is not a good patient, Dr. Krueger," Roxie said. "He was drinking whiskey and smoking cigars with Baptiste Dupoix, the gambler, and him sick in bed."

"No more smoking and drinking until we get you on your feet, Ranger," the doctor said.

"When will that be?" Cannan said.

"A few weeks." Krueger thought for a moment, then said, "Will your superiors come looking for you?"

Cannan shook his head. "No, I'm on my own. A Texas Ranger is supposed to look out for his ownself."

"Even if his life is in danger?" Krueger said.

"Yes, even if his life is in danger. He's expected to handle it. That's how it works."

Cannan moved in the bed, and immediately jagged shards of pain stabbed at him.

"Damn it," he said, breathing hard, "who shot me?"

Roxie answered that. "Feller by the name of Jess Gable. He works for Abe Hacker."

"There were two of them," Cannan said.

"According to Hacker, the other one was Dave Randall," Roxie said.

"You said, *works* for Abe Hacker. You mean he's still alive?" Cannan said.

"Barely," Krueger said. "He has a belly wound, and there's nothing I can do for him except ease his pain and make his dying easier." The young doctor's face took on a strained look as he forced himself to admit that death, his archenemy, had beaten him. "He won't last the night," he said.

"Why did they try to kill me?"

Cannan addressed his question to Roxie. She worked the saloons where whiskey-talking men freely exchanged gossip about the citizens of Last Chance.

"Hacker says Gable and Randall were rogue employees who wanted to kill a lawman," she says. "He says his men are out hunting for Randall and when they find him, they'll turn him over to the law."

"What law?" Cannan said. "I'm the only law in Last Chance. I mean, what's left of me."

The Ranger and his wife had once been invited to attend a mummy unwrapping party at a grand house in Austin. Now, lying in bed, swathed in bandages, he felt like that Ancient Egyptian feller . . . before he was unwrapped.

"Where is Gable now?" Cannan said.

"Across the street at the Cattleman's Hotel," Dr. Krueger said. "He'll die in his room, and Hacker says he'll bury him decently, for old times' sake."

Cannan badly wanted to sleep, just close his eyes and drift, but he forced himself to stay alert.

Outside the reflector lamps were lit along the street and from one of the saloons a bored piano player one-fingered the notes of a Chopin étude. An owl, perched on the top of one of the false-fronted buildings, asked its question of the night and in the distance a pair of hunting coyotes yipped back and forth.

Cannan, his voice no louder than a whisper, said, "Who is this Hacker feller, and what's he doing in Last Chance?"

"He came looking for gold and didn't find any," Roxie said.

"Then why is he still here?"

"Nobody knows."

"Is Mickey Pauleen working for Hacker?"

"Yeah, him and a bunch of other Texas draw fighters," Roxie said. "They act real big in the saloons, and spend big, too."

"Why did . . ." Cannan's voice failed him and he coughed painfully, then tried again. "Why did Pauleen kill your town marshal?"

This time Dr. Krueger answered. "Marshal Isaac Dixon was nearly eighty years old. The town gave him the job because he won a medal in the war and was wounded at Gettysburg."

"For the South?" Cannan said.

"Of course."

"So what happened?"

Krueger's face was empty. "The story is that Isaac knew Pauleen from somewhere before and ordered him out of town. Witnesses said that the marshal drew down on him and Pauleen killed him."

"Who were the witnesses?"

"Hacker's boys. The shooting took place at the livery stable and nobody else saw it."

Cannan was silent for a few moments, then said, "I'd guess the old man was lured to the stable, then murdered."

"That's not how Hacker's men tell it," the doctor said.

"What about the townspeople?" Cannan said. "Didn't they do something?"

"What could they do? It was an open-and-shut case of self-defense. And the folks around here are not much inclined to lynch a man."

Cannan was again quiet for a spell.

Then he said, "Why does he want to take Last Chance away from the people who founded it and still live here?"

"Where did you hear such a thing?" Roxie said. "I think that's enough for tonight, Ranger Cannan. You're starting to imagine things. Dr. Krueger, can you give him something to help him sleep?"

"I don't need anything," Cannan said. "I reckon I'll sleep real good on my own."

Krueger rose, snapped his bag shut and said, "By the way, your gambler friend has taken a room next to yours. He says he'll make sure you don't get your damned fool head blown off."

"Doctor!" Roxie said. "I've never heard you cuss before."

The physician smiled. "I'm only repeating what he said."

"Baptiste Dupoix is no friend of mine," Cannan said. "I should have strung him up years ago."

"Well, he still seems to like you," Krueger said. He smiled. "I'll drop by again in the morning, Ranger Cannan."

After Roxie and the doctor left, sleep would not come to the exhausted Hank Cannan. Baptiste Dupoix's words still haunted him . . .

"We're going to take it all away from them."

The pain from his wounds tormented Cannan, but worse a torment was the growing certainty that Abe Hacker planned to destroy Last Chance, with its fields and orchards, ranches, and the dreams of its people.

But why?

And how?

And when?

Cannon had no answers.

But he did know this: When the hard times came down, he was in no shape to fight them. He was stove up and weak as a kitten. Hell, he could barely get out of bed.

Despair hung heavy on Hank Cannan. He was a helpless cripple at a time when the people of Last Chance needed a fighting lawman with no backup in him.

A Texas Ranger . . .

But one who could stand on his own two feet.

CHAPTER NINE

Abe Hacker, wearing a red robe and slippers of the same color, padded along the hotel hallway, his flabby face intent.

The grandfather clock in the lobby struck two as the fat man reached the door of Room 11.

Hacker stood for a while and listened to the soft groans of pain coming from inside. He smiled. Jess Gable was doped up on morphine, or he'd be screaming by now.

Ah well, perhaps it was easier this way. Quicker, certainly.

Silently, Hacker turned the door handle and stepped into the room.

For a few moments he stood still and let his eyes adjust to the gloom.

The air was fetid, heavy with the stench of a man's ruptured bowels and the strange, elusive vanilla odor of morphine.

On the bed, Gable moaned, the pain that was beyond pain building in his belly again.

Morphine is a good friend, but ultimately a fleeting and treacherous one.

Hacker took the Scottish dirk from his pocket.

A gift from some visiting British diplomat in Washington, it was not the puny pea-sticker worn as part of Highland dress, but a heavy fighting knife with a thirteen-inch blade, forged a hundred and fifty years before from meteoritic iron by a blacksmith who was said to have sold his soul to the devil in return for the secrets of steel.

A shaft of moonlight angled through an opening in the curtains and rippled on the blade as Hacker stepped on quiet feet to the bed.

His breath hissed between his thick lips, and beads of sweat formed on his forehead. His eyes, hidden in shadow, and the whiteness of his face gave him the look of a skull.

"Jess, are you awake?" he whispered.

Gable lay on his back, and the grayness of death gathered in the hollows of his cheeks and temples. His pale lips were flecked with blood.

He made no answer.

"All right, Jess, we'll do it the hard way," Hacker said, smiling.

He raised his arm and brought the silver, disc-shaped pommel of the knife down hard into Gable's belly.

The dying gunman's eyes flew open and he shrieked in mortal agony.

Hacker's beefy hand quickly covered Gable's mouth and stifled his screams.

He brought his mouth close to the man's ear and whispered, "You couldn't even get rid of a sick Ranger for me, you yellow, worthless dog turd."

Gable violently kicked his legs and tried to rise, his frantic eyes filled with fear and pain.

Hacker enjoyed the feel of the man's open mouth against his palm, the saliva slickness of his silent screams.

A morphine syringe stood on the table beside the bed.

"Jess, do you want your medicine?" Hacker said. "Would you like that?"

The man lay still for a moment, then nodded, his wide-open eyes pleading.

"No!" Hacker said, enjoying himself. "You don't deserve to have it after the way you failed me."

Jess Gable was not a cowardly man. He made a supreme effort to fight back his pain, and his lips moved as he mumbled something into Hacker's suffocating hand.

"What's that, Jess? I didn't hear you," Hacker said.

Gable's lips moved again.

"Let me take my hand away, Jess," Hacker said. He giggled, his jowls quivering. "I'm such a good nurse, am I not?"

This time Gable managed to speak . . . just two words.

"Kill me," he whispered.

His head cocked to the side like an inquisitive bird, Hacker said, "I'm thinking about it, Jess." He smiled. "Hey, yellow belly, how's your poor little tummy-tum?"

"Please . . ." Gable said, his voice as soft as a woman's sigh.

"Well, you didn't even laugh at my good joke, and thanks to your whining this is getting boring," Hacker said. "It's time I returned to my warm bed and willing woman." He grinned. "That make you jealous, Jess, huh?"

Gable grimaced, his teeth bared against the waves of agony that broke over him with fiendish intensity.

Then, for the first time since he was a child, his lips moved in prayer.

"Well, that does it for me," Hacker said. "Jess, you really are a worthless lowlife. And I've got nobody to blame but myself for hiring you in the first place."

He held the knife low, ready for a thrust. "Nobody, but nobody, fails Abe Hacker and lives to boast of it," he said. "Go to hell, Jess!"

Hacker rammed the dirk into Gable's throat, just under the man's chin. He pushed until the blade went in to the hilt, then withdrew it again.

Wiping the knife clean on the sheet, he said, "Are you dead, Jess?"

One look at the man's face, frozen in a death mask of agony and horror, convinced Hacker that he was.

Hacker slid the dirk into his pocket, then slapped the sides of his huge barrel of a stomach.

"Now, time for a little bedtime snack, I think," he said.

Henriette Valcour woke from a restless sleep and a warning dream.

The fat man had killed again . . . but so far her Baptiste was safe. The dream had made that clear.

Still, she was fearful and rose from bed and sat by the dying embers of the fire.

Was it the fat man and his strange, blood-blackened knife that had scared her so badly . . . the dire fact that by killing with his own hand he'd gained enormously in power?

Or was it just old Jacques St. Romain with his talk of

the loup-garou ball to be held right there in her own bayou?

Earlier that day, Jacques stood in his canoe and hollered at Henriette from a safe distance, his eyes fixed on the still surface of the water.

"Las' night I seen their lanterns in the swamp, me," he said. "Over on the bank by the dead tree. When the loups-garous got lanterns, I t'ink it means they plan to have their ball in this bayou."

"Go home, Jacques," Henriette had said. "Hang a colander on your door."

"I ain't got one of them, Madam Valcour."

"You got a calendar, you?"

"Got a Union Pacific Railroad on my wall, but it's for 1882."

"It will do very well, Jacques. Nail it to the outside of your door," Henriette said. "The loups-garous will stop and count the dates, just like they count the holes in a colander. They can't add up real good, they always make mistakes and have to start over and over again."

"How come the loups-garous got to count stuff, Madam Valcour?" Jacques said.

"It's just how they are, Jacques. They'll count anything, the holes in my colander and the numbers in your calendar, and never try to get through our doors."

"Them's words of good advice," Jacques said. "Soon as I get home, I gonna nail that Union Pacific calendar to my door, me, and keep them loups-garous busy."

Then, before he paddled away, the old man said, "I got some fish an' a piece of poke loin from a hog I shot t'other day. I'll t'row them on your po'ch, Madam Valcour, but don't you go lookin' at me none, you."

"Go right ahead, Jacques," Henriette said. "I'm going inside now anyhow, me. Got a turtle in the pot."

* * *

Henriette had no fear of werewolves, poor, cursed creatures that they were, and the colander was powerful protection. The loups-garous were also deathly afraid of frogs, and there were plenty of them jumping around her home.

So let the werewolves enjoy their ball and howl at the sky. If they did not trouble her, she would not trouble them.

It was the fat man who scared her so.

He was evil and dangerous, and Baptiste was in peril as long as the man lived.

Restless, Henriette left her chair and stepped onto her porch.

Fireflies danced in the gloom of the swamp and the air was heavy with the perfume of night-blooming wild petunias. The moon was not yet full, but it was as bright as a silver coin.

If she was to be Baptiste's guardian and save him from the fat man, she needed more power.

Henriette untied her nightgown and let it drop and puddle around her feet. Naked, she tilted her face to the dark cauldron of the sky, stretched out her arms to the moon's radiance, and bathed in its mother-of-pearl light.

CHAPTER TEN

Someone rapped on Hank Cannan's door, an apologetic tat-tat-tat.

Groaning, he reached out and unholstered his Colt.

"Come in," he said. "And you'd better be grinnin' like a possum."

The door opened, and a man stuck his gray head inside. "I hope we're not intruding, Ranger Cannan," he said.

"Folks come in and out of here all the time," Cannan said.

"Then we can come in?"

"Come right ahead."

Three men filed into the room, respectable-looking citizens who seemed to have dressed for the occasion in their Sunday best.

"My name is Frank Curtis," the gray-haired man said. "I'm mayor of Last Chance. These are my associates, Ed Gillman and Ben Coffin."

Gillman was a tall, slender man with an open, pleasant face. Ben Coffin was plump, jolly, with a wide, copper-colored nose. Thin strands of pale hair were fastidiously arranged across his balding pate.

He stuck out his hand and grinned. "Coffin by name, Coffin by nature," he said. "Put it there, Ranger."

Cannan placed his revolver on the bed and accepted the man's hand.

"Ben is the town undertaker," Curtis said. "Ed owns the dry goods store across the street."

After shaking hands with Gillman, Cannan said, "What can I do for you gentlemen?"

Roxie Miller, who looked as though she'd just waked up the light of a May morning, had slipped into the room. "Please make it brief, Mayor," she said. "Ranger Cannan is very weak and he tires quickly."

Disappointment tightened the faces of the three townsmen, and Cannan figured Roxie had just said something they didn't want to hear.

"Then I'll be brief," Curtis said. "The man you shot has been murdered."

Cannan was surprised. "Who would murder a dying man?"

"We don't know. But someone did. Stuck a knife in his throat."

"We think Abe Hacker is behind this," Coffin said.

"Murdered one of his own men?" Cannan said.

"That could be the case," the mayor said.

"Motive?" Cannan said.

Curtis shook his head and the others stayed dumb.

Cannan said, "It could be he killed Gable to shut him up. Hacker may have ordered the attempt on my life."

"Because you were in the way of his plans," Curtis said.

"That's how I see it," Cannan said.

He picked up his revolver from the bed and shoved it back in the holster. "Hacker plans to take Last Chance away from you, Mayor," he said. "Have you heard that?"

"No, we haven't."

"Maybe it's not true."

"He wants something, all right," Coffin said. "That's why he's still here."

Cannan sat higher in the bed. He tried not to let the pain show.

"He came for gold. I heard that," he said.

"There is no gold," Gillman said. "There never was any gold."

"I reckon Hacker knows that by now," Cannan said.

A silence fell, stretched.

Then Curtis said, "We hoped you could investigate the matter, Ranger Cannan." His eyes flicked to the bloodstained bandage on Cannan's shoulder. "But I see now that it's impossible."

Cannan closed his eyes briefly.

Roxie was right. He tired fast.

"Mayor," he said, "how many fighting men can you raise in a hurry?"

"Two score, I reckon. But none of them are gunfighters like Hacker's boys."

"What about the ranchers?"

"They hire seasonal punchers. The Rafter-K and the Elkhorn won't sign on more until spring."

"Tom Battles and his two sons over to the Elkhorn are pretty good with guns," Coffin said.

"If they come up against Hacker's men they'll need

to be more than pretty good," Cannan said. "Baptiste Dupoix is one of them, and all by himself he's a handful."

Weak and worn out as he was, the Ranger tried to make himself think.

Finally he said, "Hacker won't try to take Last Chance by force. He doesn't have enough men to take on two score armed citizens who'll fight to keep what's theirs, even if they're not professional gunfighters."

By nature, Ed Gillman was not a talking man, but a keen intelligence showed in his high forehead and alert eyes. "Frank, he wants to take all of it, by God," he said. "This town, the fields, the tree groves, the ranches, the fur trade with Mexico . . . the whole kit and caboodle down to the last stalk of wheat."

"And cotton," Cannan said. "Don't forget the cotton. A man could make a killing growing cotton along this part of the Big Bend."

"It's thin, mighty thin," Curtis said. "Who would work Hacker's fields? His gunmen?"

"Maybe he figures he can force the people of this community to work his fields," Coffin said.

"No. As I said earlier, he'd have a war on his hands, and he doesn't want that," Cannan said.

"Then I can't figure it," Curtis said, throwing up his hands.

"Me neither," Cannan said. "But I plan to study on it."

The Ranger closed his eyes again, pain and fatigue wearing on him.

Curtis read the signs and said, with a tinge of bitterness, "You can think about it, Ranger, but you can't get up out of bed and help us."

"Not for a few weeks or so," Roxie said.

"Then look on the bright side, Ranger," Coffin said,

smiling. "You'll be up and about for our Independence Day celebrations."

As though the jolly undertaker irritated him, the mayor chose to be gloomy.

"By this Fourth of July we might all be dead or scattered to the four corners of the earth," he said.

"Mother of God, don't say that, Frank," Gillman said. But the store owner's worried expression betrayed him.

Gillman knew it could happen.

CHAPTER ELEVEN

A severe drought in the southern-steppe growing zone of Chihuahua forced the Mexican farmers north, toward the desert country.

Riding through sandy brush country thirty miles south of the Rio Grande, Mickey Pauleen learned from distressed peons that the drought was in its third year and that they were heading for the sky islands, hanging valleys in the mountains that stayed wet and cool enough to grow pines and hardwood trees.

Although it was late in the planting season, many of the peons carried seed corn with them. If the high valleys were not dry as mummy dust, they could plant their corn and expect a harvest in the early fall.

"And if there's drought in the mountains, what then?" Pauleen asked a farmer, who was trailed by a pregnant wife riding a burro and seven children.

"We will eat the burro and our seed corn and when those are gone my family will starve," the man said.

This was good news for Pauleen.

He reckoned he'd seen several hundred Mexicans

already, and their presence in great numbers this far north would help Sancho Perez's roundup.

The bandit had several strongholds scattered around the desert country, but his permanent quarters was a hacienda located among a group of low-lying hills a few miles to Pauleen's east.

Pauleen slid the Winchester from his boot and laid it across the saddle horn. Then he swung his horse toward the hills and his eyes reached out across the sun-blasted yellow desert and hoped Perez was at home and not raiding into Texas or the New Mexico Territory.

After a mile or so, three men appeared in the distance, horses and riders strangely elongated in the shimmer like gaunt knights in an old Gothic tapestry.

Gradually, as they rode closer, men and horses slowly regained their proper proportions, and sunlight flashed on silver bridles and saddles. Dust lifted from the hooves of the oncoming horses and laced away in the unceasing desert wind, and suddenly Pauleen's mouth was dry.

Sancho Perez was insane, and that made him an unpredictable and dangerous hombre.

The riders spread out, but the foremost man rested the butt of his rifle on his thigh and came on at a walk. Judging by his massive girth, he was Perez.

Pauleen felt a surge of relief.

It seemed that the bandit had decided to talk first and shoot later.

Mickey Pauleen drew rein and waited. His sober clothes were covered in a thick layer of dust, and his red-veined eyes burned in the harsh light.

Perez stopped when he was five yards from Pauleen

and his outriders came back and flanked him, their broad, peasant faces set and hard, revealing nothing.

The bandit chief grinned and revealed that his two front teeth were set with diamonds.

"Mickey Pauleen, my good fren'," he said. His black eyes flicked to the gunman's horse. "I see you are prospering since Piedgras Negras."

It was difficult for Pauleen to keep a straight face while talking to a mustachioed, stubble-chinned man who wore an Amish woman's white bonnet instead of a sombrero, but he managed it.

"That was not a good fight, Sancho," he said. "We found no army payroll, only rurales."

"*Sí*, that is so," Perez said. "The last I saw of you, you were running across the desert as though the devil himself was after you."

"And you were galloping south on my horse," Pauleen said.

The bandit laughed, a loud, rollicking bellow that shook his great belly. "Good times, Mickey, good times," he said.

"For you, Sancho, not for me."

Perez's face fell. "Ah, now Sancho is ver' sad that you did not enjoy Piedgras Negras."

He turned to his men, first one and then the other. "Is Sancho not sad?" he said.

Both Mexicans nodded their agreement and Perez sighed.

"And I am sadder still, because I am a thief and I have to take your fine horse and set you on foot again."

But before Pauleen could say anything, Perez's face brightened.

"Wait, I have a plan, and then I will not be so sad," he said.

He turned to the man on his left. "Sandoval, give my friend Mickey your horse."

The young man shook his head.

"This horse is mine, *patrón*. I will not part with him."

Perez drew his Colt and shot the man.

The young bandit's swarthy face registered a moment of surprise before he tumbled out of the saddle and hit the ground.

"See, Mickey, my fren', now you can have his horse and I will take yours," he said. He spread his hands and smiled. "I have solved the problem."

"*Viva Perez!*" the surviving bandits yelled, grinning.

Pauleen knew he had to talk fast, and the sight of the dead man on the ground loosened his tongue.

"Sancho, if you accept my proposition you can buy all the blooded horses you want," he said.

Perez scowled. "Proposition? What is this proposition? Do you try to bargain with Sancho?"

"It's from Abe Hacker," Pauleen said.

As he knew it would, the name made a difference.

"Ah, *Señor* Hacker is a ver' rich man. We have done business before."

"And you can do business again," Pauleen said.

Perez glanced at the sky, the same shade of faded blue as a washed-out pair of dungarees, and said, "We will talk at my hacienda."

He turned to the man at his side.

"Clemente, put poor Sandoval on his horse, and we will give him to his woman to bury," he said. "I am ver' sorry he died with disrespect on his lips. It makes Sancho so sad."

He grinned at Pauleen. "Now, my friend, we will go and drink some wine and talk business."

CHAPTER TWELVE

When Sancho Perez called his place a hacienda, he had not exaggerated.

It was a sprawling complex of adobe with a red tile roof and an elegant arch over the main gate. Every inch of the masonry was covered with plaster as white and even as fallen snow. The hacienda was shaded by broadleaf trees that spoke of constant watering and extensive, shriveled flowerbeds that did not.

Perez was an irrational man, and his cultivation efforts reflected his mental state.

When Pauleen rode under the arch into a large flagstone courtyard he realized that the hacienda was much older than it first appeared. Its pillared verandas and balconies suggested its original builder had been a Spanish hidalgo who'd been in the grave for at least a hundred years.

While Perez's bandits lounged outside a timber barracks block, peons in white cotton shirts and straw sombreros rushed to take the horses, and when the word got around that Sandoval was dead, the courtyard filled with crying, wailing women.

A small chapel lay at a distance from the house and the women quickly carried the body there.

Perez didn't spare the sad procession a glance as he ushered Pauleen inside.

The interior of the house was shady and cool. In the Spanish colonial style, it had substantial furniture and exposed wood beam ceilings. But native craftsmen had made the tables, chairs, and chests from walnut, cedar, cypress, and mesquite, lighter woods than the original heavy oak and mahogany.

Perez untied his sunbonnet, threw it onto a chair, and indicated that Pauleen should sit in another.

The gunman chose a massive, leather-upholstered chair by the cold fireplace, and Perez sat opposite him.

The bandit clapped his hands and within seconds a young woman stepped into the room.

"Wine," Perez said.

The woman poured wine into a pair of fine silver goblets. She served Perez and then Pauleen.

"Now go," the bandit said. Then, grinning, "Come to me tonight, Consuela."

The woman nodded, unsmiling, and said nothing.

She left the room on silent feet and Perez said, "Why did Hacker send you and not come himself?"

"I'm here because Hacker needs to win," Pauleen said. "I'm the man who ensures that he does."

"An answer of sorts," Perez said. "Where are your guns?"

"I had no need for them, Sancho," Pauleen said. "You are a great and powerful man and under the roof of your hacienda I am safe from all harm."

The flattery worked. Perez bowed his head and said,

"This is true. All are welcome here and are protected while they are my guests."

Because of the summer heat, the bandit wore only a frilled white shirt open to the waist, and woolen pants tucked into fine English riding boots. His gun belt was buckled over the vaquero's traditional red sash.

"The wine is not to your taste, Mickey?" Perez said, his obsidian eyes glinting.

"It is an excellent vintage," Pauleen said. He lifted the goblet, put it to his closed lips, and pretended to drink.

"Tell me about Hacker's proposition," Perez said.

"A dollar for every peon you can drive across the Rio Grande," Pauleen said. "It's as simple as that, Sancho."

Perez was surprised. "What peon is worth an American dollar?"

"Man, woman, or child, that is their worth to Hacker."

"How many?"

"As many as you can round up. Hacker mentioned a figure of a thousand and more if you can get them."

"That is all I have to do? Herd peons across the river like cattle?"

"Yes, but to a certain place in the river, the town of Last Chance."

"How will I feed and water so many on the drive?"

"Better they cross the border hungry and thirsty. The fields and orchards around Last Chance will look like the Garden of Eden to them."

"Ha! The Spanish monks taught me about the garden when I was a boy," Perez said. "The people were cast out by holy angels with fiery swords."

"The peons will not be cast out. They're welcome to stay and work for wages," Pauleen said.

Perez said, "A bowl of beans and a couple of pesos a day. That's all a peon needs, or asks."

"Can you round up the number Hacker needs?"

"In a normal year, it would be impossible. But the drought drives the peons north. Some have already set their eyes on crossing the Rio Grande, I think."

"By the fourth of July, huh?"

"This I will do, if I can keep them alive that long. But my fee is three dollars a head."

"You're a robber, Sancho," Pauleen said without rancor.

"*Sí*, that is my profession," Perez said. "And I am ver' good at it."

"Then three dollars it is. Bring more than a thousand and Hacker will pay a bonus."

Perez nodded. "He is a fine man." He rose to his feet, leaned into the fireplace, and grabbed a handful of fine wood ash from the grate that he scattered on his head. His black hair now streaked with gray, Perez said, "Come with me to the chapel. We will mourn for poor Sandoval who now lies so stiff and cold."

When they were still twenty yards from the chapel, Perez screamed his grief, then moaned and beat his chest with a fist as he approached the door.

"Eeeiii, poor Sandoval," he wailed. "What have I done to you?"

Inside, thick yellow candles guttering in wrought-iron brackets on the walls relieved the dimness of the chapel.

Sandoval's body, as gray and still as marble, had been washed by the women and lay naked on a bier in front of the altar. The air was thick with candle smoke and the musky tang of ancient incense.

Gray ashes mingled with the sweat on his forehead and cheeks, Perez shrieked and threw himself on the dead man. "Sandoval, forgive your Sancho," he howled. "Aaahhh . . . I am surely damned. How can God forgive me such a sin?"

Pauleen sat in a pew and listened to the bandit's lamentation, a smile tugging at his lips. The man was either acting or insane. No, he was an insane actor.

Who better than a madman to carry out his part of Hacker's mad plan to bring the Plagues of Egypt to Last Chance and thus destroy the very thing he lusted to own?

Amid the cries of Perez and the sobs of women, Pauleen came to the realization that Hacker and Perez were both loco, but in different ways.

Sancho Perez was a roaring, unbuttoned buffoon, a born criminal who could kill a man without thought and regret it a moment later.

Abe Hacker was cooler, smarter, more calculating . . . and just as deadly.

Both made treacherous friends and deadly enemies.

Pauleen made his mind up right there and then.

Once the locusts crossed the river, he'd take his money and his woman and ride. Maybe up Wyoming way where a gun for hire was always welcome.

Pauleen rose and stepped to the bier, where Perez still wept and wailed.

He tapped the bandit on the shoulder, then whispered into his ear, "July fourth."

Perez dashed away tears and nodded.

As Pauleen turned to walk away, his eyes clashed with a young woman's who stood by the bier. Her left cheek bore the deep scar of a knife wound, but her beautiful black eyes glittered as she stared at him with stark, vicious hatred.

Pauleen, the fastest and most dangerous man with a gun on the frontier, shivered—as though a goose had just flown over his grave.

CHAPTER THIRTEEN

Dave Randall had had it up to here with hiding out in the brush.

It was time to head back into Last Chance and let Hacker smooth things over, use that glib tongue of his to convince the town that Randall's part in the attack on the Ranger had been a misunderstanding.

Jess Gable was dead. Randall was pretty sure of that.

Well then, here's what he'd say: *"See, Gable tried to murder the Ranger in his bed and I made a brave attempt to stop him. Unfortunately, the Ranger mistook my intentions and cut loose. Afraid for my life, I panicked and fled into the desert."*

Randall smiled.

Yeah, that was it. That's what he'd tell the rubes, and Hacker would back up his story.

Hell, they might make him a hero and give him a gold medal or something.

Randall drank the last swallow of water in his canteen and was wishful for coffee, but had none. He was missing his last six meals, and the thought of a steak with taters and onions was mighty appealing.

Hunger only added to his hardship, and he vowed that he'd settle with the damned Ranger for putting him to all this inconvenience.

That Gable was dead didn't trouble Randall in the least. When the chips were down the man had gotten tangled in his own loop and bungled the whole thing.

Well, next time would be different.

As far as Dave Randall was concerned, the sickly, puny Ranger was dead meat. One way or another he'd see to that.

It was still an hour till noon, but the morning was hot. Already the brush flats shimmered and even the pair of horny toads that had earlier been basking on a limestone rock had sought shade.

Randall tightened the saddle cinch and was about to mount when a flicker of movement to the south caught his eye. He pulled his boot from the stirrup and shaded his eyes from the sun glare.

Originally just a speck of black moving across the tan and orange of the desert, it grew into the shape of a horse and rider. Another quarter mile and Randall made out a long-legged gray, moving at a fluid, easy walk.

He recognized the horse.

It was Baptiste Dupoix's mount. Hacker must have sent the gambler out to look for him and escort him back.

A careful man, Randall adjusted the lie of his gun belt, then repositioned himself so that his back was to the climbing sun. It wasn't likely, but there was always the chance that it was a lawman riding Dupoix's horse.

But Randall's fears were put to rest when the rider drew closer and he recognized him as the gambler, a plain blue Colt in his shoulder holster.

Dupoix wore riding breeches and a frilled white shirt. At a time when it was considered the height of bad manners, indeed scandalous, for a man to show his wrists, his sleeves were rolled up on his forearms. The rules of Victorian etiquette did not apply in the desert.

Dupoix drew rein, and after he and Randall exchanged greetings, the gambler tossed him a canteen.

Randall drank greedily as Dupoix swung out of the saddle.

After he wiped his wet mouth and mustache with the back of his hand, Randall said, "You come to give me an escort, Baptiste?"

Dupoix shook his head.

"No, Dave," he said, "I've come to kill you."

Randall looked as though he'd been slapped.

"What the hell are you talking about?" he said.

"You tried to murder Hank Cannan, Dave, and I set store by him."

Now Randall's face registered amazement.

"He's a Texas Ranger! When the hell did you start taking a liking to lawmen?"

"Cannan is a brave man, Dave. I won't step aside and see him murdered in his bed."

"Did Hacker send you?"

"No. This is my idea. I'm here to make sure Cannan isn't shot in his sleep by a treacherous snake like you. That was in your mind, huh? To kill the Ranger and make things right with Hacker."

"Yeah, that's as true as ever was. But you should have brought someone with you, Dupoix." Randall grinned, his feral, searching eyes alight. "On your best day you can't shade me," he said. "I've killed better men than you."

Dupoix smiled. "Then I guess you'll have to shuck the iron and prove that to me," he said.

Something in the gambler's hipshot, confident stance gave Randall pause. He felt a finger of sweat trickle down his back.

"Draw the iron, Dave," Dupoix said. "Get your work in."

"I never met a man who wanted to die as much as you," Randall said. "And for nothing."

He drew.

Dupoix clawed for his gun. Slow. Way too slow.

Randall's Colt leveled in an instant.

He pulled the trigger.

CLICK!

The hammer dropping on a dud round was loud in the silence.

Dupoix fired.

The gambler did not miss at across-the-card-table distance.

Dupoix's bullet crashed into the top of Randall's chest, an inch below the neck. He thumbed a second shot.

Randall took the bullet dead center.

He lifted up on his toes, cast Dupoix a single unbelieving, horrified glance, then fell flat on his face, dead when he hit the sand.

Dupoix holstered his Colt and kneeled beside the dead man.

Dave Randall had been lightning-fast on the draw and shoot, the fastest Dupoix had ever seen. The only reason he was still alive was because the man's gun had failed.

Dupoix removed the Colt from Randall's lifeless fingers and opened the loading gate. He turned the cylinder, then let the failed round drop into his palm.

The hammer strike on the primer was deep and well defined as it should be.

Frowning, Dupoix slid the round back into the cylinder.

He rotated the cylinder again so the hammer would fall on the faulty round.

He stood, thumbed back the hammer, and pointed the Colt into the air.

BANG!

The echo of the shot hammered across the flat and sent a startled covey of bobwhites exploding into the air.

For a moment Dupoix stood lost in thought.

It seemed that someone was watching out for him . . . maybe a crazy old swamp witch named Henriette Valcour.

Dupoix shook his head, smiled, and came back to earth.

A defective cartridge often worked on the second strike. There was nothing witchy about it.

It was not in the gambler's nature to leave a dead man to the buzzards.

He manhandled Randall's body across the saddle of his horse and gathered the animal's reins before he mounted.

Under a relentless sun he kneed his gray in the direction of Last Chance.

Dupoix smiled to himself again. "Thank you, Henriette," he said.

CHAPTER FOURTEEN

"Damn it, Dupoix, you should have let Randall kill the Ranger and then gunned him," Abe Hacker said, his tight little eyes blazing. "This was ill done."

"I wanted to stop him killing the Ranger," the gambler said.

"Who's side are you on, Dupoix?" Hacker said.

"You're paying my wages, Abe."

"Then I want the damned Ranger dead. He could interfere with my plans."

"How could a man who's so shot up he can't even get out of bed interfere with your plans?"

"I don't know. But I'm not a man who takes chances." Hacker waved a chubby hand. "I can deal with the rubes, but a Ranger is the joker in the deck."

"What are your plans, Abe?"

"You'd like to know, huh?"

"I've been sitting around for weeks doing nothing, drawing gun wages I can't justify."

"Yeah, well, just set tight for a while longer. Your time will come."

"What are your plans, Abe?" Dupoix said again.

As was his habit of late, Hacker was still in bed though the afternoon light was shading in to evening. He was naked, pale, and sweating like a tallow candle in the fetid atmosphere of the hotel room.

Nora sat in a chair, in her dressing gown, pretending not to notice her lover's stink as she kept her eyes lowered to a dime novel.

"You read the Bible, Dupoix?" Hacker said.

"All I read are faces across the baize," the gambler said.

"Well, I'm sure your Ranger friend has a Bible. All them do-gooders have one."

"What do I read, chapter and verse?"

"Hell, I don't know that chapter and verse stuff. Just thumb through the Book until you get to the part that talks about a plague of locusts descending on Egypt, or get the Ranger to read it to you."

"No need for that. I remember the story."

Hacker's smile was unpleasant. "Well, now you know my plan," he said.

"As far as I'm aware, there are no locusts in this part of Texas," Dupoix said.

"Well, that's where you're wrong, ain't you?" Hacker said. He nodded in the direction of the door. "Now get out of here. And remember, I want that Ranger dead. Smother him with a pillow if you have to, but kill him."

"You're the boss," Dupoix said.

And Nora looked at him and smiled.

Baptiste Dupoix tapped on Hank Cannan's door, then stepped inside when the Ranger said, "Come in."

Dupoix halted in his tracks, staring at the unwavering muzzle of Cannan's gun.

"A Colt pointing at his brisket is hardly a friendly way to greet a man," he said.

"You're not my friend, Baptiste," Cannan said.

"But I'm not your enemy. Abe Hacker is your enemy."

"A man who draws gun wages from my foe, is my enemy," Cannan said. "Isn't that how it goes?"

"Foe. I've only seen that word in poems when I was a boy."

"It fits," Cannan said. He lowered the Colt. "But you didn't come here to kill me today, did you?"

"I've already killed a man today, Cannan. I don't much feel like killing another."

Dupoix stepped around the bed, picked up the Old Crow, and held the bottle up to the light of the oil lamp.

"There's enough," he said. He poured whiskey into the glasses and handed one to Cannan. "Like old times, huh?"

Dupoix reached into his coat pocket, and Cannan tensed and moved his hand closer to his Colt.

The gambler smiled. He threw a sack of tobacco and papers on the bed.

"I don't think you cared for my brand of cigars much, so I brought you the makings. Oh, and you'll need these lucifers," he said, handing over a box of matches.

"Who did you kill, Dupoix?" Cannan said, his face like stone.

"Not one of your friends, I assure you," the gambler said. "I disposed of that fine gentleman Dave Randall."

"He was one of the men who tried to kill me," Cannan said.

"Indeed. And now they're both dead."

"Jess Gable was murdered, and not by my hand," the Ranger said.

"Can you murder a man who's already dead, or at least dying?"

"Yes, you can. Who cut his throat, Dupoix? You?"

The gambler shook his head. "Not my style. No, I suspect it was Hacker."

"Why?"

"Because Gable failed him. I mean, you're still alive and kicking, aren't you? Hacker doesn't much like that."

"You're sunburned, Dupoix. Did Hacker send you out after Randall?"

"No, it was my own idea. Dave didn't go far, and he wasn't difficult to track, even for a gambler. When it came down to getting our work in, I got lucky. Dave's gun misfired."

"It happens sometimes," Cannan said. He looked down at his fingers busily building a cigarette and said, "Why did you feel the need to kill him?"

"Because I knew he'd come back here to the hotel and finish the job to get himself in good with Hacker," Dupoix said.

"Why are you so concerned for my welfare?" A match flared, and he lit his cigarette.

Dupoix smiled. "Because I like you, Cannan. You're an honorable man and one meets so few of those in the gambling profession. Besides, you always look like a big ol' angry walrus and that makes me laugh."

Cannan inhaled deeply, then let the smoke drift out with his words. "Amusing to you or not, you know I'm duty-bound to hang you, Dupoix."

"And I may be duty-bound to gun you, Ranger. But let's not build houses on a bridge we haven't crossed yet."

"All right, we'll lay that aside for the moment," Cannan said. "Tell me if I have enough evidence to arrest Abe Hacker."

"I didn't see him do it, Cannan," Dupoix said.

"What about his woman?"

"Nora? She didn't see it, either, and even if she did, she wouldn't testify against her meal ticket."

"Anyone else?"

"Nope. Not a soul." Dupoix sat on a chair, crossed his legs, and lit a cigar. The whiskey in his hand glowed like Black Hills gold in the waning light. "Besides all that, you can't even get out of bed, Cannan. How are you going to arrest anybody?"

"I can deputize some of the townsmen."

"And leave a dozen of them dead on the ground? Too steep a price to pay for a rat like Hacker."

"You don't like him, do you?"

"No, but I don't have to like him to take his money." Dupoix sipped his drink and said, "Without much success, I've been trying to buck a losing streak that started in Denver a year ago. Right now I'm down to my last chip, and I need this job."

"The people of this town all the way up to the mayor are concerned about Hacker," Cannan said.

"They should be," Dupoix said.

"What the hell is he up to?" Cannan said.

"It's all in the Bible," Dupoix said.

The Ranger choked on his whiskey, then wiped his wet mustache with the back of his hand.

"What bible?"

"The holy one, I guess," Dupoix said.

Seeing Cannan stare at him in puzzlement, he added, "Hacker said his plan for Last Chance, its fields, orchards and ranches, is all written down in the Bible."

Dupoix smiled. "He said a do-gooder like you would have one."

"My wife has one," Cannan said. Then, scowling, "Damn it, I hurt like hell all over."

Dupoix, relaxed, watched the lazy drift of his cigar smoke. "It's from shock, Ranger Cannan. I mean Abe Hacker getting his villainous inspiration from the Good Book."

"What part, Dupoix?"

"The part that says God sent a plague of locusts to destroy the land of Egypt." Dupoix frowned. "Or was it Moses who sent the locusts? I can't quite remember."

"Whoever sent them, that's not a plan," Cannan said.

Dupoix shrugged. "Hacker thinks it is."

"A plague of locusts . . . locusts . . ." Cannan said. "Hell, I don't get it."

"Nor do I, Cannan. Unless the locusts decided that they're on Hacker's side." Dupoix smiled and rose to his feet. "Maybe this town should stock up on flyswatters."

A low mist hung low over the bayou so all Henriette Valcour saw of Jacques St. Romain was his gray head poking above the haze.

"Jacques," she called out, her voice a hollow echo, "you come over here now. I need to talk with you, me."

"I wasn't huntin' your gators, Miz Henriette," the old man yelled.

"Then what was you huntin'? The loups-garous?"

Jacques paddled his canoe closer.

"I don't bother them none, Miz Valcour, and them gettin' ready for the ball an' everyt'ing."

"You come here, Jacques."

"I ain't lookin' at you none, me. An' don't you go lookin' at me, Miz Valcour. You turn me into a frog, maybe so."

Jacques had muddy brown eyes, the whites cracked with red. His hands on the paddle were huge and muscular, a legacy of the twenty years he did on the Huntsville State Prison rock pile for murder.

"You come closer, Jacques," Henriette said. "All this shouting will bring the loups-garous."

The old man quickly paddled closer, the pearly mist opening and closing around him.

He stood in the canoe and held on to a porch floorboard to steady himself. His eyes were downcast, staring at his bare feet.

"You know dreams, Jacques," Henriette said.

A shake of the gray head, then, "I know nothin' about dreams, me. When a man has a dream his soul wanders an' sometimes it don't ever come back."

"You dream, Jacques. We all dream."

"No. Never, Miz Henriette. I tole you so."

"You read your Bible, Jacques?"

"Every day, Miz Henriette. I got a t'ing to atone for. That's what Father Jarreau say."

"You poor thing, you strangled a cheating, painted woman and you paid for it," Henriette said.

"It was a bad t'ing I done, Miz Henriette."

"Yes, it was a bad thing, Jacques."

"An' that's why I read my Bible every day, me."

"You remember the plague of locusts?"

"Oh yes, ma'am. I remember. The king of Egypt

wouldn't let the slaves go free an' God sent locusts to devour the land." Jacques shook his head. "It was a bad t'ing that king done."

"Last night I dreamed I saw locusts destroy the land and my grandson tried to stop them, but they devoured him and picked his flesh clean to the bone."

"It was a bad dream, Miz Henriette."

"What does it mean, Jacques?"

"I don't know what it means."

"You know dreams, Jacques."

"Don' ax me no more."

"What did I see in my dream?"

Jacques looked around him, into the swamp where the loups-garous lived. The mist had grown thicker and the air smelled and tasted foul, of black ooze and decay.

"Where is your grandson?" Jacques said.

"I saw him beside a great river. The locusts came from beyond the river and spread over the land and destroyed everything in their path."

Jacques closed his eyes, looking into his own darkness where the pictures formed.

Finally, after several minutes, he said, "Invaders will come across the river and your grandchild will try to stop them, but they'll kill him and flay his skin from his bones."

"Can I help him?" Henriette said.

"The dream says nothin' about he'p, Miss Henriette. Maybe you can, maybe you can't, the dream doesn't tell me."

"Who are these invaders, Jacques? It is an army?"

The black man shook his head. "No, they are a people, Miz Henriette. Like the Children of the Book who fled Egypt. They seek the Promised Land." Jacques let go of his support and sat back in the canoe. "Don' ax me any more, because I don't know any more, me," he said.

Then, before he was out of earshot the old man turned.

"But I seen the river, Miz Henriette," he said. "And it ran red with blood and dead men and horses."

CHAPTER FIFTEEN

The sound of boots thudding in the hallway woke Baptiste Dupoix from shallow sleep.

Dawn angled gunmetal light into the hotel room as he swung out of bed and stepped to the window. Outside, four horses stood tethered to the hitching rail, a paint mustang among them. Dupoix recalled that the pony belonged to a kid called Matt Husted, one of the young Texas guns Hacker had hired.

The four youngsters, all of them blue-eyed towheads, had the fresh-faced look of farm boys, and they had been raised well enough that they always walked carefully around Dupoix and called him "Sir."

But looks were deceiving.

Each wore his gun with confident ease, as though he'd been born to it, and all four had run with some pretty hard crowds and had killed their man.

Husted was the fastest with the iron, maybe as fast as Mickey Pauleen, or so the kids said, but none of them would be a bargain in a gunfight.

The four young men stepped onto the porch to the right of Dupoix's window, and then Pauleen, already dressed in the garb of a malevolent preacher, joined them.

Dupoix couldn't hear what was being said, but the kids listened to Pauleen intently, and whatever he told them, it made all four grin.

The gambler's first thought was that Pauleen was sending them after Hank Cannan—but they wouldn't need blanket rolls and booted Winchesters for that.

Then what?

Whatever was afoot, Dupoix had a stake in the game.

He dressed hurriedly, strapped on his shoulder holster, and made his way downstairs. He met Mickey Pauleen at the door.

"Early for you, Baptiste," Pauleen said, his cold eyes speculative.

"Yes. I fancy I'll take an early morning ride," Dupoix said. "Clear my head of last night's whiskey."

"There's a serpent in every bottle and it biteth like the viper," Pauleen said. "Ever hear that?"

"No, but the serpent is sure enough biting this morning."

Dupoix tried to move past Pauleen, but the man stuck his arm out, blocking his way.

"I hear tell you got witch kin over Louisiana way," the gunman said. "Is that right?"

"On the bayou folks call my grandmother a swamp witch," Dupoix said.

"Witches should be burned," Pauleen said.

"Maybe so," Dupoix said.

He couldn't see a gun on Pauleen, but that didn't mean the man wasn't carrying a hideout.

"Funny thing is, a man who sticks his nose into things that don't concern him can get burned. Just like a swamp witch, huh?"

Dupoix didn't want to push it with Pauleen. The fight for Last Chance hadn't yet begun and when it finally came down he wanted to be on Abe Hacker's side. "Will you give me the road, Mickey?" he said.

The little gunman nodded. "Enjoy your ride, Baptiste. Remember what I said about witches an' sich, huh?"

"Sure, Mickey, I'll remember," Dupoix said. "A tête-à-tête with you is so much fun, how could I forget?"

Dupoix left the livery and looped wide around town, then swung south. He passed vast wheat and corn fields crisscrossed by irrigation ditches, then the ripening fruit tree orchards where cicadas buzzed.

In the distance a couple of punchers drove a wandering Hereford bull back to their home range. The men waved and Dupoix waved back.

A couple of miles east of town he picked up the tracks of four riders and followed them into the Rio Grande and then to the far bank.

Ahead of him stretched a wilderness of scrub desert and cactus. The far mountains on each side of him stood as dark purple silhouettes against the lapis lazuli sky. The peaks looked as though they'd be cool to the touch, cascading water.

There was no sign of the four young Texans, but then the distances were already rippling, distorting the terrain.

Dupoix kneed his horse forward. The morning sun's glare was dazzling, spiking white, and he tilted his hat forward over his eyes.

He'd taken the precaution of filling his canteen at

the livery, and it sloshed with every movement of the horse.

He didn't drink. Not yet.

In the desert, once a man feels the need for water, it's better for him to drink what he has all at once and then find a place to hole up.

Dupoix wasn't that thirsty and he had no intention of riding far into the desert. There was a limit to his curiosity.

After an hour, the tracks veered west and Dupoix followed them.

A few minutes later he heard a rattle of gunshots and drew rein, his eyes scanning into a patchy wilderness of sand and ocotillo. Nothing moved and there was no further sound.

It was hard to tell in the desert, but the shots had been close, not the flat statements of rifles but the sharper bark of revolvers.

Wishful for field glasses, but having none, Dupoix stood in the stirrups and raised his hat above his head, shading his eyes.

The gambler was by nature a far-seeing man, and he was sure he spotted the four Texans in the distance, riding due south.

He waited. The kids were young, but they'd probably run ahead of enough enemies to instinctively check their back trail.

A four-against-one gunfight he was sure to lose was the last thing Dupoix wanted.

The sun was midway between the shimmering horizon and its noon point in the sky, but its heat already hammered at Dupoix and seared through the thin stuff of his shirt. Sweat beaded his forehead and trickled down his back, and his gray horse had suddenly become reluctant to move.

He decided to call it quits and head back to Last Chance. Whatever the young guns were up to, it obviously was nothing to do with Abe Hacker or his plans. Probably the young men were hunting, shooting javelinas and jackrabbits with their Colts.

But then a flicker of white about half a mile ahead of him caught Dupoix's eye.

He stared into the distance and saw a dust devil perform its dervish dance before it spun itself into a column of sand and then collapsed onto the desert floor.

The devil had passed over something and caused that brief glimpse of white.

A scrap of paper? A dead bird? An animal?

Whatever it was, it was in the direction of the shots Dupoix had heard, and he decided it was worth investigating. He pushed the gray into a reluctant walk and rode forward.

When Dupoix got within a hundred yards, the white object became clearer. He rode closer and confirmed what his eyes had earlier told him.

A body law facedown on the sand, and a few yards away sprawled a second, smaller, its brown face turned to the burning sun it could no longer feel.

Dupoix swung out of the saddle and stepped to the still corpses.

Each had been shot several times, their cotton shirts glistening red with blood. The contents of the packs they'd carried on their backs had been scattered. A few miserable possessions, blankets, clean shirts, crusts of bread, and a small rosary with blue beads lay forlornly on the sand.

Both dead were Mexican peons.

Dupoix guessed that they were father and son. The adult was a man in his forties, the boy no older than twelve or thirteen.

Judging by the lack of boot tracks, the killers had shot their victims from horseback and then rode on. It had been a casual killing, murder for no apparent reason.

The young Texas guns were the culprits. Of that there was no doubt.

But why?

Dupoix asked himself that question, and the only answer he could come up with was the obvious one—the Mexicans had been murdered for the sheer joy of killing.

A gambler learns early to conceal his emotions, and Dupoix did so now, his face stiff and without expression. He looked around him . . . looking for what, he did not know.

Help, maybe. Some people passing by who'd shed a tear for the dead, bury them decent, and say the right prayers.

But there was no one.

Now the murderers were long gone, the desert seemed empty of life, breathless, as though being crushed to death by the massive bookends of the Sierra Madres to the east and west.

To the west, far, but closer than the aloof mountains, sprawled a maze of canyons, some shallow, others as deep and dark as the basements of hell.

Dupoix watched a dust cloud rise a couple of miles south of the canyon lands. At first he thought it might be a sandstorm, but the cloud didn't move on a broad front. Instead it was strung out, like a moving cattle herd.

Was a rancher bringing up a herd from Mexico? It seemed unlikely. No sane man would make a drive across hundreds of miles of scorched, waterless desert in the middle of summer.

Suddenly Dupoix felt too used up to even speculate, the savage heat of the sun getting to him.

The dust cloud was what it was, and no concern of his.

He poured water from his canteen into his open hand and let his horse drink. When the water was all but gone, he took the last couple of swallows, then swung into the saddle. The silver that decorated the horn and pommel were hot to the touch.

Dupoix took a last look at the dead father and son, their bodies already buzzing with fat, black flies.

Somehow he felt the dust cloud near the canyons and the two dead Mexicans were connected. But he was too worn out to make a connection.

He swung his horse north, back toward Last Chance.

He'd let Hank Cannan do the thinking.

CHAPTER SIXTEEN

Baptiste Dupoix was still an hour south of Last Chance when Mickey Pauleen killed another man.

It was said later that Jake Stutter had clearly stated his intentions when he drove a buckboard into town with a rough pine coffin in the back and a chalked sign that read:

> **RESERVED FER**
> **MICKY POLEEN**
> **There's a hell of**
> **shootin goin on**

It would be pleasant to record that Stutter sought out Pauleen to avenge the death of a friend or relative who'd died under the little gunman's Colts. But that was not the case.

A driven man, Stutter felt only the need to prove that he was faster on the draw than Mickey Pauleen.

That and nothing else.

It was Nora Anderson who told Pauleen that a man

was calling him out. She took great delight in bringing him the news.

"Saw him from the window of my room, Mickey," she said.

"Who the hell is he?" Pauleen said, sitting up in bed.

"I don't know," Nora said, drawing her robe closer so her large breasts stood out in relief. "Why don't you ask him?"

Spindle-legged in his long-handled underwear, Pauleen stepped to the window, drew back the curtain, and glanced outside. After a moment, he said, "Never seen him before in my life."

Pauleen turned from the window, stretched, yawned, and said to Nora, "I was up early this morning and need more sleep. Tell him, whoever he is, to come back in an hour or so." He grinned. "Then you come and join me in bed, Nora."

"Not a chance of that," the woman said. "But I'll convey your message."

"Don't say no chance until you make a trial of it," Pauleen said. "You'll be my woman one day real soon, so you might as well get used to me, huh?"

"I'll never be your woman, Mickey," Nora said, moving to the door. "Even the thought repulses me."

"But you will, depend on it," Pauleen said, his eyes ugly. "And you'll rue this day."

Nora stepped out of the hotel and into the street.

A few early morning shoppers, mostly matrons in fluttering, white cotton dresses, were on the boardwalks, shopping baskets over their arms, determined to buy their groceries now and escape the heat of the day.

Jake Stutter stood in the middle of the street.

Behind him was the buckboard, and a black horse, its head hanging, tied at the rear.

Nora was struck by the difference between the gunman and the soft, white bulk of Abe Hacker on one hand, and the diminutive stature of Mickey Pauleen on the other.

Stutter was thirty years old that summer. He was tall, very lean, his face browned by exposure to sun, snow, and wind. The blue eyes under the wide brim of his hat were carved into wrinkles at the corners as though he was a man who smiled readily or had stared at too many far horizons.

He wore a Remington low and handy on his right hip, and looked what he was . . . a professional gun for hire who could not abide the thought that somebody, somewhere, was faster than he.

Stutter's eyes flicked over Nora, lingered on her breasts for a moment, and then dismissed her.

"Pauleen, Mickey Pauleen!" he yelled, his eyes on the glass door of the hotel that still swung on its hinges after Nora's exit. "I'm calling you out fer a damned, back-shooting, Yankee liar."

Nora stepped closer to the gunman and said, smiling, "Begging your pardon, but Mr. Pauleen is still abed. He asks if you could come back in an hour or so."

Stutter's head turned in Nora's direction, slowly, menacingly, like the gun turret of an ironclad. Through bared teeth, he said, "He asks what?"

"Looks like there's something going on outside the Cattleman's Hotel," Roxie Miller said.

She'd been arranging Hank Cannan's pillows, but now stood at the window, hugging one to her body.

"If it involves Baptiste Dupoix I don't want to know," Cannan said. He felt sour that morning after a restless night.

"I don't think so," Roxie said. "That Nora Anderson woman is talking to a man in the street." She turned and smiled at the Ranger. "The feller looks like maybe's he's a lawman and he's got a pine coffin on a buckboard and a sign on it."

"What does the sign say?"

"I don't know. I can't read it from here."

"Roxie, help me get out of this damned bed," Cannan said.

The woman shook her head, hands on hips.

"No, Ranger Cannan. I have to cut your hair and trim your mustache, so you're staying right where you're at."

"Damn it, woman, is Baptiste Dupoix paying you to torture me like this?"

"Yes he is, and I need the money, so behave yourself."

"Well what's happening now?"

"I'll take a look," Roxie said.

Jake Stutter was two hundred pounds of slow burn.

"He wants me to come back in an hour?" he said.

Nora nodded, her smile sweet. "Yes, that's what Mr. Pauleen said. He had to get up quite early this morning on business, and now he needs an extry hour of slumber."

Stutter drew himself up to his full height and a strange shudder convulsed him. Eyes bulging, head cocked to one side, he roared, "Git him the hell out here!"

"As you wish," Nora said.

Her back stiff, she stepped into the hotel.

"See anything?" Cannan said.

"Yes. Nora went back inside, and the man standing in the street looks like he's mad enough to eat bees," Roxie said.

"What did she say to him?"

"I don't know. I can't hear anything from up here."

Roxie was about to step away from the window but suddenly stopped in midstride. "Wait a minute, the hotel door just opened again," she said.

Mickey Pauleen stepped onto the hotel porch. He wore only pants, boots, his undershirt, and a sour expression.

"Who the hell are you and what do you want?" he said, glaring at Stutter. "And why are you disturbing a man's sleep?"

"My name's Jake Stutter. Ever hear of me?"

Pauleen smiled. "I reckon I once heard somebody mention a two-bit piece of white trash by that name."

Stutter seemed to take the insult in stride. "I'd watch your tongue, Pauleen, since I'm the man who'll kill you this morning. Make me angry enough and you get it in the belly. Take you a long time to die." He thumbed over his shoulder. "The coffin is reserved for you."

Stutter sounded confident, but all the while an alarm bell clamored in his head.

Pauleen wasn't wearing his crossed gun belts.

He'd carelessly shoved a Colt into his waistband,

almost like an afterthought, as though Stutter didn't rate any higher.

The tall man tensed, braced for the draw.

Pauleen would make him realize his mistake soon enough.

"I think the stranger is going to draw down on Mickey Pauleen," Roxie said.

"Help me get up," Cannan said.

"You're not going down there," Roxie said.

"It would take me until nightfall to get down there," Cannan said. "Help me to the window."

Roxie thought about that and then crossed the floor to the bed.

Cannan swung his legs over the side and stood.

Immediately his head swam and the room cartwheeled around him.

"Hold on to me, Ranger," Roxie said.

Cannan was a tall man, who tipped the scale at two hundred and twenty pounds, but Roxie was a strong, capable woman, and she helped him stagger to the window.

"Grab the window frame and I'll get a chair," she said.

When Roxie returned Cannan sank gratefully into the chair and directed his attention to the street.

He was just in time.

Even a pang of self-doubt about his gun skills can slow a man on the draw and shoot. And Stutter knew that better than most because he'd killed men whose doubt indulged became doubt realized.

Pauleen had dismissed him as a no-account and undermined his confidence just a shade, but enough.

He had to prove him wrong.

Fast.

Stutter drew.

And a moment later wished he'd died quick.

Two bullets from Pauleen's .45 slammed into the big man's belly and he staggered, screaming, then joined his shadow in the dirt.

Mickey Pauleen stepped off the porch and held his gun high.

To the crowd that had gathered, gawping at Stutter who was dying hard, he said, "Stay back. I'll kill anyone, man or woman, who tries to help this trash. Let him lie there like a dog."

"Then you'd better kill me, Pauleen," Ed Gillman, the general store owner, said. He pushed through the crowd and took a knee beside Stutter, whose face was twisted into a mask of pain, suffering an agony that was beyond any man's ability to endure.

"Son, make your peace with God," Gillman said. "Your time is short."

Blood in his mouth, Stutter grabbed the front of Gillman's white apron in a scarlet fist and pleaded, "Help me."

"I'm afraid you're beyond help," Gillman said. "But I won't let you die in the street."

"Yes, you will," Pauleen said.

He pushed the muzzle of his gun into Gillman's temple, the triple click of the cocking hammer loud in the silence. "Touch that man again and I'll scatter your brains," he said.

* * *

The moment Gillman kneeled beside the dying man, Hank Cannan had seen enough.

He made an attempt to raise the window, but it was beyond his strength. "Help me, Roxie," he said.

The woman took in at a glance what was happening in the street, and she helped the Ranger struggle the window open.

Cannan didn't hesitate.

He stuck his head out the window and yelled, "Pauleen, shoot that man and I'll see you hang!"

The little gunman hesitated, his snake eyes darting as he tried to pin down the source of the voice.

Then he spotted Cannan and grinned.

Pauleen cupped a hand to his mouth and shouted, "Ranger!" Then, before Cannan could answer, "You go to hell!"

"Leave Gillman be, damn you," Cannan said.

"Or what, sick man? You'll come down here and arrest me?"

Pauleen pushed the muzzle of his gun harder into Gillman's temple. "Git up, you," he said, his words venomous.

The storekeeper ignored Pauleen, his attention fixed on Jake Stutter. The man's agonized death shrieks were terrible to hear.

It's a natural fact that no matter how game he is, in the end a gut-shot man screams like a woman in the midst of a difficult labor.

"Mickey! No!"

Two words, as loud and authoritative as rifle shots.

Abe Hacker stood on the hotel porch, dressed in broadcloth and brocade, a massive gold watch chain across his belly.

Then before anyone could speak, Hacker said, "What happened here?"

"This trash called me out," Pauleen said.

"Most unfortunate," Hacker said. "How is he?"

"Dying like a gutted hog," Ed Gillman said.

A smart man, Hacker had sized up the situation immediately.

"Then let Mr. Gillman succor the dying, Mickey," he said. His little eyes telegraphed a warning to Pauleen. For the benefit of Gillman and the crowd of onlookers, he said, "The Ranger is right. We need no more unpleasantness this morning."

Accusation edged Gillman's voice. "Pauleen is your boy, Hacker," he said.

"Yes, and he was called out. Mr. Pauleen was only defending himself from a dangerous desperado. Look at the coffin on the wagon and read the sign. Doesn't that tell you all you need to know?"

Stutter's bellow of pain and the sudden, tense bow he made of his back attracted everyone's attention.

After a moment that seemed to last forever, the people of Last Chance heard the gunman sigh and death rattle in his throat.

Gillman closed Stutter's eyes and stood. He stared hard at Hacker.

"Why are you still in our town?" he said.

For a moment Hacker seemed taken aback by the question. But he recovered and smiled, his little eyes vanishing under folds of fat. "I'm a businessman, just as you are, Mr. Gillman," Hacker said. "I came to find gold, but discovered there was none." Hacker gave a dramatic little sigh. "Well, in business we learn to take our disappointments just as well as we take our triumphs, with a certain amount of humility and grace."

"Then why are you still here?" Gillman said, clinging to that question like a terrier to a rat.

The crowd had grown larger.

"Ah, that is easy to explain," Hacker said. "It was my intention to return to Washington in haste"—then a smooth lie—"especially since I was engaged to deliver a series of business lectures at Georgetown University."

Hacker had expected to impress the onlookers with that last, but he was met with a thin silence and stony expressions. The dead man on the ground made the atmosphere even more funereal.

He forged ahead.

"Then someone told me—was it Mayor Curtis? Yes, I believe it was—that the town planned to throw a crackerjack Independence Day party and that my good self and my associates were invited."

Hacker beamed, throwing his arms wide as though to embrace the crowd.

"How could I leave after that? Yes, Washington, D.C., throws one hell of a shindig, and I knew that I'd disappoint many students, but I could not refuse such a kind invitation."

He turned his attention to Pauleen. "Is that not so, Mr. Pauleen?"

"You got it, boss," the little gunman said, grinning.

Hacker saw Gillman open his mouth to speak, but he cut him off. "And all the expenses of our great patriotic celebration are on me," he said. Then, his voice rising, "Abe Hacker will pay every last penny."

A few in the crowd smiled and one man let out with a halfhearted "Hurrah," but Hacker's generous pledge was met mostly with a stony silence.

Pauleen had enough of Hacker's niceties, hollow as they were.

He stepped over Stutter's body, walked to the wagon, and hauled off the coffin.

He threw it to the ground, pointed at Stutter and said, "One of you rubes get the undertaker and tell him to bury that sorry piece of trash in the coffin he intended for me."

"Pauleen, you have no respect for the living, but have some for the dead," Gillman said, appalled.

"Shut your trap, storekeeper," the gunman said.

And a moment later Pauleen revealed his withering scorn for Last Chance, its citizens, and the rule of law.

He made as if to walk back to the hotel, but stopped in midstride, swung around, and thumbed off fast shots at the window where Hank Cannan sat watching the proceedings.

"Ranger!" Roxie Miller yelled as three bullets crashed through the window and set showers of shattered glass flying everywhere.

Too stunned to move, Cannan sat where he was.

But Roxie reacted quickly.

She threw herself on Cannan and drove him to the floor.

"Stay down!" she said.

But there were no more bullets.

"What the hell?" Cannan said. "And you're squashing me, Roxie."

The woman smiled. "Most men are glad to pay me for that."

"Not this one," Cannan said. "I'm a happily married man."

"So are most of the men who pay me," Roxie said.

She pushed on Cannan, eliciting outraged groans

from the Ranger, and scrambled to her feet, in the process revealing a considerable amount of shapely knee and thigh.

"Help me get up," Cannan said.

After a considerable struggle, Roxie manhandled the Ranger into bed.

"Who the hell did that?" Cannan said.

"Mickey Pauleen took pots at you."

"Why?"

"I guess because he doesn't like you, Mr. Cannan."

"Damn, was he trying to kill me?"

"No, just scare you. If Mickey wanted to kill you, he wouldn't have missed."

"He's a son-of-a-bitch and low down."

"Yup, he's all of that."

Cannan breathed hard, hurting all over.

Fragments of glass covered the floor under the window, and a few shards had reached his bed.

Roxie bent over and picked a piece of glass from Cannan's mustache. "There's nothing you can do about Pauleen," she said.

"I could arrest him for the attempted murder of a law officer."

"Yes, you could, if you had the strength to get out of bed."

"Roxie, I've got to get well again. You have to help me."

"What can I do that the doctor can't do better?"

Defeated, Cannan laid his head on the pillow. "I don't know," he said. Then, "How close is Independence Day?"

"A couple of weeks."

"I've got to be on my feet by then."

"What's the big hurry? You can watch the celebrations from the window," Roxie said.

"And get shot at again?"

"I'll talk to Abe Hacker. He stinks like a hog and treats his woman like dirt, but he can keep Mickey Pauleen in line."

Cannan shook his head. "No, let him be. I think he's the one who'll bring the locusts."

Roxie look puzzled, then concerned. "Ranger, did you get shot in the head again? Let me look."

"I didn't get shot in the head," Cannan said.

"No mortal man can bring the locusts," Roxie said. "They're a force of nature. Some say an evil force of nature."

"And so is Abe Hacker," Cannan said.

CHAPTER SEVENTEEN

By his count, Sancho Perez had rounded up close to seven hundred Mexican peons—men, women and children—and given himself a major headache.

His original plan was to stash the people in the canyons under guard; but without water, and a lot of it, he feared he'd lose most, if not all of them, before July fourth.

After a meeting with his captains, the consensus among them was that the peons must be driven east, toward Perez's hacienda.

"They're dying of thirst even as we round them up, *patrón*," one bandito said. "If we can't water them, they'll all die on us."

The idea of hundreds of thirsty, hungry, and dirty peons descending on his hacienda did not appeal to Perez, but he saw no way out.

They were still coming north in droves, fleeing the worst drought in memory, and the roundup was going well.

To throw it all away because of a lack of water was unthinkable.

Five miles south of the hacienda lay a deep limestone rock pool where the Apaches had watered their horses during spring raids into Mexico. Fed by an underground stream, the pool now met the irrigation needs of the hacienda, and Perez had four large water wagons built to ensure a constant supply.

Alarmed that he was already losing too many peons to thirst, he sent riders on fast horses to fill the water wagons and bring them back to meet his column.

Perez's prompt action would save lives, but as his men rounded up more and more people the water problem would become even more acute.

He had five wagons, but needed at least three times that number.

"So you see how it is with me," Perez said to the three young Texans who'd caught up to him on the trail. "The peons are fleeing the drought, so rounding them up is easy. But keeping them fed and watered is not."

"How many head have you lost?" Matt Husted said, his blue eyes half-amused.

"Maybe a hundred and fifty," Perez said. "But since the wagons arrived, only three or four. God is good."

Perez, his sunbonnet hanging down his back by its ribbon, sat with Husted under a hastily rigged canvas cover. A bottle of mescal stood between them.

The other two youngsters prowled the darkness looking for willing señoritas among the exhausted, hungry peons.

"Pauleen sent us to give you any help we can," Husted said.

Perez nodded and smiled. "He is ver' good man, is Mickey. Fast on the draw."

"Yeah, that's what they say," Husted said. "But he don't come close to me."

"It is all right to talk big, señor, when Mickey is not here, huh?"

The young man's posture stiffened. "Hell, I've told him to his face that I'm faster than he is."

"And yet you are still alive. Mickey is a patient man." Without waiting for Husted to speak, Perez said, "Why did you shoot the peons, father and son?"

"I already told you."

"Tell me again."

"They refused to join us." Husted took a swig from the bottle. He wiped his mouth with the back of his hand and said, "We couldn't let them get cross the river and warn Last Chance about what's coming."

"Did they even know?" Perez said. His eyes glittered.

"If they did or didn't, I couldn't take a chance."

"They were Mexicans."

"Hell, I know they were Mexicans. This is Mexico, remember?"

"You shouldn't have killed the peons, father and son. It was not a good thing."

"What's it to you, Perez. You've killed . . . what? . . . a hundred and fifty in the past week."

"I did not kill them. They died of thirst. And they were almost dead when they got here."

Husted felt the warm embrace of the mescal and how it oiled the tongue. "Killing is killing, Perez," he said. "Who cares about a couple of greasy Mexicans anyhow?"

"I do," Perez said. "Maybe because I'm a greasy Mexican."

The young Texan saw something in Perez's fixed stare he didn't like. "Back off, Perez," he said. "What's done is done."

"I said something wrong?"

"Yeah, you said something wrong, all right. You said killing a Mex is some kind of crime. It ain't. Everybody knows that."

"Oh, but it is, señor," Perez said, smiling. "When a Mex is killed by a gringo, it's a crime, a crime against the Mexican people, a crime against me."

Husted's anger flared. "You go to hell, Perez."

"No, you will go to hell, *mi amigo*." The bandit drew and fired.

His reactions slowed by alcohol, Matt Husted didn't even reach for his gun.

The bullet took him square in the chest, ripped through his heart, and exited his back.

The youngster toppled onto his side, his open, dead eyes staring into a dark eternity.

Perez stared at the body for a moment, then wailed, "Aiii, what have I done?" He rose to his feet, yanked at his long hair, pushing it above his head, and picked up the bottle.

Holding it high he screamed, "*Madre de Dios*, it was the mescal made me do it. Forgive poor Sancho!"

Perez's men had tumbled out of their blankets and now ran to their penitent *patrón*.

"I killed the gringo," he told them. "Aaah . . . I killed

him with this bloody hand I hold before you and I am surely damned forever."

The dozen bandits gathered around Perez but said nothing. They looked stunned, both by the killing and their *patrón*'s hysterical behavior.

"Manuel," Perez yelled, "shoot this wicked hand off my wrist that I can atone for my great sin!"

The man called Manuel, a scar-faced brute with carbon black eyes, shrugged and drew his gun.

"No, wait!" Perez said, thoroughly alarmed. "I think it's better I pray for this man's immortal soul and ask for God's forgiveness. I need two hands for that."

He waited until Manuel holstered his revolver, then joined hands, tilted his face to the sky, and closed his eyes.

Perez's lips moved in prayer for a full minute, then, hands still together, he opened one eye and said, "Manuel, where are the other two gringos?"

"I think with señoritas, *patrón.*"

"Then find them and kill them."

Manuel was puzzled. "The señoritas?"

"No, fool. The gringos."

Perez closed his eye.

"Sancho will include them in his holy prayers," he said.

CHAPTER EIGHTEEN

The livery stable owner, a one-legged former sailor by the name of Ephraim Slough, told Baptiste Dupoix what had happened in his absence.

The gambler did what he could to slap trail dust off his shirt and pants, then said, "Did Pauleen really try to kill the Ranger?"

"Some say he did, some say he didn't."

"What do you say?"

"I say if Mickey had tried, the Ranger would be dead right now, lay to that."

"It's how I figured it," Dupoix said.

"I'm pretty sure he planned to scatter Ed Gillman's brains, though. Ol' Ed's always had more sand than sense."

"And Hacker stopped him. Strange, that."

"Nothing strange about it, gambling man. If Mickey had killed Ed, the town would have strung him up and Hacker alongside o' him," Slough said. "Feelings are already running high over the killing of Marshal Dixon."

"Never rated Last Chance as a lynching town," Dupoix said.

"It isn't. And it isn't because the folks around here are a peaceful bunch and it takes a long time afore they get themselves worked up to a thing." Slough gave Dupoix a sidelong look and then a wink. "A thing to know," he said.

The gambler smiled. "I'll sure keep it in mind."

The door to Hank Cannan's room was wide open, but Dupoix was a careful man and he stopped in the hallway and said, "Ranger, it's Baptiste Dupoix. I'm coming in."

"Come right ahead," Cannan said. "Seems like everybody else in town is doing it."

Roxie was gone, but the Ranger sat up in bed, looking irritated, while several silent workmen replaced the shattered windowpanes and plastered over the bullet holes in the wall.

"As always, Dupoix, this is an unpleasant surprise," Cannan said.

"You got a burr under your tail, Ranger?" the gambler grinned.

"Yeah, because of that woman you're paying to torment me."

Cannan pointed to his own face. "Look at me, damn it."

Dupoix stepped back and rubbed his chin, like an art lover judging a painting. After a few moments he said, "I don't see any difference. You still look like a big ol' mad-as-hell walrus."

"The mustache, Dupoix! Don't you have eyes?"

"What's wrong with it? Well, I know there's a lot wrong with it, but what do you mean specifically?"

"Roxie cut it too short! Damn it, man, I look like I've been skun!"

"Becomes you, though," Dupoix said. "Makes you look distinguished." He nodded to the window. "I heard about that."

"Mickey Pauleen's idea of a joke," Cannan said.

"You don't think he tried to kill you?" Dupoix said.

"No, I don't. Damned lowlife made me scamper, though." Cannan glared at Dupoix. "If he had killed me what would you have done about it?"

"Given him the sharp edge of my tongue, I fancy."

"I knew I should've hung you when I had the chance," Cannan said. He picked up the makings from the bedside table and began to build a cigarette. "Notice anything about the three workmen?" Cannan said.

Dupoix shook his head. "No, can't say as I do."

"They all look alike," Cannan said.

"Must be brothers," Dupoix said.

"And they don't talk. They haven't said a word to me."

"Dumb brothers," Dupoix said.

But the mystery was solved a few moments later when the workmen gathered up their tools and lined up at the bottom of Cannan's bed.

The oldest, a medium-sized man with high cheekbones and close-cropped black hair, waved to the repaired window and wall, grinned, then he and his brothers bowed.

"Yeah, thanks boys," Cannan said.

When the men straightened up, the oldest puffed

up a little and pointed to his chest. "Polska," he said proudly. He pointed to the others in turn. "Polska, Polska."

Cannan was confused, but he managed a smile and, "And I'm right pleased to meet you Polska boys."

Then all three men reached into their top pockets of their ragged coats and flipped out identical medals that had been pinned inside.

The crosses now hanging on their chests were made of gold with white enamel and were obviously military awards.

The workmen clicked their heels, saluted Cannan with great precision, and filed out the door, one by one.

For a moment the Ranger was stunned into silence.

Then he said, "There are some mighty strange folks in Last Chance."

Dupoix laughed. "They're Polish, old soldiers by the cut of their jib, and they saluted you because you're a Texas Ranger."

"They think I'm some kind of a soldier?" Cannan said.

"I think so. Officer, even. You should be honored."

"They look tough as nails," Cannan said.

"I reckon they'll do in any kind of a fight," Dupoix said.

As though really looking at the gambler's appearance for the first time, Cannan said, "You look used up, Dupoix."

"Been out riding."

"Where?"

"Into Old Mexico."

"Hell of a place to ride."

"I followed Hacker's boys, three young Texas guns looking for trouble."

"Why? I mean, why did you follow them?"

Dupoix shrugged. "I'd nothing better to do."

"That, I very much doubt. Roxie would have entertained you, I'm sure."

The gambler ignored that and said, "Found two dead men in the desert just south of the river—well, a man and a boy."

"How did they die?" Cannan said.

"Murdered. Shot to death."

"And you believe Hacker's men did it."

"Yes, I do."

"Motive?"

"Just for the fun of it, I guess." Dupoix hefted the bottle of Old Crow. "I'll have to get you another one of these," he said.

"You drank most of it," Cannan said.

The gambler poured himself a drink. "Saw something else," he said. "A dust cloud to the west near the canyon country."

Cannan took the cigarette from between his lips.

"Don't tell me it was locusts and not a dust cloud."

"I won't tell you that, Cannan. I don't know what it was."

"A cattle herd, maybe?"

"Coming up from the dry country? I guess it's possible."

"But you don't think so."

"Now I've been studying on it, a herd would aim straight for the river. I have the feeling that whatever raised the cloud had decided to turn east."

"East to where?" Cannan said.

"The only place east of anywhere is Last Chance."

Cannan bowed his head in thought for a moment, then said, "An invading Mexican army?"

Dupoix stared at him with a "you've got to be kidding me" expression.

"Yeah, I guess not," Cannan said. "Then what?"

"Suppose it's people?"

"People!"

"Hundreds, maybe tens of hundreds of people on the move, fleeing Mexico's once-in-a-lifetime drought."

Cannan weighed that and said, "Like . . ."

"A plague of locusts," Dupoix said.

"Headed for here."

"Last Chance is the Garden of Eden, Ranger. So why not?"

"The irrigated land around here can't sustain that many," Cannan said.

Dupoix smiled. "Locust swarms arrive hungry. They devour everything in sight, devastate cropland and orchards, then move on. Behind them they leave wastelands and famine."

"How the hell do you know so much about locusts, Dupoix?" Cannan said, suddenly angry with the gambler for no real reason.

"When I was a boy, my grandmother, the swamp witch I told you about, read to me from the Bible every night before bed," Dupoix said. "She knows a lot about many things, and locusts is one of them."

"Damn it all, Dupoix, what can I do?" Cannan said.

"Nothing much until you can pull on your boots and walk."

"If thousands of people looking for land are about ready to cross the Rio Grande, I don't have that kind of time."

"No, you don't, Cannan."

Dupoix drained his glass and set it on the table.

"If it's any help, I think someone is looking to gain from all this."

"Hacker?"

"It could be. But I can't fathom his motive."

Cannan shook his head. "I can't, either."

Dupoix was not the kind to touch another man, but he did now.

He put his hand on Cannan's shoulder.

"I'll promise you this, Ranger, I won't let you be murdered in bed, and I won't stand by and watch my country invaded by anyone."

"So what will you do?"

"Find out if Hacker is involved, and if he is, why."

"I'll give you a week," Cannan said. "If you don't find out anything by then, I'm getting out of this bed and arresting Hacker, Pauleen, and the rest of the whole sorry bunch."

"On what charge?"

"Pauleen on the attempted murder of a peace officer. Hacker . . . well, I'll think of something."

Dupoix shook his head. "I won't let you do that, Cannan," he said. "Even after a week you'll still barely be able to walk. Just say the word 'arrest' to Mickey Pauleen, and he'll gun you right where you stand."

"Hell, I'm not that much of a bargain," Cannan said.

"Maybe so, Ranger, but you're not in Mickey's class. Not even close."

"And you?"

"On my best day I can't shade him. I've never shot a man in the back before, but in Pauleen's case I might give it serious thought."

Dupoix took his hand from Cannan's shoulder. "What's your wife's name?" he said.

"Jane," Cannan said.

"I've always been partial to that name. I hope you two are reunited soon. A woman should have her husband close by."

The gambler smiled and walked to the door.

"Dupoix," Cannan called after him. "Thanks." He hesitated, choosing his words carefully. "I mean, thanks for your concern."

Dupoix stood at the door and said, "I'll chide Roxie about the mess she made of your mustache, Ranger."

He closed the door, opened it again and stuck his head inside.

"I miss the walrus look," he said.

CHAPTER NINETEEN

One of the novels Mickey Pauleen had been allowed to read as a boy, because of Mr. Herman Melville's sound spiritual values, was *Moby-Dick*.

It was understandable therefore that the man lying in bed reminded Pauleen of a great white whale beached on a slimy shore, smelling rank.

"Damn, boss, you ever think of opening a window?" he said.

"No," Abe Hacker said. "Fresh air is bad for the heart. It carries too many ill humors."

Nora sat in a chair by the bed, polishing her fingernails. She spread out her hand and took a critical glance. The nails looked like scarlet talons.

"Nearly a week has passed, and I've heard nothing from the three riders you sent out," Hacker said. "I don't know what's happening with Sancho Perez."

"And what's happening here in Last Chance?" Pauleen said.

Hacker scowled. "I don't understand what you're talking about, Mickey."

"Meetings. The rubes are holding citizen meetings."

"About what?"

"I wasn't invited, but I'm willing to bet they plan to run you out of town."

"You shouldn't have threatened the storekeeper, Mickey."

"Threatened? I would have blown his damned fool head off if you hadn't butted in."

"Another killing would've been bad for business, Mickey, bad for business. We need to keep the rubes in their place until Independence Day."

"Then they'll get their comeuppance, huh?"

"Indeed they will."

"Tell me why, boss?"

Hacker looked puzzled and said nothing.

"I mean, why do you want this dunghill so badly?"

Hacker's smile was smug, unpleasant. "You know why. All right, the gold thing didn't pan out, but there's still money to be made here. All I'm doing is adding another link to my watch chain and keeping it for someone who will soon be very dear to me."

Pauleen opened his mouth to speak, but Hacker silenced him with a raised hand.

"Mickey, when I see something I want, I take it. One of the ranches I own is in Montana, the Claymore it's called. I saw that range, wanted it, took it and laid out a score of lively lads dead on the ground in the process."

Hacker selected a cigar from the cedar humidor beside him.

"Do you know why I wanted the Claymore so badly, and now this place and so many others just like it?"

Pauleen gave a slight shake of his head.

Hacker spoke behind a blue veil of smoke. "For my son!"

Mickey Pauleen was surprised, but Nora's face registered shock and disbelief.

"I didn't know you had a son, Abe," she said.

Hacker smiled. "I don't, not yet. But I intend to sire one very soon."

Nora stood and stepped to the bed, her face pale.

"Abe . . . honey . . . I don't think I can—"

"Not you!" Hacker snapped. "My son's mother will be a well-bred young lady of good family. Not a painted trollop."

Speechless, Nora returned to her chair, an agonized look on her face after Hacker's words had stabbed her heart like a knife. She'd knocked over the red bottle of nail oil as she sat, but ignored it as it stained the floor like blood.

Hacker, a sadist with deep contempt for humanity in general and women in particular, glared at Nora. "Why did you think for one moment that I'd let you bear my son?" he said.

The woman said nothing.

"Answer me!" Hacker yelled.

Pauleen had enough Southern breeding in him to say, "Boss, leave her alone."

"You stay out of it, Mickey," Hacker said, still staring hard at Nora. "Answer me," he said again.

In a small, defeated voice, Nora said, "Abe, I just thought . . ."

"You thought! You're too damn stupid to think." Hacker's cigar glowed in the dim light of the hotel room. "Before I left Washington, I made arrangements to wed into the Harbridge family," he said. "Senator Harbridge pledged me his daughter Molly in holy matrimony. She's just a slip of a lass of fifteen, but she'll provide me with a fine son."

Nora reached deep and found her backbone. She sat straight and stiff in the chair.

"I see," she said.

"Yes, a slip of a lass," Hacker said. "Not a dried-up old whore like you."

Nora rose to her feet, her face like stone.

Like a ragged cloak, she pulled what was left of her dignity around her and with considerable poise left the room.

After the woman left, Hacker dismissed her from his mind and said, "Get back across the river, Mickey. Find out what's happening with Sancho Perez. Take Hugh Gray with you and tell Sancho time is running short."

"Boss, the only gun you'll leave to guard you here will be Dupoix," Pauleen said.

"He can handle it," Hacker said.

"He's a gambler," Pauleen said.

"So what if he is?"

"He's still to show his hand."

"Dupoix draws wages from me, Mickey. He'll do what I tell him and play the cards I deal him."

"I hope you're right."

"I know I'm right. Now round up Shotgun Hugh, then hightail it across the river." Hacker waved his cigar, smearing smoke across the fetid air of the bedroom. "You'll be my eyes and my mouth, Mickey. Do what you have to do, say what you have to say, but make sure the locusts cross the Rio Grande on Independence Day."

Pauleen hesitated, turning the brim of his hat in his fingers. "Boss, that talk of getting hitched, was you joshing me?"

"Hell no. I told you, I want a son, an heir to my fortune."

Pauleen grinned. "And she's fifteen, huh?"

"Yeah, a sweet little thing."

"Can I claim Nora when I get back?"

Hacker thought about that, then said, "Sure, why not? Take her, Mickey. She's yours. Nora is starting to bore the hell out of me."

CHAPTER TWENTY

Ranger Hank Cannan swung his legs off the bed and sat for a few moments, mustering the strength and will to stand.

Finally he rose to his feet, then clutched the brass headboard as the room cartwheeled around him.

When the world steadied itself he turned and put his left foot in front of the other. Then the right. He stopped and bit his lip to stop from crying out. His half-healed wounds protested, bombarded him with pain, and beads of sweat popped out on his forehead.

Cannan was as game as they come, but this was impossible.

God, he was weak . . . feeble as a day-old kittlin. He took a tottering step. Then another. Like a ninety-year-old man walking across seaweed-covered rocks, Cannan made it to the room's far wall. For a full minute he laid his cheek against the flowered wallpaper, saliva dripping from his gasping mouth.

He turned and stared hopelessly at the wall opposite.

God help me, it's a hundred miles away . . .

Cannan took a step. He managed a second, unsteady as a drunk.

Pain took its toll of him and so did muscles atrophied from weeks in bed, but, drawing deep, he fought back and kept on going.

His long nightgown flapping around his bare ankles, Cannan reached the wall.

He rested, let the blading pains subside, and turned, his long, sad face set and grim.

Now he had it to do all over again.

Cannan had completed twenty trips across the floor and was embarking on his twenty-first when the door swung open and Roxie entered, carrying a basket covered with a blue-checkered cloth.

"Lunch—" she said. "Time . . ." then, "Ranger Cannan, what are you doing out of bed?"

Cannan stopped, glad of the rest. "Learning to walk again," he said.

Roxie, tall, beautiful, but as stern as a matron in a lunatic asylum, laid down the basket and said, "Get into bed and eat your lunch. And do it now!"

"No!" Cannan said, aware that he sounded like a defiant little boy. "I'm on my feet and, by God, I'm going to stay on my feet."

"All right, let me see you walk," Roxie said.

Cannan did his best impression of the wobbly ninety-year-old.

"Are you dead set on doing this?" the woman said.

"Hell, yeah," Cannan said.

"Then hold on to me. We'll do it together."

"But I need to walk by myself," Cannan said.

"Your legs will walk by themselves. All I'll do is help keep your balance."

Thus began an ordeal that Cannan would always remember as the greatest trial of his life.

Midway through, as pain and exhaustion racked him, the Ranger faltered, but Roxie encouraged him.

"One step at a time, Ranger," she said. "Think only of your next step."

Roxie smiled at him and tried a distraction strategy.

"Were you always a Texas Ranger?" she said.

Cannan shook his head.

"Well," Roxie said, "what did you do before you got religion?"

Pain showing in his eyes and the slickness of his sweat-stained face, Cannan made the effort to talk. But he was breathing hard.

"I worked as a store clerk in my younger years . . . then got a job as a shotgun guard for the Butterfield stage . . ."

"Keep walking and talking, Ranger, you're doing real good," Roxie said.

Cannan's sweat-soaked nightgown clung to him like a second skin.

"I . . . later . . . I was a town sheriff . . . then . . . then . . ." He groaned, his head spinning, the pain in his legs like biting terriers. "I . . . was a clerk again . . . in a mercantile. After a year of that, I joined the Rangers."

Roxie smiled at him but said nothing.

"All that was more interesting than it sounds," Cannan said.

"I'm sure it was," Roxie said.

They reached the wall behind the bed and she said, "Had enough now?"

"No, not yet," Cannan said.

They turned and began to walk again.

The Ranger managed a tight smile. "Tried to rob me a train one time in my younger days," he said.

"Well, that sounds exciting," Roxie said.

"I . . . me . . . I tried to stop the locomotive, but it rings its bell and blows past me. I heard the engineer laugh."

"Oh, I'm so sorry," Roxie said. "That wasn't a good start."

"Trouble was . . ." Cannan swayed a little and the woman steadied him. "Trouble was, the train was carrying a hunting party of Russians. Grand Duke somebody or other, and his entire entourage . . ."

"I've never met a Russian," Roxie said.

"Until then neither had I," Cannan said. "But next thing I know . . . God this hurts . . . next thing I know it seems like everybody in Russia is hanging out car windows taking pots at me with hunting rifles."

"That wasn't very nice," Roxie said, frowning.

"Well, them Russian fellers figured me for a gen-u-ine Wild West desperado . . . wanted my head to hang on the Duke's trophy wall, I guess."

"Poor Ranger Cannan. Were you hurt?" Roxie said.

"No, not hurt. But I lost a fifty-dollar hoss and the stock of a brand-new Winchester."

"That settles it," Roxie said, frowning again. "If a Russian gentleman ever calls on me to entertain him, I'll send him packing with a flea in his ear."

"After that experience, I never tried to rob a train again," Cannan said.

"And no wonder. Some people are just so inconsiderate," Roxie said. "Especially foreign royalty."

"I think we'd better stop for today, Roxie," Cannan said, breathing hard. "I'm all used up."

"Then stand right there," the woman said. Roxie

took a fresh nightgown from the dresser and a pair of white towels from the brass rail beside the washbasin. "Hands up, then bend forward."

"Why?" Cannan said.

"You're not going to bed in that sweaty nightgown."

"But I'll be naked."

"And I haven't seen a naked man before? Now be a good boy and do as you're told."

Cannan was too worn out to argue.

Roxie pulled off the nightgown over Cannan's head, dropped it on the floor, then used a wet towel to wash his sweaty body and dried him with the other.

After the woman helped him into bed, Cannan said, "How long did we walk?"

Roxie thought for a while, calculating, then said, "Oh, at least twenty minutes."

"Twenty minutes!" Cannan said. "I thought it was an hour, or maybe two."

Roxie smiled. "It felt that way to you, Ranger, huh?"

"Yes it did, and I've got to do it all over again tomorrow." He looked into Roxie's face and saw no impending comment there. "I'll be on my feet and out on the street by Independence Day," Cannan said.

He'd expected the woman to smile and shrug off his promise as wishful thinking. But Roxie surprised him.

Her face troubled, she said, "You know, maybe it's because of my Irish mother that I see and feel things . . . events that haven't happened yet, but will happen, as surely as rain follows thunderclouds."

"What kind of events?" Cannan said.

"I don't see as clearly as my mother did, but I believe it's the plague."

"A plague on the land, you mean," Cannan said.

"Yes, and many will die from it," Roxie said.

CHAPTER TWENTY-ONE

Shotgun Hugh Gray was a morose man, a former prizefighter whose grotesquely battered face showed the scar of every bare-knuckled punch he'd ever taken.

Gray quit the ring in 1885, after he took a terrible beating from the great Jack Kilrain, fighting under brutal London bare-knuckle rules before they were banned in the United States.

Too many blows to the head had left Gray mentally unbalanced.

He was not a revolver fighter like Mickey Pauleen, but a sadistic killer for hire who murdered with neither mercy nor remorse.

Silent, grim, his head like a block of rough-hewn granite, Gray was not a convivial traveling companion, and he and Pauleen had not uttered a word to each other since they'd left Last Chance.

After several hours, Pauleen drew rein at the top of a shallow ridge that looked like a petrified sand dune chiseled out of the desert floor. Below him, raked by the relentless sun, stretched a flat expanse of thorn scrub and cactus, cut through by a wide trail made by the passage of many feet. Without a word, Pauleen swung out of the saddle and inspected the tracks, including deep ruts made by heavy wagons and the hoofprints of outriders.

He returned to the ridge, took a swig from his canteen, and wiped his mouth with the back of his hand. "Tracks are headed east," he said.

Gray only grunted in reply.

Pauleen sat in silence for a few moments, thinking.

"Perez is herding the Mexicans in the direction of his hacienda," he said finally.

Gray looked at him with eyes the color of a storm cloud. "He needs to water his stock," he said.

Pauleen considered that, remembering the well-irrigated grounds that surrounded the bandit chief's lair. He nodded. "I reckon you're right. He'd lose too many head in the dry canyons."

"He must have a water source close by," Gray said.

"Hugh, you're smarter than you look," Pauleen said, urging his horse into motion.

Gray said nothing. His damaged brain ground slowly, like a millstone within a millstone, and he was thinking of señoras and señoritas.

Pleasant enough thoughts . . . that would soon thrust him into a living hell.

After thirty minutes the tracks swung south, away from the hacienda, and Pauleen followed them.

He fancied the Children of Israel must have left a similar tramped road when they crossed the desert in search of the Promised Land.

But the land the peons needed to enter was to the north, across the Rio Grande.

The thought made Pauleen frown. They were headed in the wrong direction.

A single rider trotted out of the hacienda gate and Pauleen and Gray drew rein and let the man get closer.

"*Buenos días, señores,*" the bandit said.

"Buenos días," Pauleen said. "Where is Sancho?"

"Ah, he is at the spring to the south, *señor,*" the bandit said. "Just follow the tracks."

"How many people?" Pauleen said.

"A great many, señor." The bandit waved a hand. "As many as the stars in the sky, I think."

"You see anything of three young white men riding together?" Pauleen thought for a moment, then said, "Pistoleros?"

The Mexican shook his head. His skin was very dark and pocked. "No. I have not seen such men."

Pauleen touched his hat brim. "Obliged," he said.

He kneed his horse forward, but Gray lingered. "Women at the spring?" he said to the bandit.

"*Sí,* many women, señor."

"Pretty?"

The Mexican shrugged. "Some pretty. Some not."

Gray nodded and followed Pauleen.

Behind him the bandit gazed at Gray as he left and nodded to himself.

That one will bear watching.

The area around the limestone bluff was crowded with people, like an encampment of nomads who'd wandered into the desert and lost their way. Pauleen estimated they were a thousand in number and maybe more, and farther to the south a dust cloud lifted, signaling more arrivals.

A dozen of Perez's men used their rifle butts to push back the frantic crush of humanity crowding close to the natural water tank.

But the aquifer that fed the spring lay deep underground, and the flow was weak.

As Sancho Perez knew, it took an entire day to fill a water wagon, and the level in the limestone tank was half what it was when the peons first arrived. He ran around like an obese, cursing Moses in a sunbonnet, attempting to shove people into some semblance of a line while his men doled out water one small clay cup at a time.

But most did not even get that much as pushing from behind jostled the cups from the avid mouths of drinkers, and half the precious water spilled onto the sand.

Maddened by thirst, hundreds of people rushed for the tank, and Perez had to flee to avoid the wild stampede. The noise from the crowd rose to a harsh, whining growl . . . a primitive cry of fear and despair.

The riflemen guarding the water were swept aside and frenzied men jumped into the tank, more and more of them, until the displaced liquid cascaded wastefully over the side.

Ignoring the distraught pleas of their wives and children, men drank deep, fighting one another for space, cursing and punching, and now glittered the honed iron of drawn blades.

Mickey Pauleen had seen enough.

His face empty, he slid the .44-40 Winchester from the boot under his knee. Pauleen threw the rifle to his shoulder, sighted on the biggest man struggling in the tank, and fired.

He didn't wait to see the Mexican go down.

He shifted his aim to another man, fired. Then again . . . aim, fire!

The blood of the three dead peons slid across the surface like scarlet fingers . . . then slowly stained the water red.

Appalled, the crowd drew back, cringing in the face of death.

"Sancho!" Pauleen yelled. "Don't just stand there wringing your hands. Order them to sit and then water them one at a time."

Perez stared at the man on the horse, distant enough that he wavered in the heat haze.

Pauleen held the Winchester upright, the butt on his right thigh. Outlined by dazzling sunlight, he looked like the wrath of God.

"Damn you, do it!" the little gunman roared. Pauleen pushed his horse forward, Hugh Gray, shotgun in hand, riding close behind him.

Perez shook himself and finally responded.

He had no idea how long the peons would remain cowed, but now was not the time to take chances. He ordered his riflemen into the crowd, then yelled to his other bandits to give everyone a full cup of water, half that amount for children.

The bodies were dragged out of the tank and cups filled.

Pauleen rode up and glanced at the red-tinged water.

He grinned. "Look, Sancho, I've turned the water into wine," he said.

"Ver' good, Mickey," Perez said. "You make a funny joke."

The Mexican smiled, but inside he seethed with resentment, and his growing hatred for gringos, how they killed his people like animals, spiked at him. "They may not stay, Mickey," Perez said.

Pauleen glanced over the peons, sitting or lying on their backs, spread over a couple of acres of ground.

"They'll stay," he said. "They're thirsty, hungry, and exhausted. If they had any fight in them to begin with, it's long gone."

"*Sí*, long gone," Perez said. "Is so sad."

Pauleen's eyes lifted. "Looks like there's more a-comin', Sancho," he said.

The bandit's gaze moved to the sun-spangled water where it sprang from the limestone cliff. "I hope the water lasts, Mickey," he said.

"It's probably been here for a thousand years," Pauleen said. "It'll last a thousand more."

Perez turned his head and stared silently at the approaching dust. Then, spreading his hands, "Poor Sancho. How can he handle so many?"

"Kill a few. The rest will fall in line," Pauleen said. He swung out of the saddle. To Gray he said, "Help Sancho's men keep an eye on the greasers."

"Sure thing," Gray said.

Pauleen watched him leave, then took off his hat and ran his fingers through his damp, thin hair. He replaced his hat and said, "Sancho, I sent three guns to help you. Did you talk to them?"

Perez shook his head. His face looked like a round, red apple just beginning to go bad. "I never saw them, Mickey."

"Strange, that."

"Not so strange. The desert has a hundred ways to kill young men."

"How did you know they were young?"

Perez didn't miss a beat. "There are no old pistoleros, Mickey."

Pauleen let it go. For now. "Looks like a couple hundred coming in," he said, staring beyond Perez.

"The drought to the south is bad, many dead, peons and animals."

"Get them watered and bedded down with the rest. Talk to them tomorrow when they're in a mood to listen."

"What do I tell them?"

"That golden fields of grain, fruiting orchards, and fine homes wait for them over the river—fat cattle, too. Tell them whatever the hell you want, but get them across the river on July fourth."

"Not so long a time," Perez said.

"I know, but get them there, Sancho."

The bandit watched his mounted men settle the newcomers, a couple of other bandits already carrying cups of water among them.

This lot was in much worse shape than the others. They'd come from farther south and were living skeletons, faces as thin as paper, their clothing in tatters. The Mexicans threw themselves on the sand, too weak to stand or even cry out for water.

A woman among them broke into a piercing scream, then held out a limp baby to the man beside her.

The man wailed and held the baby close. The baby did not move or make a sound.

"Keep them alive, Sancho," Pauleen said, his eyes cold. "Can you feed them?"

"With what, Mickey? How to cook tortillas for so many, huh?"

"Well, do the best you can. Just keep them alive for another few days."

CHAPTER TWENTY-TWO

A lantern cast orange light onto Sancho Perez's round face, giving him a look of a pumpkin man from a child's nightmare.

As was his duty as a host, a bottle of mescal stood upright in the sand between him and Mickey Pauleen, even though the little gunman would not drink.

Out in the moaning, muttering night, half of Perez's bandits guarded the peons, working two hours on, two off. It was a hardship for the men, but it helped quell Sancho's uneasiness.

"A great host will cross the river," he said. "Never fear."

Pauleen nodded. "You've done well, Sancho."

"Will Abe Hacker let them stay?"

"Of course. Then, after a while, most will return to Mexico."

"But Hacker will take possession of a ravaged land."

"He has money. He can bring the land back quickly. The Big Bend country will support vast cotton fields, and the peons that remain will work them for him."

Pauleen glanced at the starlit sky.

"Understand this, Sancho—to Hacker, the land around Last Chance is a small matter, just another business property," he said. "He wants much money and many worldly possessions to leave his son."

"But he has no son."

"He plans to make one."

Perez laughed. "Hacker can't make a son. His belly is too big . . . like mine."

Pauleen sighed and shook his head.

"Where there is a will there's a way, I guess."

"I'd like to see that," Perez said, grinning. "Abe Hacker on top of a young woman."

Pauleen thought of Nora. "I reckon he manages," he said.

Perez let his mirth subside, then took a drink from the bottle.

He burped loudly, cocked his butt and farted, then said, "The people of Last Chance will fight, I think."

Pauleen shook his head. *Perez, you're an ignorant, greaser pig.* "The rubes have grown too fat," he said. "They've forgotten how to fight. If they ever knew."

"Ahhh . . . this is true. People who live in towns grow soft and weak."

"They don't all live in town. Maybe the ranchers will stand."

Perez smiled. "If they do, my compadres will take care of them."

"I'd like to take a couple of your men back to town with me," Pauleen said.

"Why?"

"As an insurance policy, Sancho, on account I don't know where the three men I sent to you are. Who among your men are fastest with the iron?"

"You will leave me short, Mickey."

"Damn it, you've got fighting men acting as sheep-herders. You can spare me a couple."

Perez sighed dramatically.

"Ver' well, Mickey. To you, my dear friend, I can deny nothing. I will give you—"

A scream bladed into the desert silence like a thrown lance.

Out in the moon-dappled darkness a shotgun roared, followed by another scream and the shouts of angry men.

"Rebellion!" Perez yelled, his face alarmed.

He and Pauleen wakened the sleeping bandits, who cursed as they scrambled groggily for their weapons.

Rifles at the ready, the bandits formed a semicircle around Perez and Pauleen and stared into the night.

"Do you see anything?" Perez whispered.

"*¡Mire!*" one of the younger bandits yelled, excitedly pointing with his rifle.

Every eye shifted to that patch of night.

The darkness parted and two bandits appeared, their rifles slung as they dragged a man across the desert, his toes gouging the sand.

It was Hugh Gray, his left cheek bloodied by four parallel talon marks.

The bandits threw the groaning Gray at Perez's feet and one of them babbled in rapid Mexican Spanish that was too fast and colloquial for Pauleen to under-stand.

After the man stopped speaking, Pauleen said, "Sancho, what the hell?"

Perez's anger flared. He kicked Gray in the face and screamed, "Pig!"

"What happened?" Pauleen said.

Perez's red-rimmed eyes were bulbous, and saliva flecked his lips. "He lured a señora into the desert, promised her food. He tried to take advantage. When her husband came to her assistance, this man shot him."

"Well, his name is Hugh Gray, and Hacker will deal with him when we get back to Last Chance," Pauleen said. He looked at the bandits around him, smiled, and said, "Excitement's over, boys. Go back to sleep."

No one moved. The surrounding Mexicans were grim-faced, a powder keg waiting to explode.

"The woman's husband is dead," Perez said. "I will deal with this man."

"Mickey," Gray said, raising his head, turning his raked cheek to the moonlight. "Look what she did to me."

"Yeah, I see it," Pauleen said. "And that pretty much evens things up, I reckon."

To Perez he said, "Sancho, I'll see to it that Hacker fines this man fifty dollars. You can give the money to the widow."

The bandit ignored that and yelled, "Get the gringo dog to his feet." When that was done, Perez said, "Strip him! Then tie his hands behind his back!"

Gray's angry face was distorted in the moonlight. He cursed as relentless hands tore off his clothes and he tried to kick out at Perez.

The bandit backhanded Gray across the face and the huge jeweled ring he wore on his middle finger opened up a gaping cut at the corner of the man's mouth.

Blood running down his chin, naked, Gray pleaded

with Pauleen. "Mickey, you ain't gonna let greasers do this to a white American, are you?"

The black eyes of the bandits around him glittered with hostility, and Pauleen knew it would be dangerous to push it.

"Sancho," he said, "how much for Gray?"

"Restore the peon to life. That is my price."

"You don't give a damn for these people. A white man is worth saving."

"Not if he killed a Mexican."

"Five hundred dollars," Pauleen said. Then, desperately, "In gold."

"I tire of you, Mickey," Perez said. "I warn you not to weary me any longer."

Pauleen was beat and he knew it.

Perez was insane, but right now he was also dangerous. The little gunman let it go.

"You should have kept it in your pants, Gray," he said.

Gray spat at Perez, then said, "Damn your eyes, then shoot me and get it over."

The bandit's voice was low, level—ominously quiet.

"Give this gringo pig to the women," he said.

It took a while for those words to sink into Gray's slow brain.

But once they did, he shrieked in mortal terror.

Beyond the limits of the lantern light, beyond the small music of the water tumbling into the tank, stood a line of Mexican women, young and old, still and silent, as menacing as tigresses.

The moon hung high behind them, silvering their shoulders and the tops of their heads, here and there glinting on steel.

Bandits dragged the kicking, screaming Gray toward

the wall of women . . . it opened, parting slowly like a great gate.

Gray, thrown to the ground, screamed as the gate closed . . .

And the ravening pack descended upon him.

To Mickey Pauleen, how long it took several hundred women to kill a man became a matter of academic interest.

To his surprise Gray's screams choked off after just half a minute, and the women stepped away about twenty seconds afterward, leaving a bloody, mangled thing on the sand.

There would be nothing left of Gray worth saving, but Pauleen stepped closer to take a look.

Around the torn carcass, which looked as though it had been set upon by wolves, stood the circle of women, their still-savage faces spattered with blood, arms scarlet to the elbows.

When Pauleen drew close, hostile eyes that glowed like candlelit amber in the gloom turned to him. He saw the gleam of bared teeth and felt a sudden stab of fear, an emotion strange to him.

"Mickey, I think you better go now. Step away, but don't turn your back on them." Perez stood at Pauleen's elbow. "You are the one who brought the gringo, and your life is in peril," he said.

Pauleen needed no convincing.

He slowly backed away, trying not to hurry as his fear demanded.

Wasting no time getting into the saddle, he saw two Mexicans already mounted, slim young men with hard, violent faces and low-slung guns.

"These men will go with you, Mickey," Perez said. He glanced anxiously over his shoulder at the women. "I will see you again when I cross the river."

Pauleen nodded and gathered up the reins. Perez put a restraining hand on his leg.

"Last Chance has a bank, yes?" the bandit said.

"Yeah, it has."

"Tell Hacker it is Sancho's bank, huh?"

"We already made a deal," Pauleen said.

"The bank was not mentioned. Now I mention it."

"I'll talk to Hacker."

"And I will talk to him . . . when I ride into town with my men."

Pauleen recognized the implied threat.

"Then so be it," he said.

His lips drew into a thin, white line.

It seemed that Hacker had made a deal with the devil, and his price was steep.

CHAPTER TWENTY-THREE

Ranger Hank Cannan had not expected a reply to his letter this soon, if at all.

But there it was in his hand, in his wife's fine copper-plate, all the way from El Paso by stage in a stained, travel-worn envelope.

Cannan read the letter again, as though the words might miraculously change.

They did not.

My Dearest Henry,

How distressed I was to learn that you are sorely wounded and confined to a sickbed.

Thus, I believe it is a matter of the greatest moment that I hasten to your side in your hour of need, and, by my Loving and Tender Administrations, restore you to good health.

I have therefore undertaken to hazard the journey from El Paso to Last Chance on the Butterfield Stage to arrive—Oh, most fortunate happenstance!—on the afternoon of July Fourth, the day of our Great Nation's independence.

Until then, my dearest one, you will be always in my thoughts and prayers and I am most eager to once again behold your Noble and Manly countenance.

> *I am,*
> *Your Respectful and Loving Wife,*

Then, with a fine flourish . . .

> *Jane*

Cannan only lifted his eyes from the paper when the door opened and Roxie stepped inside.

"Good morning! Are we ready for our walk?" she said, smiling.

Without a word, Cannan passed her the letter.

Roxie read it, then said, "That's wonderful. I'm so happy she's coming here."

"I'm not," Cannan said. "As soon as she steps foot in Last Chance her life will be in danger."

"I don't think so," Roxie said. "There's been town committee meetings and the agreement reached is that Abe Hacker can stay till the day after the Independence celebrations, and then he must leave."

"Has anyone told him that?"

"Yes, of course. And he's agreeable. Mayor Curtis says Hacker is even donating a couple of hogs, a barrel of whiskey, and three barrels of beer."

Cannan shook his head, a quick, jerky gesture that communicated his frustration. "What the hell is Hacker up to?" he said.

He swung his legs out of the bed. "Mickey Pauleen was about to kill Ed Gillman, remember?" he said.

"It's forgotten," Roxie said. "The town wants Hacker and his gunmen to leave peacefully. No more dead men."

"Hacker and Pauleen won't leave, because I plan to arrest them," Cannan said. "They'll hang for the murder of Sheriff Isaac Dixon or spend the next twenty years in Huntsville."

"Ranger, you'll throw your life away, and your wife will be here to toss the first handful of sand onto your coffin."

"I'll do my duty," Cannan said, his face stiff.

"I don't know if I want to help you walk," Roxie said.

"Then I'll do it myself."

"I never asked you this before, Ranger . . . are you good with a gun?"

"Fair."

"Fair doesn't cut it."

"I'll have right on my side, and I'm big enough and mean enough to take my hits and keep on a-comin'."

"You've already taken too many hits."

"I'm willing to take more. A Texas Ranger doesn't eat crow for any man."

Roxie sighed, a frown creasing her beautiful face. "Ah, well, on your feet, Texas Ranger Cannan. Let us promenade."

She helped the lawman stand, and said, "I really don't know why I'm doing this."

"Because you've fallen for my very obvious charms and manly features, Roxie," Cannan said.

The woman smiled. "That'll be the day, Ranger," she said. "That'll be the day."

Baptiste Dupoix stood on the porch of the Cattleman's Hotel and anchored a post with his shoulder. He lit his morning cigar and smiled as he watched Hank Cannan's tottering form walk back and forth behind the window, a resolute Roxie doing her best to keep him upright.

His eyes flicked to the livery stable.

A few minutes earlier he'd seen Mickey Pauleen ride into town accompanied by a couple of Mexican hard cases, and now the three gunmen walked toward him.

"You on guard?" Pauleen said.

Dupoix smiled. "And a good morning to you, too, Mickey. Feeling out of sorts, are we?"

Pauleen ignored that and said, "Gray is dead."

"He'll be sadly missed by those of us who knew and loved him," Dupoix said.

"Cut the comedy, Dupoix. With Gray gone, we're mighty thin on the ground." He thumbed over his shoulder in the direction of the unsmiling Mexicans. "That's why I brought along these two."

Dupoix touched his hat to the Mexicans, their faces shadowed under huge, ornate sombreros. They didn't respond.

He turned his attention to Pauleen. "How did Gray die, Mickey? Or did you just mislay him in the desert?"

"He tried to screw the wrong señora."

"Careless of him," Dupoix said. "And also of you, of course."

The gambler liked to play a dangerous game.

Teasing Pauleen was like prodding a rattling diamondback with a toothpick, but he enjoyed it immensely.

The little gunman didn't take it well. "I don't like you, Dupoix," he said. "You talk like you're John Wesley Hardin, but you got nothing to back it up."

Dupoix smiled. "But I try, Mickey. I really do try."

"Don't push me any harder or I'll surely make you try."

An unusual thing for him, Pauleen wore his crossed gun belts, the worn, walnut handles of the holstered Colts low. A killer with fast hands, that morning he was a man to step around.

Dupoix smiled at him, his cigar between his teeth. "Mickey, I'll remember what you said. Those were words of wisdom, the first I've ever heard you utter."

Dupoix was on the prod, but Pauleen was a realist with nothing to prove. He knew he was faster than Dupoix, but the distance between them was less than five paces. The gambler was game and a big man. At that range he'd take his hits and get his work in.

Pauleen hesitated, unwilling to play a dead man's hand, and threw in his cards.

To the Mexicans, he said, "You boys go get breakfast and then come back here. You'll bed down tonight in Gray's room."

He was met with blank stares.

Pauleen repeated the order in hesitant Spanish. The young men got the gist of it and left.

Dupoix bowed and waved toward the hotel entrance. "I give you the road, Mickey," he said. Then, because Pauleen had put a match to his short fuse, "For now."

CHAPTER TWENTY-FOUR

The dream of the great Texas river in flood had been a terrible dream.

But Henriette Valcour had no time to deal with it now.

The sin-eater demanded all her attention.

He had come to her door in the middle of the night, a small, slight man with an ashen face and huge, haunted brown eyes.

To Henriette, the stench of mortal sin was a palpable assault that left her head reeling, and she sensed the nearness of a dead soul, as black as midnight.

Her immediate reaction was to send the little man away.

Soon she must interpret her dream and determine the danger that faced Baptiste.

But the man read her face and cried, "Mercy, Madame! Mercy for my sins!"

He had not said he was a sin-eater, but Henriette knew.

"How many mortal sins have you taken on yourself?" she said.

"Hundreds . . ." the man said. "Thousands . . ."

Out in the dark swamp a thing howled.

The little man's eyes widened in fear and he opened his mouth in a silent scream. The inside of his mouth was as black as soot.

"It is only the hungry loups-garous, but they will not harm you," Henriette said. "Yours is poisoned meat."

She told the man to come inside and set him in a chair by the fire.

Henriette did not offer him food or drink.

He had devoured so many dreadful sins that he would desire neither.

She knew she could not help him, but she listened.

After a while the man recovered enough composure to tell his story.

His name was Jacob Littlejohn, he was sixty-nine years old, and once he'd been a respectable clerk in a New York countinghouse, making a full five hundred dollars a year.

But after ten years he'd tired of dusty, mind-numbing tedium, and quit his desk to see the world.

Six months later, starving, he was asleep on a park bench in Baltimore town on a cold winter night when . . .

"I was wakened from fitful slumber by a man wearing a dusky greatcoat, a vast muffler of the same shade around his neck. He wore a black slouch hat pulled low over his eyes, and he seemed to be in a somewhat agitated state of mind. The night was dark and I was trembling, both from cold and fright."

"And did the man talk to you?" Henriette prompted.

"Yes, he did. He said he was sorry to see me in such a state and asked how my life had come to this sorry pass."

Suddenly Littlejohn threw back his head and wailed.

"O my sins! My mortal sins tear me apart!"

"You are a poor, lost creature," Henriette said. "Damned for eternity like the loups-garous."

"Oh dear God, must that be my fate?" the man said.

"No. I will save you if I can," Henriette said.

"I was told you are a swamp witch of great fame."

"I am only an old woman with the wisdom of years."

Henriette used an iron poker to push a log farther into the fire. The log sent up a scarlet shower of sparks.

She said, "The man who wakened you in the Baltimore park told you to become a sin-eater. Is that not so?"

"Yes. He told me by taking on the sins of others I would become a success and never have to sleep on a bench again."

Littlejohn screeched, like a man in agony.

"Thrice-cursed liar, he damned me for eternity!"

"Did he tell you his name?" Henriette said.

"Edgar."

The old woman smiled. "Yes, Edgar. He died the very night he spoke to you, after he'd sowed one last mischief."

"You knew him?"

"I knew him. Edgar Allan Poe practiced the black arts, and we were mortal enemies." Henriette shook her head. "Can it be that he's been gone this two score years?"

She spat into the fire. "Ah well, that for him."

Littlejohn threw his hands out in an odd, desperate gesture. "Can you take my sins from me, witch?" he said.

"How old are you?" Henriette said.

"Near seventy."

"Then, poor thing, I will help you."

The woman rose and found a clay cup. She poured in goat milk and then a pinch of powder from a jar on the shelf.

She stirred the mixture and handed it to Littlejohn.

"Drink. This will make your soul as white and pure as the liquid in the cup."

"It will wash out my mortal sins?" Littlejohn said. "All the deadly sins I took from those who committed them?"

"It will give you the peace that your tormented soul has not known since the dreadful night you met Edgar."

Littlejohn drank eagerly, and when he'd drained the cup, Henriette said, "You must go now. I will point the way back through the bayou."

The man rose to his feet and danced a little jig.

"I feel as though a great weight has been lifted from me," he said.

"It is the weight of your sins leaving," Henriette said.

She refused Littlejohn's offer of payment, because his money was tainted.

Jacob Littlejohn had no lantern, but Henriette gave him one. She stood on her porch and pointed out a route to the man she said was a shortcut out of the bayou, well away from alligators and the loups-garous.

In fact, she knew it would lead Littlejohn deeper into the swamp.

But the poison she'd mixed with the goat milk would kill him quite quickly and without pain.

Henriette watched the bobbing lantern until it disappeared into the darkness.

Killing the man was a tender mercy.

Littlejohn had lived his allotted threescore and ten,

and a clean death in the swamp was better, far better, than a descent into the haunted insanity that had killed Edgar.

As to how God would judge Littlejohn, rotted as the man was with mortal sin, she did not know.

All she could do was trust that the Good Lord would be merciful.

Henriette reverently crossed herself, and then went back inside.

Now she could finally take time to recall the details of her dreadful nightmare.

The moon rose high above the swamp and made delicate lace triangles of the spiderwebs at the corners of Henriette's porch. Water lapped against the pilings, but whether caused by the ripple of a passing alligator or a loup-garou she neither knew nor cared.

In the dream, she stood on the bank, her arms raised, but the tide that engulfed the great river was too mighty to hold back.

She saw Baptiste being swept away, others with him, as a fine town and its fertile land was laid waste by a great flood.

The fat man with the massive belly saw all this and was mightily pleased.

He stood on a hillock, his hands on his sides, and rocked back and forth as he laughed.

Henriette cursed him, but the fat man only laughed louder.

Then she woke. In stark terror.

The old woman reached for the whiskey jug beside her chair and drank deep.

Now she knew the meaning of her dream . . .

She did not possess the power to stop what was about to cross the great river.

Even Henriette's magic could not save her grandson from the evil to come.

CHAPTER TWENTY-FIVE

The moon hung high over the darkened town of Last Chance as a tall man with the hesitant gait of an infirm, elderly person left the Big Bend Hotel and angled across the street toward the livery stable.

It was only two in the morning, but the saloons were shuttered, the sporting crowd apparently saving themselves for the Independence Day celebrations three days hence.

The only night sounds were the chink-chink of Hank Cannan's spurs and the whisper of the winnowing wind that clove through the gloom.

He stopped several times, breathing hard, and let the stabbing pain in his side lessen.

Then, his lips drawn back from his clenched teeth, he struggled on.

Blown sand drifted around Cannan's boots as he mustered his strength and pulled open the door of the stable. Its rusty iron hinges squealed in protest.

Shielded from the moonlight, the stable was murkier than the street, and Cannan let his eyes adjust to its almost total darkness.

But men with horses in their care are a restless breed, and a lantern immediately flared to orange life in the livery's office.

Cannan stepped into the rectangle of lamplight cast by the window and stood still, the Winchester in his hand held low by his side.

The office door opened slowly and a shotgun with a bell-shaped muzzle appeared.

Then a man's voice, creaky, shrunken with age.

"Mister, this here blunderbuss is both wife and child to me. She's loaded with cut-up tenpenny nails and she don't miss, lay to that. Be ye a hoss thief?"

Already irritated by the pain in his side, Cannan snapped, "No, you crazy old coot. I'm here to get my bay."

"This late?" the man said. "Then ye be a night rider and up to no good, I'll be bound."

"Damn it, man, I'm a Texas Ranger and I need my horse."

"The feller that rode into town all shot to pieces?"

"Yeah. That was me."

"Hell, I heard you'd passed away recent, or were close to it."

"Close enough," Cannan said. "Now bring that light out here while I saddle my horse."

The door opened wider, and a white-haired man wearing a naval coat with brass buttons stepped close to Cannan.

He held the lantern high and studied the Ranger from the top of his hat to the toes of his scuffed boots.

"Big cove, ain't ye now?" the old man said.

He laid the blunderbuss aside.

"What takes ye out at four bells, young feller?" He

indicated with the lantern. "You got blood on your belly, plain to see."

"My side," Cannan said. "Old wound opened up. Where's my horse?"

The old sailor gave the Ranger a shrewd look.

"You on Ranger business, if you please, matey?"

"You could say that."

"Your big stud is feisty. Penned up for too long."

Another appraising glance, then, "Beggin' your pardon, cap'n, but you can't handle him tonight."

"I'll make a trial of it," Cannan said.

"Then I'll help ye saddle him. And God help you."

As the old man fetched his saddle, Cannan said, "My name is—"

"Aye, I know who you be. And mine is Ephraim Slough, an old sailorman who lost his left pin to Moroccan pirate rogues off the coast o' Tangier in the summer of '68. I were master's mate aboard the *Sally Hudson* in them days. She were a fine sloop-of-war, was the old *Sally*, and fast as the wind."

"It's a pleasure to meet you," Cannan said. Suddenly he felt weak and dizzy, the stable floor shifting under his feet.

"You just set on the nail keg by you, cap'n, and I'll saddle your horse," Slough said.

Cannan nodded and sank gratefully onto the keg. He felt like hell, and his apprehension grew when Slough led out his tall, rawboned bay.

The stud, fire in his eyes, was "up on his toes," neck arched, raring to go.

Slough held tight onto the reins as the horse tried to rear and said, "Ranger, are you sure—"

"Yeah, I'm sure. Just hold him until I get up on his back."

"Ranger, beggin' your pardon, but you got more sand than sense."

"Right now I've got neither," Cannan said.

He slid his Winchester into the boot, then, after a struggle that drained what little strength he had, mounted.

"Ephraim," he said, "you see anything going on in this town you think is strange or even a little out of place, you tell me, huh?"

The old sailor knuckled his forehead. "I surely will, cap'n. You can depend on me."

CHAPTER TWENTY-SIX

Hank Cannan let the bay have his head and left town at a hell-for-leather run.

He then swung north, as though headed for the Chisos Mountains, but after the bay ran himself out and slowed to a tired trot, then a walk, Cannan headed back toward the river.

He was physically drained from the ball-bouncing ride and from the newly opened wound in his side that pained him considerably and oozed blood like rust-red pus.

But Cannan forced himself to grit it out.

There was something wicked across the river that threatened Last Chance, and it was his duty as a Ranger to seek it out and destroy it.

Despite his misery, Cannan smiled, mocking himself.

It was big talk from a near-cripple who was only fair to middling with a gun and could barely sit his saddle.

Still, he had it to do. That was the Ranger way and he knew no other.

The moon-glow lighting his way, Cannan rode to

the bank of the Rio Grande, just west of town, and drew rein.

Around him the brush desert was silent, empty; though dried dung told him that cattle had come this way.

He stared across to the opposite bank and saw only darkness.

Nothing moved. No sign of a threat.

Thanks to Roxie, he had the makings, and he took time to build and light a cigarette, thinking things through, even though his bodily pains clamored for attention and exhaustion weighed on him like a wet cloak.

After a while, Cannan made a decision.

The threat, whatever it was, would not present itself here. A crossing would be difficult because at that spot the rippled water ran deep.

If an army of Mexican bandits chose to attack across the river, they'd opt for shallows where their horses would not be slowed.

Cannan flicked his cigarette butt into the sand, then rode north, away from Last Chance.

He found a couple of places that seemed shallow enough for an easy crossing, but they were so far west of town that any invaders would have to attack across a half mile of open ground, vulnerable to rifle fire all the way.

Cannan backtracked and then found what he was looking for.

Last Chance sat close to the river, and about fifty feet beyond a disused, tumbledown jetty stretched an elongated sandbank, about two acres in extent.

Water flowed sluggishly around the barrier with

scarcely an eddy and whispered softly onto both banks, wide, half-moons of firm sand.

Here, Cannan decided. The attack would come here.

He kneed the bay into the river and crossed to the Mexican side. At no point did the water rise higher than his stirrups.

The moon had dipped lower in the night sky, but there was enough light to reveal only empty desert before it faded into darkness and distance.

Cannan listened into the silence, but all he heard was the rising wind blowing shrouds of waist-high sand across the desert floor. Like an incoming tide washing footprints from the beach, the wind busily erased any tracks that might have been made in the past few days.

But of signs left by a Mexican force preparing to invade across the Rio Grande there were none.

Cannan arched his back, trying to work out kinks.

He was done. Used up. Sapped.

And for what?

The answer was . . . nothing.

He was no closer to discovering what danger threatened Last Chance than he did when he first got out of bed and dressed himself in the early hours of the morning.

Maybe it really was locusts coming up from the drought-stricken south.

And maybe it was nothing at all.

Hank Cannan built and lit a cigarette, but only to postpone for at least a few minutes the agonizing trip back to the livery stable. No sooner had the match flared than a sound reached him . . . a faint mewing, like a kitten in distress.

Cannan listened into the night . . . there it was again . . . somewhere ahead of him in the gloom.

As was his habit, the Ranger asked himself a question aloud.

"A kittlin out here?"

But a cry reached him that no animal could make, the weak wail of a human child.

Cannan tossed the cigarette away and urged his horse forward.

After a few yards he drew rein and listened.

But for the wind . . . silence.

Was that what he'd heard, the sound of the west wind that now pushed hard against him?

No, there it was again, and very close.

Definitely a child, and a baby at that.

The last thing in the world Cannan felt like doing was to climb down from the saddle, but he gritted his teeth and made the effort.

When his boots hit the sand, a wave of pain followed by a sudden weakness sucked the life out of him and left him wide-eyed and gasping. He leaned against the horse, and the left side of his washed-out blue shirt was black with blood.

It was a measure of his dead-on-his-feet distress that Cannan prayed he was dreaming and would soon wake up to Roxie forcing her vile gruel into his mouth as she chided him for smoking too much and overindulging in strong drink.

But this was not a dream.

It was real, and the Ranger knew it.

Cannan gathered up the reins and stepped . . . staggered . . . stumbled forward, leading the spooked bay.

The baby, if that's indeed what it was, had been

silent for a while, but the Ranger had its whereabouts pretty much figured. Figured so well in fact that he nearly tripped over the child . . . and its mother.

The woman was lying on her right side, her baby pulled close as she shielded the child from the stinging sand. Cannan, a huge, looming presence in the darkness, leaned over her and said, "Howdy, ma'am."

For a moment the woman didn't respond, but then she opened her eyes, saw the Ranger and shrieked, hugging the baby even closer. The child began to squeal like a baby pig caught under a gate, and its mother shrieked even louder.

Surprised, appalled, Cannan took a step back but tripped over his spurs and hit the ground hard on his butt.

The woman rose to her feet, the baby in her arms, but she seemed too weak or intimidated to run away. Instead, she shrank from Cannan, a look of horror on her ravaged but still beautiful face.

"My dear lady, I mean you no harm," the Ranger said.

This brought no response from the woman, only a whimper of fear.

Cannan's fall had jolted pain through his entire body, but now, as his head cleared, he saw that the woman was Mexican. Her black hair, once waist length and glossy, hung stiffly over her shoulders, tangled with burrs and windblown sand.

"You've been through it, lady," Cannan said.

Like most Texas Rangers he knew a little Spanish and he told the woman he was her friend and that she would come to no harm.

At least, that's what he hoped he'd told her.

"Agua," the woman said. She pointed at the baby, then herself.

Cannan, whose home range was farther north, all the way into the New Mexico Territory, was not desert savvy enough to have brought along a canteen, and he silently cursed himself for a greenhorn.

But aloud, in his halting Mexican, he told the woman that the Rio Grande was close and he would take her there.

Then, patting the dusty flank of the bay, Cannan pointed at the woman and indicated that she and the baby should—he used the Spanish *"hagasé de a bordo"*—get onboard.

But the señora hesitated, a strange, hunted expression on her face. She turned her head slowly, looked behind her, and let out a gasp of fear.

Cannan saw what the woman saw. Two men rode through a curtain of blowing sand and tattered moonlight, rifles across their saddle horns, one of them leading a saddled horse.

Cannan had been a lawman long enough to recognize a pair of hard cases on the prod when he saw them.

He was half dead on his feet. His shoulders sagged, and his face settled into its habitual gloomy expression.

"I don't need this," Hank Cannan said aloud. "I really don't need this."

CHAPTER TWENTY-SEVEN

The two riders were thin men who wore wide sombreros, cartridge belts across their chests, and ferocious scowls.

Both dismounted, and the younger of the two glanced at Hank Cannan, summed him up, and then dismissed him.

It was not an easy thing to do to a man that stood six-foot-four and weighed close to two hundred and twenty pounds, but the Mexican did it.

Cannan decided that the young Mexican was confident and most likely that had to do with the ivory-handed Colt that hung low on his right thigh.

The older man, a bowlegged, round-shouldered, simian brute with the eyes of a reptile, ignored Cannan completely and strode toward the stricken woman. Without a word, he backhanded her hard across the face, and the woman fell to the sand, the baby still in her arms.

The infant screeched, its little face red, and reptile-eyes tore it from the woman's arms and dropped it on the ground. The Mexican stood over the child. He pulled his gun, thumbed back the hammer—

Cannan drove at the man, a headlong, low dive for his waist. But the Ranger instantly regretted it. He felt as though he'd collided with a granite column.

Weak as he was, Cannan's feeble effort had no effect, and the Mexican didn't even move . . . except to slam the barrel of his gun into the Ranger's head.

Hank Cannon woke with a thundering headache and figured he'd been led astray by Baptiste Dupoix and had indulged in too much Old Crow.

Roxie would be real mad at him.

Hell, but not that mad . . . A hard kick to the ribs was no way to wake a man.

"Hey, gringo, on your feet!"

Cannan groaned and let his eyes open to slits. Blue dawn light immediately bladed into his brain, and his mouth tasted as though he'd just eaten rotten fish.

Another kick, harder this time.

"Get up or I'll shoot you, gringo."

Cannan opened his eyes wider and looked up at a huge Mexican with a belly the size of a killing hog. He was dressed in the usual bandito finery but wore a lady's sunbonnet on his massive head.

With the slowness of an ailing, run-down man, Cannan sat up, then staggered to his feet. The desert spun around him, and he felt like he was about to throw up over the big Mexican's boots.

The big man said, "Ah, my men brought you here and it is good to see you looking so well, my fren'."

"Where's the woman?" Cannan said.

"She is with Sancho. Safe and sound."

"And her baby?"

Perez shrugged. "I do not know. Somewhere in the desert, I think."

Perez wailed and threw his arms skyward. "Aiii . . . poor Sancho is so sad. But Conchita should not have run away from him because maybe the girl baby was his."

He shrugged again. "Or she was somebody else's. Who knows?"

As Cannan's head cleared he became aware of two things: the man facing him might well be mad, and beyond him lay a vast encampment of people, men, women, and children, herded together under guard.

Most had rigged up makeshift shelters against the burning sun, but a few others sat around in a stupor, seeing nothing, doing nothing.

The Ranger was about to ask about the captive Mexicans, but Perez cut him off.

"Did Hacker send you, hombre?" he said.

Cannan thought quickly, then said, "Yes, yes he did."

Perez's left eyebrow crawled up his forehead like a black, hairy caterpillar.

"My compadres tell me you are all shot to pieces," he said. "Why would Hacker send me such a man?"

"I had a brush with the law a couple of months ago," Cannan said, his lie smooth. "Mr. Hacker"—he thought the *Mister* was a nice touch—"told me to give you whatever help I could."

"Hacker is good to Sancho Perez. He is my very best fren'."

The bandit frowned.

"For all your great size, my men say you did not do well when you tried to save Conchita," Perez said. "But perhaps you are a fine pistolero, huh?"

Now was the time to drop names, Cannan decided. "Mickey Pauleen thinks I am."

Perez grinned, the diamonds in his teeth glittering in the shade of his sunbonnet.

"If Mickey thinks you are, then it must be so. He is also my very best friend. Sancho is happy to have so many friends."

Perez turned his head and said something to the men behind him in Mexican that was too quick for Cannan to understand.

He felt a quick spike of panic.

But the apelike man he'd tried to tackle to save the woman and her child stepped forward and returned Cannan's Colt and rifle.

"What is your name, *hombre?*" Perez said.

"Hank Cannan."

The Ranger realized he'd replied without thinking. A stupid mistake!

But Perez's face did not change, revealing no recognition.

"Well, Señor Cannan, you will help drive the peons across the river on your Independence Day when your gun will be of great value to Sancho."

The Ranger didn't take time to think that through. Not yet.

Instead he said, "I will be honored."

"Good! Then we are compadres," Perez said. "You are my friend."

He waved a hand. "There is coffee and tortillas."

"First I'd like to find the baby," Cannan said.

"Huh?" Perez said. The bandit was totally baffled.

Cannan glanced at the copper-colored sun just skimming the horizon. "She might still be alive."

"She is dead," Perez said. "They coyotes have found her by now."

"I'd like to make sure," Cannan said.

"Why does a gringo care about a Mexican child?"

"I feel responsible for her," Cannan said.

Then the Ranger banked on the bandit's mental instability.

"She should be buried decently and prayers said over her. You could be her father, Señor Perez."

For a moment the bandit looked stunned. Then he tilted back his head and screamed, so loud it reached the captive Mexicans and a sea of brown faces turned in his direction.

"This is why Abe Hacker sent you!" Perez shrieked. "To remind poor Sancho of his duty. Yes, find the *niña* and bring her back to her loving father, that he may lay her to rest." He grabbed the scowling, simian bandit and pushed him toward Cannan. "Go with him Esteban," Perez said. "Bring Sancho back his dead daughter that his poor broken heart may mend."

The man called Esteban's reptilian eyes flashed and he gave his boss a "what the hell?" look.

But Perez either didn't notice, or ignored it.

"Esteban, as devout a son of the Church as ever was, will aid you in your holy and righteous quest, *Señor* Cannan," he said.

Perez threw his arms heavenward again and cried, "May God in Heaven forgive me for leaving my only child to demons and the wild beasts." Then, tears in his eyes, "Go, Esteban, bring the *caballos.*"

With ill grace, the squat bandit spat at Cannan's feet and turned away, but Perez's voice stopped him.

"And Esteban, if you see any business of the monkeys kill the gringo."

This order was much more to the bandit's liking. He grinned, and in English, so Cannan would understand, he said, "You can depend on it, *patrón*."

Perez stepped forward, threw his arms around the Ranger, and hugged him close. Cannan smelled the man's rank sweat.

"You are my new best fren', Señor Cannan," the bandit said. "Tonight we will share a bottle of mescal and talk of many things."

"Maybe I should go after the child myself," Cannan said when he was finally free of Perez's bear hug. "I can cover more ground alone."

"No, I would not think of it," the man said. "Esteban will keep you safe. I have already lost my very own baby, and I don't want to lose my new fren'."

Cannan was cornered and he knew it. His plan to find the baby and ride for Last Chance had no chance of succeeding so long as Esteban with him.

Cannan felt ill, very ill, and he was weak, no match for a man with the body and strength of a gorilla and who was fast with the iron.

Then he remembered a saying of his wife, "God will provide."

The Ranger hoped she was right, because there was sure as hell nobody else around.

Esteban brought the horses and effortlessly, as though he was a child, helped Cannan into the saddle. The bandit smiled at the Ranger, knowing that his little demonstration of strength had hit home, and then he also mounted.

He passed Cannan a canteen, then said, "Let's ride, gringo."

As they left the encampment and the vast host of unmoving Mexicans, Perez threw himself on the sand, his sunbonnet askew, and loudly begged the Virgin Mary to forgive him for abandoning his child.

The corners of the Ranger's mouth twitched.

The man was as mad as a hatter . . . but did that mean Abe Hacker was also insane?

Or was the fat man crazy like a fox?

Then, in a moment of blinding revelation, the fog cleared from Cannan's brain and he figured Hacker's plan.

The insane Sancho Perez, like a trained monkey, was the bringer of the locusts . . .

But Hacker was the organ-grinder.

CHAPTER TWENTY-EIGHT

As was his habit, Ed Gillman opened up his store just before dawn. Then, as he had done for years, he fired up the stove and put the coffeepot on to boil. Early customers always made a beeline for the coffee before transacting their business, and Gillman never hurried them.

Normally he would next go outside and pull down the blue and white canvas awning, but that morning the tap of a molasses barrel had sprung a leak and spread over the wood floor like an ink stain.

The interior of the store had not yet shed the night darkness and Gillman lit a lamp against the gloom.

He brought the lamp to the molasses barrel and discovered to his relief that it was a simple fix, a matter of digging out crystallized sugar from around the stuck tap handle.

When that job was done to his satisfaction, Gillman wiped his hands on his white apron and poured himself coffee.

The morning brightened and he blew out the oil

lamp that produced a ribbon of black smoke, as straight as a string.

Gillman knew he'd be busy later as folks stocked up for the Independence Day celebration. His shelves groaned under the weight of coffee beans, spices, baking powder, oatmeal, flour, sugar, dried fruit, hard candy, eggs, milk, butter, fresh fruits and vegetables, honey, crackers, cheese, syrup, dried beans, and a plentiful supply of cigars and tobacco.

Partitioned off from the main-store, another room offered bolts of calico and gingham cloth, pins, needles, thread, ribbon, celluloid collars, undergarments, suspenders, hats, and shoes (to be let go at cost).

Gillman also sold rifles, revolvers, ammunition, lanterns, rope, crockery, pots and pans, zinc bathtubs, and farming items.

But his pride and joy was the Apothecary Department, a wall of stacked shelves that offered soaps and toiletries, lavender water, and elixirs. Gillman anticipated that his best seller would be *Doctor Thom's A to Z Curative, Guaranteed to Positively Cure Any Ailment from Acute Bronchitis to Zygomycosis.*

However the storekeeper fancied that its main use on July 5th would be H for hangover.

Gillman set down his coffee cup and took one last glance around the store. Everything seemed to be in its rightful place. The floors were swept clean and the corners free of spiderwebs. Satisfied, Ed Gillman smiled.

It was going to be a crackerjack day!

To the west, the sun rose and donned its finery, a dazzling morning robe of pearl-pink, pale crimson, and jade. The light tinged every building in Last Chance with a coral glow, and out in the surrounding fields and orchards, flocks of noisy birds greeted the new-aborning day.

Ed Gillman, humming a selection from the latest Gilbert and Sullivan operetta, hooked the awning with the pull pole . . .

And his head blew apart.

It had been a difficult shot, but a good one, judging by the sudden eruption of Gillman's blood and brains that spattered the boardwalk and the window of the mercantile. Mickey Pauleen smiled as he lowered Abe Hacker's customized .45-70 Marlin Model of 1881 . . . a fine rifle and, by God, a fine cartridge.

He'd fired from a flat, brushy area to the east of Cattleman's Hotel. There had been no one on the street at the time, and Pauleen enjoyed an open line of sight along the boardwalk to Gillman's store. A lack of wind and the brightening dawn light had made things easier, but still, it had been a hundred-yard kill, excellent marksmanship by any standard, and Mickey was mightily pleased.

After he watched Gillman drop, Pauleen ducked into the hotel by the back door and went straight to his room.

He saw no one.

A couple of minutes passed, then somebody rapped quietly on his door.

"Who is it?" Pauleen said, drawing his Colt from the holster hanging on his bed.

"You know who it is."

"Come in, boss."

Abe Hacker, in his robe, opened the door just wide enough to allow passage of his great bulk, then closed it behind him. "I heard the shot," he said.

Pauleen grinned. "I dropped him like a sack of doorknobs."

"Are you sure?"

"The .45-70 damn near took his head off," Pauleen said.

Outside boots pounded on the boardwalk and men yelled to one another, the common cry, "Ed Gillman's been murdered!"

"Damned two-bit grocer won't trouble us again, Mickey," Hacker said. "To hell with him and his town meetings and rubes poking their finger in the air demanding that I be run out of town." Hacker slapped his great belly and puffed up a little. "A bunch of small-town hicks trying to put the crawl on Abe Hacker. That'll be the day."

"The fourth of July is day after tomorrow, boss," Pauleen said. "Perez is ready to go."

"I know when it is, Mickey."

"Yeah, of course you do."

Hacker put his hand on the doorknob as the shouting outside was joined by the wail of women.

"We'll kill some of them before we leave, Mickey. Despite all the promises of goodwill they made to me, they agitated for my ouster behind my back. I don't like that. I don't like it at all."

"We can blame the killings on the Mexicans," Pauleen said.

"Yes. Yes of course. Let Perez and his bandits take the blame."

"I planned on killing Perez," Pauleen said. "I can't stand an uppity greaser."

"No. There's no profit in that. When I come back to claim this place, all legal and aboveboard like, you can kill him then."

Pauleen grinned and sang, "Oh I wish I was in the land of cotton . . ." Then, "Where's Nora?"

"I can't loose her to you just yet, Mickey."

"Why the hell not?"

"I'll keep up appearances for a little while longer."

"Appearances for who? Don't you think the rubes know who gave the order for Gillman's death?"

"They can't prove it."

"A hemp noose hanging from a tree limb don't much care one way or the other."

Hacker gave Pauleen a baleful glare. "When did they last lynch a man in this hick town?"

"There's always a first time."

"Not with sheep, there isn't. Hell, they don't have the cojones to stand by and watch a man dangle."

"I want my woman," Pauleen said.

"And you'll have her, Mickey. Very soon, trust me."

"You reckon now that Gillman's gone we got this town cowed?" Pauleen said.

"They won't move against us any time soon. And the day after tomorrow they'll be hotfooting it out of here so fast, it won't matter."

"Sancho wants the bank."

"What Sancho wants isn't necessarily what he gets."

"He'll have a lot of men with him, boss."

Hacker smoothed the satin lapels of his robe. "Once the Mexican"—the fat man grinned—"immigrants are here I leave it up to you to take care of Sancho. You were right, Mickey, he has to go. And the Ranger across the street with him."

"What about Dupoix?"

Hacker waved a negligent hand. "Kill him at your convenience. He doesn't figure in my future plans."

CHAPTER TWENTY-NINE

The desert was an inferno of heat that burned sweat from a man's body and, like the exhaust from a blast furnace, the air was hard to breathe and scorched the lungs.

Around Ranger Hank Cannan, the rippled sand stretched into infinity, a vast sea of brush, prickly pear, ocotillo, and dozens of other species, even more vicious, that stabbed and stung and slashed.

To the west, the canyon lands shimmered in the distance, looking like rocky mesa cut through and through by a gigantic saber.

"Enough of this, Cannan," the man called Esteban said. "The *niña* is long dead."

"We'll search just a while longer," Cannan said.

"You are a fool," the Mexican said.

"A fool who needs a miracle," Cannan said.

Esteban glanced at the burned-out sky, then consulted his watch. "Gringo, you got another fifteen minutes."

Cannan smiled. "You're a giving man, ain't you?"

"I don't like you and I don't trust you," Esteban said,

his lizard eyes ugly. "If we quarrel, I'll take you back to Sancho Perez over your saddle."

In his present weakened state, Cannan was no match for the Mexican, and he sure as hell wasn't as fast on the draw and shoot. Bearing these melancholy facts in mind, the Ranger nodded. "Then fifteen minutes it is," he said.

Esteban had a way of stretching his mouth, as though he intended to swallow a jackrabbit whole, but Cannan took it as a smile. "Go one minute over and I'll shoot you, gringo," he said.

The Ranger said nothing. Esteban was on the prod and there was no use in antagonizing the man further.

Five minutes passed, the only sound the soft footfalls of the horses and the creak of saddle leather.

The wind had been blowing when Cannan ran into the woman and her child and all the tracks had disappeared. But using the faint purple outline of the Chisos Mountains as a guide, he hoped he rode in the right direction.

He could barely stay in the saddle, and Esteban watched him like a cold-eyed buzzard, searching for weakness. Cannan had no idea why he stuck to the search. No baby could survive the cool desert night, then the heat of the day, without water.

Or milk. Wasn't that what babies needed? If it was, he had none of that. And Esteban didn't even have the milk of human kindness.

Cannan smiled at that thought as his burning eyes reached out into the arid land. Then he answered the question in his mind. He stuck to the hunt for the child because he was a Texas Ranger and it was his duty. It was as simple as that and there were no ifs and buts about it.

But right about then the Ranger star in his shirt pocket weighed him down like an anvil.

"Five minutes left, gringo," Esteban said.

"Time flies when you're having fun, don't it, Esteban?"

"You are pleased to make a joke, Cannan. Don't make another."

The second hand of the Mexican's watch was ticking toward the twelve-fifteen mark when Hank Cannan heard a soft, thin wail just ahead of him. Was it the baby? Or maybe a wounded jackrabbit? Or his own tormented imagination?

But Esteban's sudden stiff posture in the saddle told him that the Mexican had heard it, too.

The Ranger half-fell from the saddle, righted himself, and led his horse forward.

"What, you think you will find a baby?" Esteban said. "It is the sound of a quail."

"Maybe so," Cannan said.

The sand under his feet was soft. And he staggered a little.

All he wanted to do was fall on his face, sink into the desert's warm embrace, and sleep . . . sleep . . . sleep . . .

Then, behind him, the Mexican said, "Yes, it's the baby. Hah, it is as dead as a stone. Now we will go back."

Cannan ignored the man, dropped the reins, and stepped toward the little bundle on the sand. He took a knee beside the child and lifted her in his arms.

She whimpered like a sick puppy. "She's alive," Cannan said.

"Then strangle her and let us be on our way," Esteban said. "I'm hungry and I'll tell Perez that the child is dead."

"Toss me your canteen," Cannan said.

The Mexican thought about that, then grudgingly complied.

The infant was wrapped in a crocheted shawl that had fallen across her face and protected her from the worst of the sun. But she was very weak, her kitten-mew barely audible.

Cannan wore a yellow bandana tied loosely around his neck, one of a dozen presented to the Texas Rangers by an army officer, Second Lieutenant James G. Sturgis, who'd later died at Little Big Horn.

The Ranger treasured the bandana, though it was now faded to a dull straw color and frayed in places. Cannan soaked a corner of the bandana in water and held it to the baby's mouth. The little tyke sucked greedily and opened her black eyes and the Ranger grinned.

Still smiling, he turned to Esteban and said, "I think she's going to be all right."

The child was hungry, because she'd shifted her attention from the water and her wet little mouth sucked on Cannan's knuckle.

"Damn thing stinks," the bandit said. "Leave it where you found it."

"It's a baby and babies do stuff," the Ranger said.

"How the hell would you know?"

"I've been around babies before. Plenty of times."

"We're not taking it back, Cannan," Esteban said. "We have too many of them as it is, stinking up the camp."

"She can ride with me," Cannan said.

"Stand aside, gringo."

The words, flat, ice cold, and menacing. Hank Cannan felt their chill. He turned his head.

Esteban had his gun up and ready. Sunlight flashed

on the nickeled barrel. "Stand aside," the Mexican said again.

"For God's sake, she's only a baby," Cannan said.

"Get away from it or my first bullet goes through your head." Esteban sat his saddle like a gorilla on a pony. His eyes held nothing but death.

Cannan's hands dug into the sand and he rose unsteadily to his feet.

"You'll burn in hell for this," he said, stepping closer to the mounted bandit.

Esteban smiled. "Of course I will." He shrugged. "It will be but a step from one hell to another."

The Mexican thumbed back the hammer, and Cannan threw the handful of sand he'd picked up into the bandit's grinning face. Cursing, Esteban shook his head to clear grit from his eyes.

Cannan drew and fired.

The Mexican's horse, sensing its rider's distress, reared at that instant, and the Ranger's shot went wild.

Blinking and rubbing at his eyes, Esteban thumbed off a shot. A miss. He swung his horse around and trotted away.

Cannan, no confidence in his skill with the Colt, holstered the revolver and stumbled to his horse.

He yanked the Winchester out of the boot just as Esteban, his vision cleared, screamed a high-pitched war cry and charged at the gallop. The Mexican's gun spat flame and a bullet split the air near Cannan's left ear.

But, levering and firing from the hip, the big Ranger was a good hand with a rifle. Esteban took a hit in the chest . . . then another . . . and a third . . .

A scarlet bib appeared on his white shirt, and he left the saddle at the gallop. The Mexican crashed onto the ground and sand erupted around him as though he'd dived into a rock pool. Not a man to take chances, Cannan pumped two more shots into the man.

The baby, terrified, screamed her little lungs out.

As gray gun smoke drifted around him, looking more than ever like a dejected walrus, Cannan shook his head and said, "You're in a hell of a fix, Hank, with a dead man and a baby an' all."

But, used up as he was, he had it to do.

The Mexican's bloody body sprawled twenty-five yards away and his horse stood nearby. Just getting there would be a chore.

First the kid needed attention. She sucked more from the bandana, but then started in to screaming again. Trying not to inhale, the Ranger removed the baby's soiled loincloth—he had no idea what its proper name was—and then washed her butt with the warm water from the canteen. The child screamed the whole time and Cannan figured he wasn't doing it right, but all this was new to him.

After washing his hands and drying them with sand, he stood, told the baby to hush, which she didn't, and stumbled toward the Mexican. Esteban's eyes were wide open, but the man was as dead as he was ever going to be. Cannan slowly shook his head, made a tut-tut-tut sound, then said, "Damn it, you let yourself get all shot to pieces and left me holding the baby."

His face clenched in the stiffness of death, Esteban neither saw nor heard nor cared.

It took Hank Cannan all of thirty minutes to man-handle the dead Mexican's body across his saddle. Twice he had to let the man thump back to the sand when the baby's cries became particularly clamorous.

The second time he covered the child in sand up to her neck to keep off the sun, but the real problem was that she was hungry.

And there was nothing he could do about that.

After Cannan finally draped Esteban across his saddle and roped the dead bandit's feet to his wrists, he was tuckered beyond exhaustion. But he had no time to rest.

The baby had suddenly gone silent, ominously quiet, and he had to get her to Last Chance . . . and fast. Groaning with every movement of his body, his head pounding like a hammer on an anvil, Cannan picked up the baby and climbed into the saddle.

It wasn't going to work. He couldn't lead the Mexican's burdened horse, rein his own mount, and hold the baby all at the same time.

The Ranger pondered the problem, tugging at his great mustache, and finally came up with a solution that made him smile. "Crackerjack, Hank," he said. "Just crackerjack!"

Fortunately, he had his saddlebags with him, but unfortunately, he had to climb down from the saddle again. He held the baby in the crook of his left arm, so her head hung one way, feet the other, and made it safely to the ground.

The child fitted an empty saddlebag perfectly, but the flap lay on top of her head and might be abrasive. Cannan solved that problem by making a headscarf of the yellow bandana, tying it under the child's chin.

Outraged, the baby immediately started to bawl again, and the Ranger took that as a good sign.

CHAPTER THIRTY

It was mid-afternoon when Ranger Hank Cannan rode into Last Chance with a dead man and a squalling baby.

A curious crowd immediately gathered and a skinny, stern matron, who looked as though she lived on a diet of scripture, gunpowder, and prune juice, stepped off the boardwalk. She threw up her hand and said, "Halt!"

Cannan, on the ragged edge of a faint, drew rein and said nothing as the woman grabbed the baby from the saddlebag.

She removed the bandana, tossed it at Cannan, and demanded, "What have you done to this infant?"

The Ranger, his eyes half shut, said, "She's hungry."

"Hungry indeed! Why didn't you feed her?" the matron said.

"I didn't have any milk. But there's beef jerky in the other saddlebag and I guess I could have fed her that. But I forgot about it."

The woman gasped and took a step back, highly affronted. "Beef jerky!" She turned and called to a woman on the sidewalk, "Did you hear that, Caroline?"

"Yes, I did," the woman said. She stomped her ankle boot on the boardwalk. "The very nerve!"

"Can . . . can you get her milk?" Cannan said, his head drooping. He felt as though he was on a painted horse on a carousel ride as the town spun dizzily around him. He thought he saw Roxie wearing a dress the color of a candy cane and Baptiste Dupoix standing tall and elegant beside her, showing white teeth as he lighted a long cigar, thin and black as a licorice stick.

But Cannan wasn't sure.

Men crowded around the bandit's body and demanded to know the dead man's identity and what happened and where. The prune juice woman held the wailing baby to her narrow chest and called out Cannan for "a frontier tough, a child abuser, a ruffian, and a low person."

The Ranger's world spun round and round him at breakneck speed, but suddenly the carousel came to a dead stop.

Cannan fell headlong off his painted horse.

He hit the ground with a thud . . . but didn't feel a thing.

"You really must stop falling off your horse in the middle of Main Street, Ranger Cannan," Baptiste Dupoix said. "It's embarrassing, and folks are getting mighty tired of picking you up."

"Where am I?" Cannan said.

"In bed where you belong. Roxie says she'll take a stick to you if you try to escape again." Dupoix put a new bottle of Old Crow on the bedside table, then said, "Who's the dead hard case?"

"His name is . . . was . . . Esteban. He worked for a bandit by the name of Sancho Perez."

"A gun?"

"Yeah, class."

"But you killed him?"

"I got lucky."

"Better lucky than fast."

"You could say that."

"The baby?"

"It's a long story."

"Mrs. Agatha Spooner has the squalling tyke, and she says she'll keep her at home until you're safely out of town."

Cannan frowned. "Hell, I did the best I could. What do I know about babies?"

"Damned little, according to Mrs. Spooner." Dupoix held up the bourbon bottle. "Drink?"

"I sure need one. Are the makings still in my shirt pocket?"

"Right here on the table, and so is your soldier-boy bandana. I picked it up off the street right after they picked you up."

Dupoix tossed the makings on the bed and then poured two glasses of liquid amber. "Tell me," he said, passing Cannan his drink.

"Tell you what?"

"Everything."

"Suppose I've got nothing to tell?"

"Then suppose I call you a liar? Your mustache bristles when you're lying and when you have a good poker hand. Did you know that, Hank? Saw you do that in the hell-on-wheels town."

"Damn it, are you sure I didn't hang you, Dupoix?"

The gambler smiled. "Spill it, Ranger."

"You work for Hacker." Cannan lit his cigarette. "Why would I tell you anything?"

"Because right now I'm the worst enemy and best friend you've got."

"That doesn't make any sense."

"Nothing about Last Chance makes any sense."

Cannan drank half his glass of whiskey and let its golden glow embrace him like the wind of a tipsy angel. Then he said, "I know the locust swarm."

"Mexicans," Dupoix said. "Just as I told you." Dupoix lit a cigar. "I saw their tracks in the desert, remember? It was as though a pharaoh's army had passed that way."

"I wasn't sure I believed you. I figured maybe Hacker had concocted a big windy."

"You believe me now."

"Damn right I do. I saw them with my own eyes, more people than I could ever count."

"They'll come across the river, starving, and lay waste to the land and sack the town," Dupoix said. "Then, when it's over, Hacker will pick up the pieces."

"How do I stop them?" Cannan said.

"You can't, big man."

"You're right, I can't. I can't gun down hungry Mexicans who'll step over their dead and keep on a-coming because they're desperate." Cannan drank again and drew deep on his cigarette. "The Texas Rangers would hang me."

"Or the Mexican government would."

"Then I can't win."

"Seems like."

"I can lock up Hacker, put him out of the locust business."

Dupoix smiled. "That won't work." He answered the question on Cannan's face. "Through Mickey Pauleen and Sancho Perez, Hacker told a couple of thousand ravenous people they were bound for the Promised Land," Dupoix said. "Mickey says Perez can barely hold them as it is, and once they start moving they won't stop at the river."

"And the best crossing is right here, at Last Chance."

Dupoix nodded. "Yup, Ranger, we're the Red Sea."

The gambler poured more bourbon, then glass in hand, stepped to the window. It was gone four o'clock, yet the day's heat was still intense. But the street outside was busy, and shirtsleeved men jostled women carrying packages and parasols. A piano player was already at work in one of the saloons and outside the greengrocer's a young female assistant held a struggling urchin by the back of his neck and cuffed his ear, apparently for apple-stealing, since the rosy evidence was still in the boy's hand.

"Folks getting ready for Independence Day," Dupoix said, without turning.

"If only they knew," Cannan said.

"They'll know, because you'll tell them."

"Will they stand in a line on the bank of the Rio Grande and shoot into hungry women and children?"

"A few will. Most won't."

"None will, especially not on Independence Day. Those are decent people out there, and they won't betray the principles that makes this nation of ours great."

When Dupoix turned he was smiling. "You should run for politics, Hank."

"I believe in America and Americans. To slaughter innocents is not our way."

"And that suits Abe Hacker just fine."

Cannan made no comment on that, but he said, "You going to drink the whole bottle by yourself?"

Dupoix poured the Ranger another glass. "Mickey Pauleen doesn't talk to me much, but I've listened in on conversations between him and Hacker. And I spoke to Nora Anderson just before you rode into town with your baby girl."

"She isn't my—"

"And I can give you something to think about."

"Let me hear it."

"It may be nothing."

"Let me hear it."

"Trivial, perhaps."

"Damn you, Dupoix, let it out. I'm clutching at straws here."

"Sancho Perez has a burning hatred for gringos."

"I reckon that's obvious."

"He's also crazy."

"I know. I spoke with him."

"He's also a very proud man."

Cannan looked up from the cigarette he was building. "You're giving me nothing, Dupoix."

"Pride goes before destruction, a haughty spirit before a fall." The gambler grinned. "That's from the Bible, Proverbs, I believe, or so I recall my grandma Henriette told me."

"I'm not catching your drift. In fact, you're running around in circles like a dog chasing its tail."

"If you can induce Sancho to attack across the river before he sends over the Mexicans, you might be able to end this thing."

Cannan let his exasperation show. He was weak, light-headed, and angry.

"So what do I do? Stand on the bank of the Rio

Grande and say, 'Sancho, I know you're tetched in the head, so would you please attack me so I can shoot you down?'"

"Why is it," Dupoix said, "that the bigger the man, the dumber he is?"

"You ain't exactly runtified your ownself," Cannan said.

"Hank—may I call you Hank?"

"Seems to me you've been doing it. And no, I sure ain't calling you Baptiste."

Dupoix let that go. "You play to his pride, Hank," he said. You tell him he's a coward who's hiding behind the skirts of women, too scared to face real American men."

Dupoix stared at Cannan over the top of his glass.

"Sancho will not want to lose face in front of his men."

"Hell, that's as thin as a rail," the Ranger said.

"It's all you have."

Dupoix watched Cannan as the big man considered the implications of what he'd just said.

The gambler prodded him. "You won't stop the Mexicans, nothing can stop them now, but killing Perez could make the situation more manageable."

"And Hacker and Pauleen?"

"Figure that one for yourself," Dupoix said.

"And you, Dupoix? What about you?"

"Figure that for yourself as well."

Cannan sat upright in bed, then wiped whiskey off his mustache with the back of his hand. He opened his mouth to speak, but Dupoix got his words in first.

"Your bride will be here day after tomorrow," he said.

"Yeah, I'm aware of that."

"Then you know what you should do?"

"No, but I'm sure you'll tell me."

"Get her back on the stage and go with her. Leave this whole, sorry mess behind. Buy a house with a white picket fence within the sound of a church bell and enjoy married life together."

"I can't do that, Dupoix."

"I know, the brave Texas Ranger can't turn his back on trouble."

"Wrong, I'm not brave. Right, I'm a Texas Ranger." Cannan was silent for a few moments, then said, "Dupoix I need a favor."

"From me? The man you aim to hang?"

"Yeah, from you. We'll forget the hanging thing for now."

"That's white of you. All right, a favor, but with very narrow limits. I'm still drawing wages from Hacker."

"Visit the cattle spreads. Tell the ranchers that when they come into town for Independence Day they can wear their best goin' a-courtin' suits, but I want them well armed. Tell them to bring rifles and plenty of ammunition."

"Most of the seasonal hands are paid off," Dupoix said.

"There will be enough," Cannan said. "What's left are good men and they'll stand."

"You're pushing it, Hank," Dupoix said.

"With the ranchers?"

"No, with me."

"You already told me you wouldn't stand by and see Last Chance and all it stands for destroyed. Hell, we're defending our corner of the United States of America. Doesn't that mean something to you?"

"More than you know," Dupoix said. "But when I take a man's wages I ride for the brand."

"A man can be loyal to the wrong cause. How many southern boys wore the blue?"

"All right, I'll do this for you, Ranger, since you can't ride," Dupoix said. "But afterward, I go my own way. Understand?"

"You've stated your intentions and I respect them."

Cannan eased his aching back against the pillows. He felt worn out, as though he'd been up the trail and back.

"As far as I know, the ranches—"

"I know where they are," Dupoix said. "Two to the west, one east of us."

Cannon nodded. "I appreciate this, Dupoix."

"Now you've run out of favors, Hank."

"Tell those boys to get in early," the Ranger said. "I don't know when Perez will open the ball."

Dupoix smiled without humor. "You'll know, Hank. Trust me, you'll know."

CHAPTER THIRTY-ONE

Abe Hacker was a brooding man.

Fully dressed, a diamond stickpin in his cravat, he stared morosely out at the street where late-afternoon shoppers gathered their final Independence Day supplies.

The fun would start tomorrow morning, but the noise of firecrackers would soon be replaced by the reports of rifles and revolvers.

Hacker squeezed his cigar and decided that all in all things had gone well.

He was sure the Texas Ranger—what was his name?—suspected something, but a bedridden man could do little. Besides, he'd ordered Mickey to gun—Cannan, yes, that was the name—gun him once Sancho Perez hit town.

As for the rubes, the death of Ed Gillman had them well and truly cowed. If he could be killed, so could they.

Ah well, as he'd said before, wolves fight, sheep don't.

Nora stirred in the bed and muttered restlessly in

her sleep. Hacker admired the dramatic curve of her hips under the sheet, but only for a moment. He was about to take a new bride and throw Nora to Mickey.

He was finished with her.

Best not allow the witch to rouse him at this late stage.

Hacker squeezed his cigar and smiled.

Indian clubs! Yes, that was the ticket. As soon as he got back to Washington he'd buy a pair of Indian clubs and get in shape for his coming marital exertions. He needed a strong son, and strong sons are sired by strong men. A few sessions with Indian clubs and he'd be more than ready for his young bride.

Hacker licked saliva from his thick lips. It would be a memorable wedding night.

A tap at the door interrupted his titillating reverie. Irritated, Hacker snapped, "Come in!"

Mickey Pauleen stepped inside, wearing his guns. "Dupoix just rode out of town," he said.

Hacker consulted his watch, then snapped it shut. "It's five o'clock. Where is he headed at this time of day?"

"You tell me, boss," Pauleen said. His eyes flicked to the bed. "She sick?"

"No, she's just taking a nap."

"Plumb wore her out, huh, boss?" Pauleen said.

"Please, Mickey, no crudity," Hacker said. "You know how it offends me."

"All right, what about Dupoix?"

"Follow him. If he's up to no good, kill him."

"How about I kill him anyway? We don't need him any longer."

"Yes, indeed. Sancho will take care of all my business." Hacker thought for a few moments, his cruel mouth pursed. Then, "Yes, kill him, Mickey. I never trusted him anyway."

Like a hungry buzzard, Pauleen's attention moved to Nora again. "Remember, I want that," he said.

"And you'll have it, Mickey. Just be patient for another day."

The little gunman nodded. "One other thing, boss . . ."

Hacker nodded. "Speak."

"When I get back, we'll discuss her dowry."

Hacker was taken aback, his three chins falling at the same time. "What the hell are you talking about, Mickey?"

"I'm taking Nora off your hands. You should pay her dowry."

"You don't pay a dowry for a whore."

"You will. Or me and her will invite ourselves to your wedding." Pauleen's grin was vicious. "I'll get her to wear the dress I like. The bright scarlet silk. Show off Abe Hacker's former woman to all them senators and their ladies and the like."

Hacker squeezed his cigar. "You trying to blackmail me, Mickey?"

"No, not in the least. I just want my due. A dowry is my due."

Hacker let his black anger subside. It wasn't good for his heart. "We'll discuss it when you get back," he said.

Pauleen said, "That's fine with me, boss. But let me warn you, I'm talking tall dollars here, five figures, not a grubstake."

"Don't warn me, Mickey," Hacker said. His piggy eyes hardened and his voice iced. "Don't ever again warn me about anything." Pauleen wore the guns, but

Hacker had the power. "Take a step back, Mickey," the fat man said. "A big step back."

The gunman knew that this was not the time or place to push it. He backed down. "We'll discuss the dowry when I return," he said.

"No, we'll discuss your crude attempt at blackmail when you return," Hacker said. "Then, if I feel like it, we'll argue the dollar value of an aging whore."

The fat man waved a dismissive hand. "Now go kill that tinhorn gambler."

Abe Hacker felt that Mickey slammed the door behind him just a little too hard.

No matter. Perez would take care of him.

The fat man frowned.

Hell no, he should reserve that pleasure for himself.

The Remington derringer in his vest pocket would take care of that little chore. Especially if Mickey didn't see it coming.

The fat man smiled.

How simple . . .

A fatherly pat on Pauleen's back, then POW! POW! Two .40 caliber balls into the man's head.

The plan pleased Hacker greatly, and he would put it into effect when Mickey returned. The rubes would pass off the racket of the shots as firecrackers or some drunk rooster shooting at the moon, starting his Independence Day celebrations early.

But Pauleen had left him with a mathematical problem that he now turned over in his mind. The sight of Nora, sitting up in bed, regarding him with damp, wounded eyes, could only help with his calculations.

Hacker presented himself with the problem: How much was a past-her-prime whore worth in American dollars?

Fifty . . . a hundred . . . less?

The fat man tried, but couldn't come up with a figure.

Then he had an idea. "Nora, get up and take your clothes off," he said.

"Why, Abe?" the woman said, sniffing back a tear.

"I want you to dance for me," Hacker said.

CHAPTER THIRTY-TWO

The last thing in the world Baptiste Dupoix had expected was a summer rain . . . and a heavy one at that.

Once past the grain fields he'd picked up a wagon road that stayed close to the river, in some places coming within twenty yards of the bank, at others swinging wide past acres of mesquite and its attendant bluebonnets.

With still no sign of a ranch house in sight, ragged gray clouds drifted in from the canyon lands, dragging behind them the snarling black mass of a thunderstorm.

Within a few minutes the heavens opened and Dupoix found himself drenched to the skin.

He swung his horse into the scant shelter of a mesquite, prepared to wait out the storm. The gray seemed in total agreement with that plan.

Ten minutes later, as the storm raged, the big stud suddenly pricked its ears and turned its attention to Dupoix's back trail.

A rider, veiled by rain, headed in the gambler's direction.

Blinking against the downpour, Dupoix slid the Winchester from the boot under his knee.

He recognized the slender, significant form of Mickey Pauleen.

Like himself the little gunman had made no provision for rain, riding head bent and miserable through the lashing downpour.

Dupoix had a gambler's instinct, but he was not about to take his chances with a named draw fighter like Mickey Pauleen. He was too fast . . . too certain . . . too dangerous.

The man had obviously seen him ride out of Last Chance and the fact that he followed did not bode well.

Pauleen suspected nothing, chin sunk on his chest.

Dupoix levered a round into the chamber of the rifle, his face set and grim.

Something wicked this way comes . . .

The distance was fifty yards, and he'd sight through an iron-colored murk of mist and rain, but Dupoix, a good hand with a rifle, knew he could make the shot.

He had never murdered a man in cold blood before, but he'd squeeze the trigger and live with it later.

Dupoix threw the Winchester to his shoulder.

Thunder cracked, then roared like the detonation of a hundred barrels of gunpowder, followed an instant later by the serpent hiss and sizzling dazzle of a lightning strike.

Momentarily blinded by searing light, Dupoix lowered his rifle.

After his eyes adjusted, he saw Pauleen sprawled on the wet ground beside his stunned horse.

The gambler put it together.

The strike had hit close, killing Pauleen, but for some reason Dupoix couldn't understand, spared his mount.

Now wary of the lightning, the gambler replaced the Winchester in the boot and stayed where he was.

He would pay his last respects to Mickey after the storm passed.

But Dupoix didn't get that opportunity.

Pauleen suddenly jumped to his feet, shook himself off, and sprang into the saddle of his startled horse. He swung his mount around and took off at a fast gallop, his legs flapping as though all the hounds of hell were after him.

At first Dupoix was surprised, but then what he'd just seen tickled his funny bone, and he laughed loud and long, ignoring the storm that crashed and growled around him.

The lightning had put the crawl on ol' Mickey, and he wouldn't slow down until he hit the barn in Last Chance.

Dupoix wiped tears from his eyes.

If for nothing else, the sight of a terrified Mickey Pauleen, hatless, flapping his chaps for home was well worth the trip.

Mickey had intended to kill him. Dupoix had no doubt about that.

And the order could only have come from Hacker.

There was a limit to the gambler's loyalty to the brand and the fat man had pushed it too far.

It was time to cut the ties.

Besides, Dupoix had recently outrun his losing streak at the tables, and the cards were finally falling his way.

He glanced at the darkening sky where the storm clouds had given way to a single sentinel star. It was a good omen, the star, since it pointed the way to N'Orleans and the steamboats.

Dupoix smiled.

That's where his future and his destiny lay.

CHAPTER THIRTY-THREE

In the ticking aftermath of the storm, Dupoix followed the wagon road, and the day shaded into evening before he saw the Elkhorn ranch house in the distance. The structure itself seemed fairly modest, but nonetheless it was a cabin that stood tall enough to blot out a major proportion of the starry sky behind it.

To the front, four rectangles of yellowish orange light marked the windows and a lantern glowed above the door.

Dupoix, his eyes accustomed to dark places, noted the usual corrals and scattered outbuildings, including what he took to be a long bunkhouse with low walls but a steeply pitched shingle roof.

A man stepped out of the house and looked around as though he'd lost his way. The man saw Dupoix, stuck his hands in his pockets, and sauntered toward him.

Since the passing of the Apaches the land had been at peace, and the rancher, if that's who he was, carried no firearms. When he was a couple of yards from Dupoix he stopped and said, "Howdy."

He was a sandy-haired man, showing gray, short and

stocky with a horseman's bowed legs. His ragged cavalry mustache hung over his top lip, and his good-humored eyes held a smile and no hint of suspicion.

"Howdy," Dupoix said, sitting his saddle as courtesy demanded.

"What can I do for you, mister?" the man said.

"Name's Baptiste Dupoix and—"

"Good God, boy, who saddled you with a name like that?"

"My ma and pa, I guess."

"I'm Luke Wright and you're on my spread." The rancher grinned. "An' my handle ain't near as heavy a burden as your'n."

"I guess not," Dupoix said.

"State your business," Wright said.

"I'm here on the behest of a friend of mine. Texas Ranger Hank Cannan."

"Heard of him," Wright said. "All shot up and like to die was what I was told."

"He's recovering."

"Glad to hear it. What can I do fer him?"

"He needs your help, Mr. Wright."

"Call me Luke. What kind of help?"

"It's a mite long in the telling."

"Then light an' set. My old lady has coffee on the bile."

Dupoix's boots squelched in mud as he followed Wright toward the ranch house.

"That's a nice-looking stud you got there," the rancher said. "Never much cared for grays myself, got a mighty strong smell about them, a bad thing when the Apaches raided this way."

Then, before Dupoix could answer, "The barn is out

back, plenty of hay and a sack of oats, if you'd like to take care of your hoss first."

"I reckon not, Luke, I won't stay long. I have another ranch to visit."

Wright shrugged. "Suit yourself . . . uh, Baptist."

"Baptiste."

The rancher opened the door.

"Whatever you say."

Dupoix stepped into a cozy cabin, clean and polished as the plump, middle-aged woman sitting by the fire could make it.

She looked up at Dupoix and smiled.

The two men with her didn't.

One was a healthy-looking man in his early forties, the other a frowning hard case with a tough face and a gun on his hip.

Wright made the introductions. The woman was his wife Julia; the healthy man was his foreman, Aaron Park, who seemed friendly but wary of strangers.

"And this is—"

"George Cassidy," the tough-faced man said quickly.

Then, to Dupoix's surprise, a huge, friendly smile lit up Cassidy's face.

"Best you know it, Mr. Dupoix, I'm on the scout. I've gotten myself as far from the Wyoming Territory as I can."

"In my younger days I rode some owlhoot trails myself," the gambler said. "I treat a man as I find him."

"George was in the train-robbing profession but had a little difficulty," Wright said. "But he's headed back to Wyoming in a couple of days and I'll miss him. He's a good steady hand."

Dupoix was surprised. "You came all this way just to go back?"

"Yeah, but I plan to lay low and go straight," Cassidy said. "A friend of mine has a long-standing offer of a job at his butcher shop in Rock Springs and I reckon I'll take it."

It seemed that Cassidy was a talking man, so Dupoix smiled and said, "Glad to hear it, Mr. Cassidy. As far as I know, the butchering business is booming."

"Folks need meat. My friend told me he'll call me 'Butch,' because I'll be a butcher, like. He said the lady customers would love it, but I don't hold with that."

"No, George is a much better name," Dupoix said. "George Cassidy has an almost genteel ring to it."

Wright waved to a chair.

"All right, um . . . ah . . ."

"Baptiste," Dupoix said.

"Yeah. Set and tell me what help the Ranger needs and—"

"Luke Wright, you'll do nothing of the kind!"

Julia, her gray-streaked brown hair tied back in a bun, rose to her feet, stepped to Dupoix's side, and wagged a finger at her husband. "Can't you see the poor man is soaked to the skin? He needs to get out of those wet clothes or he'll catch his death."

"I'm just fine, ma'am," Dupoix said, thoroughly alarmed.

"Nonsense, Mr. Dupoix. You come with me."

The gambler looked pleadingly at Wright, but the man shook his head and smiled.

"You better do as Julia says. She's used to getting her own way."

An affable man, Cassidy said, "I'll put your horse in the barn, Mr. Dupoix."

"There's no need, I'm moving on soon."

"You're not going anywhere in wet clothes," Julia said. "If I let you leave our home in that state, Luke would take a stick to me."

Privately Dupoix thought that Luke didn't give a damn one way or the other, but when Cassidy left to put up his horse, he surrendered himself to Julia's motherly attentions.

"Just disrobe and drop your clothes on the floor," Julia said.

She laid a folded tan blanket on the bed.

"Wrap that around you when you're ready to come out, then I'll put your clothes in front of the fire to dry."

"Ma'am there's no need to—"

"But there's every need," Julia said. "I declare, Mr. Dupoix, what a singularly odd thing to say."

After the door closed behind the woman, Dupoix sighed and stripped down to his gambler's ring. His watch and holstered Colt he left on a dresser. This was obviously a guest room and it smelled musty.

Dupoix wrapped the blanket around him and, his bare feet padding on the wood floor, stepped into the living room.

CHAPTER THIRTY-FOUR

George Cassidy was back from the barn, but neither he nor the other two men in the room made any comment or even raised an eyebrow at the strange apparition that suddenly appeared among them.

A well-bred crowd, Dupoix thought as he sat back in his chair.

But this time a steaming cup of coffee was on the table beside him and Wright said, "I sweetened it up with some whiskey . . . ah . . ."

"Baptiste." Julia must have had a hand in this, Dupoix decided. It seemed that she'd reminded her husband of his southern hospitality.

Wright iced the cake when he offered the gambler a cigar and waited until it was drawing well before he spoke.

"All right, what's going on in Last Chance that I don't know about?" he said.

"I'll make it as short in the telling as I can," Dupoix said.

Using as few words as possible, he told how the millionaire Abe Hacker had come to the Big Bend country in search of gold. "Hacker didn't find gold, but he plans to claim the land for himself and turn it into an immense cotton plantation," Dupoix said.

"What about the farms, the town, the people?" Wright said.

"They'll be swept away by a plague of locusts."

The rancher gave Aaron Park and Cassidy a puzzled, sidelong look, then said, "We're not catching your drift."

Dupoix told him about the thirsty, starving Mexicans amassed across the Rio Grande and Hacker's plan to drive them across the river on Independence Day.

"A bandit by the name of Sancho Perez—"

Wright was startled and jumped erect in his chair. "Hell, me and Aaron traded shots with Perez three, four years back, the spring of '86 I reckon, when he and his boys raided into Texas north of here," he said.

Park said, "Yeah, it was over to Blue Creek. He murdered four Chinese teamsters traveling with a woman, then skedaddled back across the river."

"We never did find that woman," Wright said.

"Perez will drive the Mexicans across the Rio Grande tomorrow," Dupoix said.

Cassidy dropped words into the stunned silence that followed. "On Independence Day? How many Mexicans?"

"A thousand at least. Maybe close to twice that by this time."

"Hell, it is like a plague of locusts," Wright said.

"They'll swarm over the land, drive the Americans away, and pick the fields and orchards clean," Dupoix said. "Then, when it's all over, Abe Hacker will use his contacts in Washington to score a deed to some prime real estate for his cotton."

"No town, no nothing," Park said. "He'll get it cheap."

"Unless we stop him," Dupoix said.

"How do we stand against thousands?" Wright said.

"Including women and children," Dupoix said. "Whatever Hank Cannan has in mind it isn't going to be easy."

"How many men do you have so far?" Cassidy said.

"At the moment just two. Texas Ranger Hank Cannan and me."

"It ain't enough," Wright said.

Earlier Julia had set up some wrought-iron contraption in front of the fire and now Dupoix stared at the melancholy sight of his patched drawers steaming in the heat.

Finally he said, "That's why the Ranger sent me to you, Luke."

"What did the other ranchers say?" Wright asked.

"You're the first."

"When will the Mexicans cross the river?"

"I don't know, but probably when the Independence Day celebrations are at their height and everybody is having a good time."

"Late afternoon, huh?"

"That would be my take on it."

Luke Wright thought things through for a spell, then his frowning face cleared as he appeared to come to a decision.

"Up for some night riding, Aaron?" he said to his foreman.

Park's smile made him appear even healthier. "I've done it plenty of times before, boss, back in the day."

Wright looked at Dupoix and smiled. "It's always

good to have reformed outlaws riding for the brand. Gives the ol' homestead snap."

"What do you want me to do?" Park said.

"Give my compliments to Clem Bates and then to Jim Hungerford. Tell them what you've heard here and ask them to bring whatever hands they have and meet me here at first light."

"Anything else, boss?" Park said.

"Yeah, tell them to come ready for a fight."

Park rose to his feet. "I'd better get going," he said.

"Aaron, you've got some long riding ahead of you," Wright said. "Take my paint mare. She's got plenty of bottom to her and she'll run from sunup to sundown."

"I'll be back by dawn," Park said. "Depend on it.

"I reckon you'll be tired out, Aaron. Will you be ready for a scrap?"

Park grinned. "Used up or no, I'm always ready for a scrap."

After the big foreman left, Dupoix said, "How many can you bring, Luke?"

"Me and Aaron. I got two hands out in the range but it would take all night to find them. They'll be in some-time after noon tomorrow for the celebration."

Wright read the disappointment on Dupoix's face. "You can see how it is with me," he said.

Cassidy stood. He looked as immovable as a granite rock. "You can count me in, Luke," Cassidy said.

Wright shook his head. "George, you got enough problems of your own. This isn't your fight."

"Begging your pardon, Luke, I may not be in good with the law, but I say an attack on my country is my fight."

"The man has a point," Dupoix said.

He smiled at Cassidy, removing any possible sting from his words. "How good are you with the iron, George?"

"I get by, I guess. I've never killed a white man."

"I hope you never do," Dupoix said.

"All right, that makes three," Wright said. "Clem Bates has a grown son and he keeps on three hands during the summer. I reckon Jim Hungerford can bring himself and another two or three. Jim's a good man, scouted for the army and fit Apaches."

Wright did the arithmetic.

"With you and the Ranger . . . um . . ."

"Baptiste."

". . . that counts a dozen, near enough."

"How many men does that Perez feller have?" Cassidy said.

"I don't rightly know, but a sight more than a dozen," Dupoix said.

Wright suddenly looked old. "Bandits," he said. "Pistoleros. And we got cowboys."

"Will they stand, Luke?" Dupoix said, his eyes suddenly worried.

"Sure, they'll stand and they'll die on their own ground if they have to. But punchers aren't gunfighters."

"What are you telling me, Luke?" Dupoix said.

"Just don't expect too much," Wright said. "That's what I'm telling you."

CHAPTER THIRTY-FIVE

Mickey Pauleen left his horse at the livery, then went straight to his room. He seethed with impotent rage and badly wanted to kill somebody.

The little gunman stood in front of the full-length mirror. A printed sign attached to the top of the frame read:

GENTLEMEN should adjust their clothing *Before* leaving room

Well, his fly wasn't unbuttoned, but otherwise his reflection stunned him.

The left side of his face was bright scarlet, the right white from shock. Pauleen figured he looked like a harlequin clown in a circus show.

His shirt was tattered, charred at the edges, as were his pants. Worse, he'd lost half of his mustache and the few wispy strands that were left smelled like scorched wool.

Cursing, Pauleen unbuckled his guns, then stripped to his underwear. He'd never been a drinking man, but he poured himself a whiskey to steady his nerves and threw himself into a chair.

To his surprise his left hand holding the glass trembled, and he seemed to have lost his sense of taste. The Old Crow had no more flavor than water.

Well, the hell with it.

Pauleen got to his feet, smashed the whiskey glass against the wall, and stepped to the window.

Across the street, in the shifting light of the reflector lamps, a couple of men hung red, white, and blue bunting across the front of the Big Bend Hotel. One held the banner like a load of laundry while the other tacked it in place.

A brewery wagon drawn by a matched pair of gray Percherons trundled past, making late deliveries to the saloons, and a towheaded boy sat beside the driver and dangled his legs.

Pauleen turned away scowling. The peaceful scene irritated him.

He was a man who thrived on chaos, violence, upheaval, the roar of gunfire, the shrieks of dying men, blood, darkness, shadow, the sulfur stench of evil.

All those things were bread and butter to Mickey Pauleen.

He looked forward to tomorrow with keen anticipation . . . eager to see the blood of dead men smoke and gold-banded widows scream and scream and scream . . .

Feeling marginally better about himself, Pauleen shaved off what remained of his mustache and hated his naked top lip. He dressed hurriedly in a collarless shirt and gray coat and pants.

He'd lost his hat when the lightning struck, but he had another, brand new in a box, a white straw boater with a black and red ribbon that he'd intended to wear when he accompanied Hacker to Washington. But since tomorrow was Independence Day, he decided to break the hat in for the happy occasion. As it happened it fit badly as boaters always did.

The hat was a little too large and the brim rested on top of Pauleen's ears and gave him the look of a particularly poisonous toadstool.

But the little gunman's vanities rested elsewhere, and he was perfectly satisfied with his appearance.

Now as the moon rose higher in the night sky it was time for Mickey to go a-courtin' . . . his bizarre, brutal, brothel-bargaining for the sullied dowry of a fallen woman.

"Well, did you kill him?" Hacker said.

Pauleen shook his head.

"No."

"Why the hell not?"

Pauleen's anger was sudden.

"Damn you, I got hit by lightning!"

"If you'd been hit by lightning you'd be dead."

"It was close."

Pauleen turned the left side of his face to Hacker, who sat in his usual chair by the window.

"Look at that," he said.

The only light in the room came from the dim lamp by the bed, but Nora said, "I see it. You're bright red."

"A lightning strike does that to a man," Pauleen said.

Hacker stirred in his chair. "Where is Dupoix now?"

"I don't know. Maybe the lightning done for him."

"Or maybe it didn't," Hacker said. "There's something going on here I don't like, Mickey. Where was Dupoix headed and why?"

Pauleen was irritated. He wanted to discuss Nora, not Dupoix.

The gauzy lamplight was kind to the woman who sat up in bed, her long hair tumbling over her naked shoulders, as she filed her nails. She looked almost beautiful.

No, Pauleen told himself, she *was* beautiful.

And she was his.

Hacker interrupted the little gunman's thoughts.

"There are ranches out that way, Mickey. Did the Ranger send Dupoix for help?"

"What kind of help? All the hands were paid off last spring and the ranchers are old men. Perez and me can take care of them."

"I know, Mickey, I know, but still, it troubles me."

More than that troubled Hacker.

The derringer was in the breast pocket of his robe, but he couldn't use it. Dupoix might come looking for him, and, like it or not, for now Mickey was his only protection. The two Mexicans he'd gotten from Perez owed him no loyalty and couldn't be relied upon to defend him.

It also annoyed Hacker that Pauleen hadn't once called him "Boss" since he'd gotten back. The man was too arrogant by half and would have to be slapped down. Put in his bloody place, as the British said.

But not tonight, Hacker decided. There was no use antagonizing Pauleen when the end was so close.

"I'm still thinking about what we discussed, Mickey," he said.

Pauleen's cobra head turned to the woman on the bed. He touched his tongue to his top lip.

"Right now I'll take her off your hands for nothing."

Hacker smiled, like a benign uncle. *Right, Mickey,*

and how long before the blackmail started? "No, a bargain is a bargain. You take legal possession of the woman tomorrow." Hacker's smile grew even more sincere. "I'm a man of my word."

Nora's nail file hovered above the fingers of her left hand and she stared at Hacker.

"Abe, I am not one of your properties to be bought and sold," she said.

"Oh really, my dear? I thought you were."

"Then you were wrong."

"And how do you expect to get out of this place when I'm gone?"

"I'll find a way."

Hacker shrugged, his chins quivering.

"You could always sell yourself to the Mexicans, I suppose, make a few pesos that way."

"You're going with me, Nora," Pauleen said. Then, his eyes ugly, "You'll be my woman for as long as I want you."

Nora fixed Mickey with a stony Medusa stare. "You'd last less than a week, little man, before I killed you," she said.

"Stop!" Hacker said, slapping a hand on the arm of his chair. "I will not have talk of violence on the eve of our great nation's birthday." He turned to the woman. "Nora, I plan to settle a generous dowry on you so that you and Mickey can live the rest of your lives in comfort and happiness." *And if you believe that you're even more stupid than I thought.* "Now," Hacker said, "let us have no more crossness and ill-chosen words."

He made a great show of looking out the window. "Mickey, see how fairly the moon has risen and how brightly it shines."

Pauleen and Nora's eyes were still locked in combat,

but without turning away the gunman said, "Yeah, I see it."

"Good, because I want you to ride out, and take those two useless Mexicans with you."

Now Pauleen directed his full attention to Hacker. "Ride out? I just got struck by lightning."

"A near miss, dear boy," Hacker said. "No real harm done."

"Ride out where?"

"Under the light of the moon you will cross the river and meet with Sancho Perez. Tomorrow you will lead the charge into Last Chance. I want no last-minute slipups."

"Damn it, Perez knows what he has to do."

"I want you there, Mickey." Hacker silenced Pauleen's objection with a raised hand. "This cotton plantation will be my son's first fiefdom and I will be very generous to the man who ensures he inherits it, Mickey." The fat man smiled. "Do you understand?"

"How generous?"

"We talked five figures for the woman. My boy, we will start our discussion at that price and go up from there."

Pauleen glanced at Nora, an odd mix of lust and contempt on his face. "Suppose I don't plan to keep her for long?" he said.

"No matter. When we get back to Washington I want your strong arm by my side, Mickey. I have enemies and sometimes enemies need to be . . . ah, eliminated."

Hacker looked out the window again, pleased with himself. It was easy to promise the moon when all he planned to offer was green cheese.

"Your new hat becomes you, Mickey," he said. "Very

spiffy. Don't you think so, Nora? . . . Ah, well, 'No answer was the loud reply.'"

Hacker rose to his feet.

"Go now, Mickey, get it done. By this time tomorrow night you'll have your woman and more money than you ever dreamed."

By this time tomorrow night you'll be dead.

Pauleen nodded. "Now we see eye to eye . . . Abe . . . make sure you don't get in the way of a bullet."

"And you, too, Mickey. You, too."

Abe Hacker didn't know it then, but by sending Pauleen away he'd made a fatal mistake.

Unlike the twitching, gibbering Mickey, the fat man slept soundly.

And throughout the long night he would not hear a thing . . .

CHAPTER THIRTY-SIX

"Ridin' late ain't you, Mr. Pauleen?" Ephraim Slough said.

"What's it to you, gimp?" Mickey said.

"Nothin'. Just askin'."

"Don't ask, or you'll get my boot in your teeth, old man."

"Your hoss is baked, Mr. Pauleen," Slough said. "That ain't askin', jes' sayin'."

"Well, if I'm heading back out, so is he."

"Hoss is in no shape fer—"

An instant later Slough stared cross-eyed at the muzzle of the Colt shoved into the bridge of his nose. "One more word and I'll blow your damned head off," Pauleen said. "I ain't in the mood for sass and backtalk."

"Then what happened?" Hank Cannan said.

"I didn't say one more word," Ephraim Slough said.

"Was he alone?"

"Naw, he had two Messkins with him. Mean as hell, they looked too, cap'n, lay to that."

"They head for the river?"

"You're right as ever was."

Slough had wakened Cannan from a sound sleep after he'd hotfooted it from the livery, figuring the Ranger would want to know about Pauleen's second, and very late, night ride.

According to Slough, Mickey had left the stable shortly after Dupoix and then returned looking as though he'd been dragged through a cactus patch backward. What that portended Cannan could not guess, though as sleep cleared from his head his concern for Dupoix grew.

But right now he had other, more urgent matters at hand.

Cannan, who'd never asked help from another man that involved being handled, swallowed his pride. "Ephraim, can you help me out of this damned bed and into my duds?" he said.

"Surely, cap'n," Slough said, grinning. "Just like you was one of me old shipmates, like." The old sailor had only one leg but he'd walked pitching decks and proved nimble enough as he helped the big Ranger get out of bed and dress.

After Cannan buckled on his gun belt and picked up his rifle, Slough said, "What course are we settin', cap'n?"

"The mayor's office."

Cannan looked down at the little sailor from his great height.

"Hold on to me," he said.

* * *

"Ranger Cannan, why are you pounding on my door at this time of night?" Frank Curtis demanded. "And what are you doing out of bed?"

"We have to talk, Mayor," Cannan said.

"What about?"

Curtis wore a long blue-and-white-striped nightgown and held a lit candlestick high.

"This town and the lives of its citizens are in mortal danger."

"Then you'd better come in," Curtis said.

"But . . . but how can we stop that many?" the mayor said.

"Maybe we won't have to if we can lure Sancho Perez into a fight," Cannan said.

"My God, but it's thin, Cannan, mighty thin."

Polly Curtis, a handsome woman who carried her late forties well, looked frightened.

"How many Mexicans, Ranger Cannan?" she said.

"My dear, he's already told you," her husband said, his own fear making him irritable.

"Maybe as many as two thousand, Mrs. Curtis," Cannan said.

The woman gasped and touched her throat.

Ephraim Slough slammed a fist into his open palm.

"Damn their eyes! Oh, fer a couple of ironclads on the river to give 'em a broadside of canister or two. That would soon settle their hash."

"Ephraim, you can't fire cannons into women and children whose only crime is that they're starving to death," Cannan said.

"Well, then what the hell do we do?" Curtis said. "Welcome them with open arms?"

"Maybe," Cannan said.

Curtis slammed back in his chair. "Are you out of your goddamned mind?"

"Yes, Mayor, I probably am," Cannan said.

Polly said, "When will this attack happen, Mr. Cannan?"

"Damn it, Polly, he told you that as well," Curtis said.

"When I was still half-asleep, dear," Polly said.

"Probably in the mid-afternoon when the Independence Day celebrations are well under way," Cannan replied.

"And everybody's drunk," Slough said.

"Only we won't be drunk," Cannan said. "We'll only pretend to be drunk."

Curtis let out a frustrated little yelp. "Polly, brandy, if you please," he said. "The man talks in riddles."

"Mayor, I'm not in the best of health and I don't have much time for any kind of talk," Cannan said. "But will you answer me one question?"

"Yes, I guess so."

"Sancho Perez has at least forty bandits, all of them first-rate fighting men. If I can trick him into attacking across the river, will the citizens of this town fight?"

"What a most extraordinary question," Polly said, gasping a little.

"It is indeed, my dear," her husband said. He stared firmly into Cannan's eyes. "In defense of their homes, their wives and children, and their nation, of course they'll fight. Could they do otherwise and still hold their heads high in the company of men?"

"Did patriots such as we not answer the call to resist

Northern aggression for those very reasons my husband has stated?" Polly said. "Sir, I am surprised at your most disrespectful and hurtful inquiry."

Cannan had touched a nerve and he found it gratifying.

"I meant no offense," he said. "But a great many lives are at stake and I had to be certain."

"Then rest assured, Ranger Cannan, that our men will fight and, should the need arise, their womenfolk will stand shoulder to shoulder and die with them," Polly said.

At that moment Mrs. Curtis looked as though she could storm the Bastille singlehanded, bare-breasted, flag in hand.

Curtis poured Cannan a brandy, told him he looked like death warmed over, then added, "I'll get my rifle."

"No, not yet," the Ranger said. He sipped some brandy, took the makings from his shirt pocket, and held tobacco sack and papers where Polly could see them.

"May I beg your indulgence, ma'am?"

"Please do, Mr. Cannan. I am well used to Mr. Curtis's pipe."

The Ranger built a cigarette but before lighting it he said to Slough, "Ephraim, go from house to house. I want every man who can walk to meet the mayor and me on the riverbank."

"I'll go with him," Curtis said. "This time of night, some might take a little persuading."

Slough cackled. "Armed to the teeth, eh, cap'n?"

"No. Tell them to leave the guns at home for now. Instead each man must bring a shovel. And pickaxes too if they've got them."

Curtis looked puzzled.

"What are you up to, Cannan?"

"I'll explain it when we're standing on the bank of the Rio Grande," the Ranger said.

He drained his glass and stood.

"One more thing, step lively, but keep as quiet as you can. There's a man in this town I don't want wakened."

"Hacker?" Curtis said.

Cannan nodded. "Hacker."

CHAPTER THIRTY-SEVEN

A low wail carried through the moonlit desert like a never-ending note on a violin string, the thin cries of Mexican men, women, and children camped hungry and thirsty in an uncaring wilderness.

As Pauleen rode closer to the distant campfires, his two companions decided to leave him. The bandits spurred their horses, whooped and hollered, and waved their sombreros, glad to be among their own kind again away from the gringo town and its strange sights and smells.

Pauleen followed at a walk on his tired horse.

The ride from Last Chance had been a short one and Perez was much closer to the river, which was as it should be.

The little gunman frowned.

Sancho must have his hands full keeping the peons from the Rio Grande, unless they were too weak from hunger to make the effort.

But apparently a few had tried.

Pauleen passed a sprawled body, shot in the back. Then another. A gray-haired woman, stark in the moonlight, lay dead in a clump of brush. She too had been shot.

As he rode on, Pauleen glanced at the bodies with all the interest and compassion he would have given shotgunned jackrabbits. Mickey was a man without a conscience and within him his soul had withered and died years before.

Sancho Perez, flanked by the two pistoleros who had just ridden in, greeted Pauleen like a long-lost brother.

"Mickey, my good fren'," he said. "How good to see you again. Come, let Sancho embrace you."

Pauleen gave the fat Mexican a perfunctory hug and said, "You've changed hats, Sancho."

"Ah, *sí*. This fine sombrero is my hat of war. Sancho only wears such a hat when there's fighting and killing to be done, no? And you wear a fine new hat, too, my fren'. We are brothers."

He waved a hand, grinning.

"Come, Mickey, sit by the fire and tell me why you are here."

Before he sat and accepted a cup of coffee, Pauleen glanced around the encampment. Every one of Perez's men stood guard over the sullen, moaning mass of Mexicans. Most of the peons looked more dead than alive.

"I'm here because Hacker sent me to help you with tomorrow's attack," he said.

Perez beamed and the firelight made the diamonds in his teeth look like rubies. "What a loving, generous fren' is Señor Hacker. Sancho is touched to his very soul."

The bandit dashed away a tear, picked up a bottle, and was about to put it to his lips when a peon wailed and yelled something about his hungry son.

Perez scowled and made a show of striking out with the bottle. "Ah, shut up!" he yelled.

He looked at Pauleen and smiled.

"That's what I tell them, Mickey. Shut up! They don't understand it, but it keeps them quiet."

"How are they?" Pauleen asked, concerned that Perez might lose too many.

"Fine. Not so thirsty, but ver', ver' hungry."

Pauleen looked at the sea of faces hollowed by moonlight. "Starving?" he said.

"*Sí*, Mickey." Perez made slashing claws of his hands. "Hungry like wild animals!"

"Good," Pauleen said, grinning. "When they reach the river and get a whiff of the good Independence Day cooking smells they'll go mad."

Perez slapped his thigh and laughed. "You and me, Mickey, my fren', we will have fun tomorrow. Plenty of bang-bang and whiskey and women."

"And food, my friend," Pauleen said. "If there's any left after the locusts have passed."

Perez patted his huge belly. "Oh, sure. Sancho likes his grub, no?"

The good humor suddenly drained from Perez's face. "Mickey, did you tell Señor Hacker about the bank? That it belongs to Sancho?"

"Of course I did. Because you're his best friend, Hacker says it's all yours, every last dime."

Perez tilted back his head and yipped like a coyote. "What did poor Sancho ever do to deserve such a wonderful fren'?" he said. "Ah, my heart is broken that I can never repay Señor Hacker for all he has given me. Sancho is so very sad."

Pauleen spoke to the bottom of a mescal bottle.

"There is something you can do, Sancho."

Perez took the bottle from his mouth so quickly he spilled down the front of his shirt. "Tell me, amigo. Tell poor Sancho what he must do. He gets very confused on the eve of battle."

Pauleen's grin made his face a mask of firelit evil. "Yes, I will tell you, Sancho. Make sure that no living thing, I mean man, woman, child or dog, leaves Last Chance alive."

Perez shrugged, disinterested. "That is easy to do."

"Survivors would complicate matters, Sancho, understand?"

"I understand, Mickey."

"The town was destroyed by bandits raiding from Mexico. There were no white men involved. Do you understand me, Sancho?"

"Do you take Sancho for a fool? What does it matter to me to wipe out a gringo town? Mexican rurales and Texas Rangers already want to hang me, but they can only hang Sancho once."

"Then we understand each other very well," Pauleen said. "Mr. Hacker will be pleased."

"He is truly a great man. He will be *presidente* one day."

Pauleen glanced at the bone-white moon, but said nothing.

CHAPTER THIRTY-EIGHT

Hank Cannan stood on the bank of the Rio Grande tired to the bone.

The night's activities had exhausted him more than he first realized and his wounds, though healing, were as yet gaping mouths that fed on his stamina.

He needed rest, but foresaw little opportunity for it.

The three Polish brothers, carrying shovels like sloped rifles, were the first to arrive and they came to a heel-clicking halt. The oldest stepped forward, saluted and said, "We await your orders, my general."

No one in Last Chance had ever been able to pronounce the brothers' last name, and even Miss Adams the schoolmistress, who spoke French, German, and a little Chinese, had never been able to make a go of it.

Cannan didn't try.

He stepped back a few yards from the water to where the ground was a mix of shingle and black, irrigated soil, and chopped down with his arms.

"A trench right here, boys," Cannan said. He placed his open hand at his mid-thigh. "This deep. You *comprende*?"

"Yes, my general," the oldest brother said.

He said something to the others in Polish, and then dirt flew as the three began digging.

One by one, then in twos and threes, the men of Last Chance, some accompanied by their womenfolk, emerged through the marbled moonlight, shovels in their hands.

A few complained about the earliness of the hour, but thanks to a talk from Mayor Curtis all understood that the town would soon be fighting for its very existence and the lives of its citizens. There would be plenty of time for sleep later.

Cannan sent only one man home, a deranged old coot, his wife tugging at his coattails, who thought he was manning the trenches at the Siege of Vicksburg and saw Yankees everywhere.

The rest remained and with no further complaint worked until the trench was dug. The earth mounds were then carried away and scattered so that the ground looked undisturbed from the far bank. The trench ended up a hundred yards long and three to four feet deep.

There was already some seepage into the trench from the river, but Ben Coffin the undertaker, who had an intimate knowledge of such things, said the water would present no major problem for at least the next twenty-four hours.

And then he said, adding his habitual sense of gloom. "If Last Chance has that long."

The moon dropped lower in the sky and the night grew a little darker.

Beyond the far bank of the Rio Grande lay a great

ocean of blackness, but a far-seeing man could have detected a faint red glow to the southeast had he looked hard enough—though he may well have decided it was all in his imagination.

"Well, Ranger Cannan, what next?" Frank Curtis said.

The mayor leaned on his shovel and his shirt was transparent with sweat.

"I count fifty men I can depend on," Cannan said.

"There's twice that many here," the mayor said.

And indeed the riverbank seemed crowded with groups of men talking and smoking, leaning on their shovels.

"Half of them are too old or too young," Cannan said. "When the shooting starts, I don't want boys and graybeards."

Curtis said nothing, but stared fixedly at the Ranger in the half-light, his eyes questioning.

"I won't bury boys, Frank," Cannan said.

"Fifty. It hardly seems enough."

"It's a force I can handle."

"How do I know, Cannan? Hell, how does this town know what you can or can't handle?"

"It doesn't. I don't know myself."

"There are men in Last Chance who could maybe do better. Men who fought Apaches like Billy Brennan and—"

"Frank, we do it my way or we don't do it at all," Cannan said.

Curtis opened his mouth to speak, but the Ranger yelled, "Billy Brennan! You here?"

A voice from the darkness.

"I'm here."

"It's Cannan. I need to talk with you."

Brennan, a tall, heavy man with blond hair and blue eyes, had an arrogant look about him, like an authoritarian foreman on a building site.

"What can I do for you, Ranger, apart from digging ditches?" Brennan said.

Cannan smiled tightly and said, "Mayor Curtis says you fit Apaches."

Brennan hesitated a moment, then said, "Well, I didn't exactly fit them, but I seen plenty of them red devils when I was a civilian contractor with the army."

"Where did you see them, Mr. Brennan?" Cannan said.

"Fort Apache, the San Carlos, places like that."

Cannan nodded. "How would you save Last Chance?"

Brennan grinned. "Glad you asked me that, Ranger, because I've been studying on it."

"Go ahead, Billy," Curtis said.

"Well, sir, I'd get everybody out of here. Take all the water we can carry and head north until we reach a settlement. Like in the old days, when the men form an armed guard around the women and children and the wagons. But before we leave, we burn the town, the fields, the orchards, leave nothing behind for them thieving Mexicans."

"You mean abandon the town?" Curtis said. "Destroy everything we've worked for?"

Brennan saw the doubt in the mayor's face. "Hell, you asked me and that's how I see it, Frank."

"Thanks, Mr. Brennan," Cannan said. "You've given us something to think about."

After the man left, Curtis said, "Do it his way and we'd all be dead by sunset."

Cannan said, "Anybody else fit Apaches that you'd care to recommend, Mayor?"

Curtis shook his head. "We do it your way, Ranger."

Cannan sat on the bank and gathered the men around him. He sat because he no longer had the strength to stand.

As briefly and simply as he could, he laid out his plan and then, as in any gathering of Americans, he waited for the cussin' and discussin' that was bound to follow.

To Cannan's surprise, Billy Brennan's scorched-earth policy attracted no support and the only objections raised to his own plan were from the oldsters and boys left out of the fighting unit.

And they were noisy ones at that.

But Mayor Curtis, with a politician's gift for placating an angry crowd, raised his hands and spoke.

"You didn't give Ranger Cannan a chance to finish what he was saying."

Cannan, who was all talked out, looked up at the mayor in surprise.

"The younger and older men will form themselves into a reserve regiment under the command of"—Curtis picked a name out of the hat—"Ephraim Slough."

The old sailor stumped his way forward, his wooden leg muddy, and knuckled his forehead. "Thank'ee kindly, Mayor," he said. "'Tis a great honor, I'll be bound."

"When the church bell rings the alarm, where will your regiment muster, Colonel Slough?" Curtis said.

"Oh . . . ah . . . that will be outside the Last Mile Saloon, an' beggin' your pardon, Mayor."

"Did the soldiers of the reserve regiment hear that?" Curtis said.

One urchin blew a raspberry but there were also shouts of "Good ol' Stumpy," and one gray-haired rooster did a passable imitation of Slough's strange, rolling walk to the amusement of all.

His voice covered by the general mirth, Curtis leaned over and whispered to Cannan, "Well, that worked a charm."

The Ranger smiled. "You get my vote, Frank." Then, "Send the men home so they can get a few hours rest."

But Cannan had his eye on the boy who'd blown the raspberry, an impudent-looking creature with carrot-red hair and a pugnacious face freckled all over like a sparrow's egg.

He guessed the child to be about twelve but his eyes were older by at least a hundred years.

"Hey, you!" Cannan yelled. "Stay right there."

"You talkin' to me?" the boy yelled back.

"Yes, you. Come here."

The child stuck his hands in the pockets of his ragged knee-pants and strolled over, whistling.

He stopped in front of Cannan and truculently demanded, "What the hell do you want?"

The reward for his impertinence was a pinched ear from the horny finger and thumb of the returned Mayor Curtis, a wheelwright by trade.

"You watch your tongue, my buck, when you speak to a Texas Ranger," the mayor said. He looked over the squealing child to Cannan. "His name is Andy Kilcoyn and his widowed mother is a respectable sewing woman, but she can do nothing with him."

"Well, let him loose, Frank. And you, Andy, quit that caterwauling. I need to talk with you."

The boy rubbed his offended ear and said, "What about?"

"Tomorrow—or is it today already?—whatever it is, stay close to me during the celebrations."

"For why?" Andy said, looking sullen.

"Can you ride a horse?" Cannan said.

"I should say I can."

"He's stolen enough of them," the mayor said.

"Only borried," Andy said.

"Then come sunup, you'll stay close to me and keep my horse close to you," Cannan said."

Andy cast a wary glance at the scowling Curtis and said, "The big American stud in the livery?"

"Yes him. Can you stay on him?"

"Better than you can," Andy said, "Ma says every time you ride into town you fall off your hoss."

The boy nimbly ducked the cuff Curtis aimed at his head.

Cannan grasped Andy's arm. "Tomorrow, when the Independence Day celebration is in full swing, Sancho Perez—you heard me talk of him?"

"You've talked about him all night. I'm not stupid, mister."

"No," Cannan said, "you're a real bright boy. Now listen, before the attack on Last Chance starts, Perez will send a rider with a glass to scout the town. Got that?"

"You want me to shoot him? I don't have a gun."

"No. I don't want you to shoot him. But after the spy is gone, you'll ride across the river on my horse and keep watch."

"For what?"

"A dust cloud. As soon as you see a dust cloud rising

into the air, you light a shuck back across the river and ring the church bell."

"I should hope I won't," Andy said, horrified. "Pastor McRae will kick my butt."

"No, he won't. I'll tell him what to expect."

Cannan looked into the boy's green eyes.

"Can you do what I've asked you to do? It might be dangerous, Andy."

Without any hesitation, the boy nodded. "I can do it."

"Good, then we'll meet tomorrow morning about eight outside the Big Bend Hotel."

"See that you do, boy," Curtis said. "And if you do exactly what Ranger Cannan told you I'll promise you'll get paid two dollars."

The flicker of hurt pride that crossed the boy's face surprised Cannan.

"Mayor, I'll do my duty like everyone else, for my mom and all the other people in Last Chance. I don't want money."

Cannan and even the flinty-eyed Curtis were much affected by the boy's comment.

Then Cannan remembered the unofficial Ranger's star he'd had made in El Paso. He reached into his pocket, then said, "Andy, raise your right hand."

The boy did so.

With great solemnity, Cannan said, "Do you, Andy Kilcoyn, swear to uphold the duties of an acting, unpaid Texas Ranger?"

"I do," the boy said.

Cannan pinned the silver star on the threadbare cotton of the boy's shirt.

"Welcome to Company D of the Frontier Battalion, Ranger Kilcoyn."

"Grows like a weed, that boy," Curtis said looking after Andy as he left.

"Frank, seems to me he sprung up a foot in just the last few minutes," Cannan said.

CHAPTER THIRTY-NINE

Abe Hacker was too excited to sleep.

The clock in the hallway struck two, then tenaciously ticked away the seconds of the new day.

The fat man rolled like a soft slug and struggled out of bed onto his feet. His great, white belly hanging in front of him like a flour sack, he shrugged into his robe and took the chair beside the window.

Hacker gazed out at the moon-dappled darkness and smiled to himself, his face smug.

Today . . . yes, it was really today! Huzzah! . . . Last Chance and all it stood for would be history.

Then the Big Bend river country, say thirty-five linear miles of fertile floodplain, would be the basis for his son's vast cotton plantation. The gin would be where the school now stood and the big, four-pillar plantation house would be built nearby.

Hacker saw himself smoking a cigar of a morning, standing on the porch beside his tall, stalwart son. Together they'd gaze out on cotton fields stretching as far as the eye could see, white and smooth as a December snowfall.

He nodded to himself.

It was good for a man to have a dream, especially one he makes come true.

Nora lay in bed asleep, her hair spread across the pillow like a fan.

Hacker glanced at the woman and grimaced.

He didn't want her there. He wanted his teenaged bride in his bed, wide-eyed awake, waiting, and preferably pregnant.

A little thrill of anticipated pleasure ran through Hacker as he directed his attention to the window again. Ah, well, the girl and all that went with her would come soon enough.

"What the hell?"

Hacker's eyes nearly popped out of his head.

Men moved in the street, rubes carrying shovels, walking back from the river.

The fat man cursed under his breath. What mischief was this? Surely the idiots weren't digging in for a fight?

Questions without answers irritated Hacker. If there was something going on he must know about it, then, with Mickey gone, he could pay some local hick to carry the word to Sancho Perez.

Hacker stuck his feet in his slippers then patted the breast pocket of his robe and made sure the derringer was still there.

If anyone questioned him, he would say he couldn't sleep and was out for a breath of fresh air.

The rubes were a suspicious bunch and wouldn't tell him anything. He'd have to find out for himself.

By the time Abe Hacker made his way out of the hotel, the street was shadowed and empty and streamers of mist crept ghostlike between the shuttered buildings. A large flying insect thudded into the window to his right, dropped to the timber floor of the porch, and spun in circles, buzzing.

Hacker tapped the derringer again, then stepped into the street, his small, porcine eyes searching into the distance.

Nothing moved and there was no sound.

The air smelled of damp earth and the orange and grapefruit trees down by the river, their odors released by the heat of the day.

His doctors had warned Hacker that night air was bad for the heart and lungs, but the men he'd seen were coming from the direction of the Rio Grande and he must go there.

Hacker was halfway across the street when a high, shrill voice stopped him in his tracks.

"Hey you, stay right where you are."

A ragged, red-haired boy stepped toward him from an alley opposite, then demanded, "Why aren't you in bed?"

The urchin walked closer and his freckled face wrinkled into a pugnacious frown.

"You weren't down by the river," Andy Kilcoyn said. His face cleared and he grinned and pointed. "I know. It's because you're too fat."

"And who are you, boy?" Hacker said, his voice like silk.

"Texas Ranger Andy Kilcoyn, that's who." He pointed to the star on the front of his shirt. "So watch your step, mister."

"Is that so?" Hacker said. "And a fine Ranger you are, keeping such a strict night watch."

"Why are you out in the dark when you should be in bed?" the boy said.

"I could ask the same question of you."

"I'm on duty. Ranger Cannan needs me by his side first thing in the morning and I mean to be on time."

"Ah, dutiful indeed," Hacker smiled. "Admirable dedication, my boy."

He looked around him. Only the mist moved and the town was as silent as a cobwebbed tomb.

"Well, off to bed with you, mister," Andy said. He wished he had a big, bone-handled Colt in his pants like Ranger Cannan.

"I'm afraid I can't," Hacker said.

"Why not?"

"I couldn't sleep so I took a walk to get some fresh air," Hacker said. "But I'm a very sick man and I need your help getting back to my hotel." He smiled. "Would you be so kind?"

"I should think a Ranger would," Andy said. "Here, mister, just you lean on my shoulder and you'll be fine."

Hacker put his hand on a thin shoulder that spoke of too many missed meals and felt mightily pleased with himself. He'd question the boy and save a walk to the river, which could only be bad for his heart. And perhaps the boy could be persuaded to carry a message to Perez.

The space between the Cattleman's Hotel and the adjoining store was too narrow to be called an alley, but it was dark, misty—ideal for Hacker's purpose.

With surprising speed and strength for a man of his massive bulk, he grabbed the back of the boy's neck and pushed him into the narrow passageway.

He slammed Andy so hard against the wall of the store the boy let out a gasp of pain and surprise.

"Listen to me, you little worm," he growled. "I want some questions answered."

Hacker's fat forearm rammed into the side of Andy's head, forcing the right side of the boy's face into the rough timber wall of the store.

"What was going on by the river?" he said. "And what is the plan?"

"I don't know," Andy gasped.

The pressure of the fat man's forearm made it hard for him to talk, and blood trickled from his abraded mouth and oozed down the wall.

"Cannan. It's Cannan, isn't it? What does he plan to do?"

"A . . . Texas . . . Ranger . . . never . . . tells . . ."

"Tell me, you little dung heap. Tell me the plan."

"Go to hell," the boy whispered.

Insane with anger, Hacker pulled Andy toward him by the front of his shirt and backhanded him across the face. It was a vicious, brutal blow with a half-clenched first by a man of immense strength and it smashed the boy's right cheekbone and eye socket.

Andy's shock and the unbearable, smashing pain from the blow manifested itself in a terrible scream torn from his throat.

Horrified by the boy's sudden and massive eruption of blood and panicked that someone might hear him shriek, Hacker grabbed the boy's head and pulled his face hard into his belly.

"Shh . . . shh . . ." Hacker whispered. "There now . . . there now . . ."

Andy Kilcoyn, the newest acting, unpaid Ranger

in Texas, smothered to death in Abe Hacker's sweating fat.

Hacker felt the boy go limp as all the light and life that had been in him fled like the shutting off of a gas lamp.

He let Andy drop, staggered back until he bumped against the hotel wall, then stared in gape-mouthed horror at his bloodstained hands.

Veins popped out on Hacker's forehead and breath wheezed in and out of his chest in short, shallow gasps. He felt as though he'd stepped out of himself, an onlooker uncertain of what to do.

He had not meant to kill the boy.

It had been an accident.

He didn't know his own strength.

The boy should have answered his questions, told him what he wanted.

It wasn't his fault.

Nobody would blame him. How could anyone be expected to know that the damned kid was so fragile? Besides, the boy was a useless ragamuffin, a nobody who would have fallen to the guns of Perez's men anyhow. It was a justifiable homicide.

Hacker's cartwheeling brain stopped its mad turning and jolted to a halt on a single thought: Get rid of the body.

He stumbled through the gloom, a thin shroud of mist parting around him, and made his way to the end of the passage.

Behind the store, thrown carelessly in a jumbled heap, lay a pile of empty packing cases, including,

Hacker noticed, a large tea chest stamped with the word CEYLON.

The fat man stepped back to the dead boy and dragged the body to the tea chest, panting from the effort.

Small and undernourished, the child fit into the chest quite well.

Hacker then kicked the box over on its side and covered it with packing cases.

No one would find the corpse until the cases were removed . . . and that could be never.

Hacker leaned against the wall of the hotel and let his breathing return to normal. He told himself that the boy's death had been unfortunate, but by and large, he was quite happy.

Very happy, in fact.

He was as pleased as punch that his heart had stood up so well to all the fuss and bother.

Huzzah! And again, Huzzah!

Not even a twinge of pain, not so much as a tingle in his left arm. It all boded well for his upcoming nuptials and political future.

As to what happened by the river, let it go to hell. Sancho Perez would deal with it.

Hacker shouldered himself off the timber wall.

This was not the time to push his luck.

CHAPTER FORTY

Abe Hacker let himself back into the hotel.

His hands covered with the dead boy's blood, he had to use a corner of his robe to wipe a red stain off the shiny brass door handle. He went directly to his room, glad that no one had decided to make a nocturnal trip to the outhouse.

Nora sat up in bed and when Hacker stepped inside she looked at him in horror, then tossed the sheet aside and jumped to her feet.

"Abe, were you shot?"

"No. It's nothing," Hacker said.

He poured water from the pitcher into the basin.

"You're covered in blood," Nora said. Her face was very pale.

"I told you it's nothing," Hacker said. "Damn you, go back to sleep."

The water in the bowl turned red.

Nora took a step back. "My God, Abe, what have you done?"

Hacker turned his head to the woman. In the low

lamplight his eyes were wild, his fleshy face masked by demonic shadows.

"I killed somebody," he said.

Nora shrank from him. "Who, Abe?" She stared at the bloodstained front of his robe. "Who did you kill?"

"Does it matter?"

The woman said nothing but her wide eyes signaled her alarm.

"It was a boy. A troublemaker. Just a ragged gutter-snipe."

"A child?" Nora said.

"I didn't mean to kill him. It just happened. He wasn't strong."

Nora was appalled, horror and disbelief vivid in her eyes.

"You murdered a child?"

"He was nothing. A bug I squashed underfoot. Can't you understand that?"

For a few moments Nora stood petrified, her mouth open but empty of words.

Finally she said, "You're a monster, Abe. You're . . . evil."

His hands dripping rust-colored water, Hacker advanced on the terrified woman.

"You'll keep your trap shut or the same thing will happen to you." He pulled the derringer from his pocket. "I warn you, Nora. Don't try my patience."

But Nora Anderson had been raised hard, and her early adult life had been spent in the cribs where every day was a struggle for survival. She had sand, and Hacker gravely underestimated her. "You're a child murderer, Abe, and if I stay silent about it I'd be just as guilty and evil as you are," Nora said.

"Don't make a move toward the door or I'll kill you, Nora," Hacker said.

His eyes, lost in folds of fat, glittered.

"Abe, there's something I should have told you a long time ago," Nora said. She grabbed her robe. "Go to hell!"

The woman made a rush for the door, but Hacker, like many grossly obese men, could be as light on his feet as a ballet dancer.

He grabbed Nora just as she turned the handle and dragged her away from the door. As the woman cried out, Hacker, cursing, violently threw her across the room.

Nora stumbled and as she fell her head crashed into the top of the brass bed frame. She sprawled onto the floor, stunned, but tried to rise.

Hacker was on her like a cougar on a whitetail doe. His meaty hands circled Nora's neck and his thick thumbs dug deep.

The reality of killing up close and personal left Abe Hacker horrified.

He had ordered men killed before, but those were assassinations and death kept its distance. But the killing of the boy and now Nora was a new experience for him, apart from Jess Gable, who had been a dead man already.

The murders lay heavy on him, not because of a guilty conscience, but because the blood was on his hands.

Damn it all, he was a businessman, not an assassin.

Hacker paid lesser men to perform that chore, men like Mickey Pauleen.

He toed Nora's body. The woman lay still and was

not pretty in death. Her face had contorted grotesquely in her final agony and her eyes were open, accusing.

Hacker looked away, shut that image from his mind.

He laid the derringer on the bedside table and took off his stained robe. Outside a coyote, hunting close, passed Hacker's window like a gray ghost, a bloody, kicking thing hanging from its jaws. Farther away a woman cried out in her sleep, then the tranquil tick of the hallway clock testified that all was well.

Abe Hacker forced himself to think.

Two killings in one evening and yet another body to hide and through no fault of his own.

Recently it seemed that the whole damned world was against him.

Naked, he threw himself down on his chair by the window, scowling.

Think . . . think . . . think . . .

All would be well by late tomorrow afternoon. That much was certain.

Yes! He'd wrap Nora's body in his robe and stuff her under the bed. Plenty of room there!

Now Hacker's mind reached longer into the future.

He'd leave Last Chance when the town was burning and the slaughter of the rubes was well under way. He and Mickey would harness the pair of mules to the wagon that had originally brought them here and head upriver. Once they found a settlement a quick wire would set his friends in Washington scrambling to get him back home to his bride and his future.

The wagon parked behind the livery had not yet been supplied with food and water, but Mickey could enlist a couple of Sancho's men and take care of that. Hacker sat back and beamed.

There, that wasn't so difficult.

He rose to his feet and dragged Nora into the middle of the floor by her feet. He picked up his robe and began to wrap the body in it.

Damn, she was heavy! Nora had put on weight, no doubt because he'd treated her so well these last few years. Finally, with an effort that left him exhausted, Hacker managed to shove Nora's body under the high brass bed.

Her elegant left hand remained exposed, and he pushed it under with his foot.

Worn out from his exertions, Hacker rolled onto the bed and lay on his back. His massive belly made him look like a man trapped under a beer barrel.

He shifted his weight and the bed creaked.

Now he did it more purposefully, rolling back and forth.

Now the creak became a screeching squeal of protesting brass and steel.

Hacker rolled faster . . . faster . . .

"You like that, Nora?" he said. "You like my lullaby?" Hacker laughed.

He laughed until tears rolled down his cheeks and wet the pillow.

CHAPTER FORTY-ONE

Ephraim Slough was not a sleeping man.

Too many four-on, four-off watches on men o' war had disrupted his slumber in the past and he'd gradually lost the habit of it.

Thus it was that when he restlessly prowled around at the back of the livery, a dark, jumbled and cobwebby place, he found the chair. Slough realized that he'd made a valuable find.

He dragged the chair out of its hiding place and instantly caused a clattering avalanche of old harnesses, timber boards, and empty paint cans.

But once the chair was exposed to the lamplight, Sough's suspicions were confirmed. It was indeed a treasure.

He did a little wooden-legged version of that jig mariners call a hornpipe, and then, after he used a rag to dust off the chair, examined his find more closely.

It was a superb wheelchair with a hickory and oak frame and wicker seat and back. It had two iron, rubber-tired wheels to the front and a smaller version at the rear. A discreet little brass plaque screwed into the top of the frame declared that the chair was made by *Jas. Brougham & Son, Market Street, Boston, Mass.*

Slough thought the contraption superb, and just the thing to get Ranger Cannan around come the fight on the river.

The only trouble that Slough could see was that Cannan was a big man and the chair itself weighed close to sixty pounds. It would take another big man, and strong, to push it. Slough rubbed his stubbled chin, thinking it through.

There was only one candidate, big Simon Rule the blacksmith. But Rule had already been chosen by Cannan as one of his fighting men. Also on the downside, the smith was inclined to surliness and very down on demon drink and had often made Slough himself the object of his temperance tirades.

But Rule was the only man in town who could push the chair with Ranger Cannan in it, so no matter how distasteful it may be he was the obvious choice.

The wheels squeaked a little and Slough used his oilcan until they turned smoothly. Then he stepped back and admired the chair again.

It was a fine chariot for a Ranger and would sure help him get around come morning.

But Slough was not a man to do things by half.

He rolled the chair out of the livery to take it for a trial spin. It pushed very well empty, and Slough walked it along the street, alone but for himself, the restless mist, and the waning moonlight.

As he approached the Cattleman's Hotel the wheels began to squeak again.

Slough stopped but the squeaking continued, loud and increasingly frantic. Then he realized the noise was the steady shriek of a bed coming from the front room of the hotel.

Slough's jaw dropped.

What was going on inside, and now he heard a man's laughter rise above the screech . . . screech . . . screech . . . was indeed a heroic copulation.

Awed, Slough removed his hat, bowed his head in silent homage to the industrious stud, and turned the chair around.

Suddenly feeling inadequate, Slough got ready to retrace his steps to the livery when he saw the last of the moonlight glint on something lying in the narrow alley that separated the hotel from the general store.

The old sailor was ready to dismiss the gleam as moonlight on an empty bottle or can, but to satisfy his curiosity he let loose of the chair and stepped closer.

What he stooped to pick up was a five-pointed star that he'd seen before, pinned to the shirt of Mrs. Edith Kilcoyn's mischievous son, Andy.

Slough shook his head. Had the boy lost it already, or thrown it away? The latter seemed unlikely. The star was solid silver, the words TEXAS RANGER picked out in gold. As a piece of jewelry it had not been cheap to make and Andy, a street urchin, would appreciate its value.

The boy had lost it then.

But what had he been doing at the Cattleman's Hotel?

Slough peered into the alley but saw only darkness.

He put the star into his pocket and stepped to the wheelchair again.

The bed in the front room was now silent and Slough gave a second, perfunctory bow in the direction of the window before walking back to the livery.

* * *

The same moonlight that illuminated Ephraim Slough's path streamed through Henriette Valcour's window and bathed the old woman in mother-of-pearl radiance as she sat by the fire.

Her lamp was not lit because she'd hung the flag outside her door to mark Independence Day and a loup-garou, attracted by the thirty-eight stars, had squatted on the porch and tried to count them.

But such a number was well beyond any werewolf's ability and he'd continually lost his way and had to start all over again. Finally, after three hours, he'd bellowed his frustration like a bull alligator out in the swamp and had scurried away.

Henriette waited a while to make sure the loup-garou was gone. While not clever, they were sly and very dangerous, especially if they'd recently lost count.

Finally the old woman rose to her feet and stepped onto the porch.

The feral smell of the loup-garou lingered. The flag was undisturbed.

A gray fog hung on the swamp like a fallen rain-cloud, and out in the darkness Henriette heard a splash, followed by another.

"Jacques St. Romain, is that you out there?" she called.

The old black man's voice sounded hollow, like a bass drum in the darkness.

"I sure am, Miss Henriette."

"You fishing?"

"No, Miss Henriette. I trying to shoot me a wild hog fo' dinner today, me."

"You can't see in this mist."

"I kin hear a hog, smell him, too. Got me my forty-five."

"Jacques, you see a loup-garou at my door?"

A long pause, then the old man's voice carried flat across the swamp.

"I sure didn't, Miss Henriette. Is that why you sound troubled?"

"I can't see you, Jacques."

"You don't need to see me an' I don't need to see you to know you feel bad."

"I have a troubled mind, me."

"You havin' them visions again, Miss Henriette?"

Moonlight tinted the fog lighter gray in places but was so thick the old woman could barely see her front door.

"I see blood and murder and the deaths of children," Henriette called.

She heard the splash of oars and again there was a long pause before Jacques St. Romain answered, his voice echoing through the mist. "Don't you go tellin' me that now, Miss Henriette. I don't want to hear that."

"I mean no harm to you, Jacques," Henriette said. "You're a good man."

"I'm leavin' now, me," the old man yelled. "Got my hand on the cross around my neck so nothin' can harm me 'cause the Good Lord will watch over me."

"Jacques . . ." Henriette called.

But the old man had disappeared into fog and distance and a solemn silence settled on the bayou but for the croak of frogs among the roots of the cypress trees.

Henriette stepped back into the cabin, lit a lamp, and made herself tea.

She sat, cup in hand, and stared long and hard at the doll on the table beside her, the one she'd made in the shape of the fat man who so haunted her dreams. The old woman finished her tea, laid the cup on the table, and picked up the doll and a pin.

For a while the pin hovered over the doll's chest, but finally Henriette sighed and set down both doll and pin.

To thrust at the fat man's heart and bring about his death would deplete her power and she'd need all her strength to save Baptiste.

She couldn't be left weak and helpless when the battle—Henriette could not tell from her vision what it was—began when the sun was high in the sky.

It would be then that her grandson would be in the greatest peril. The fat man who had murdered the child would have to wait.

His time would come.

CHAPTER FORTY-TWO

The coming of the dawn of Independence Day woke two men in Last Chance at the same moment.

One was Ranger Hank Cannan, the other Abe Hacker.

The sky was a riot of color, cobalt barred by vivid scarlet, jade, and fish-scale gray, like an impressionist artist's vision of a medieval tournament. Buildings cast long shadows on the street, shop windows tinted red, and the morning air was fresh, July 4, 1887, coming in clean.

Abe Hacker woke to horror, the remembrance of what had happened in the night returning to him in jagged, bloody shards, one painful piece at a time.

Hacker lay still, his eyes open, listening. But the dead make no sound.

"Nora?" he whispered.

The room was still. Nothing moved, as though frozen in time.

Five minutes passed . . . then ten . . .

Hacker stared at the ceiling.

Two murders. Two bodies.

One in this very room.

Hacker's gasp of apprehension was almost a sob.

Please, Sancho, come soon and free me from this hell!

He made an effort, rolled off the bed and glanced nervously at the floor . . . then shrieked.

Nora's hand, white as marble, the long nails blood-red, again lay exposed on the rug. Her forefinger was bent, as though beckoning Hacker to join her. The fat man stared at the dead hand with revulsion, then rage.

Like a man possessed, he stomped on the hand again and again as though it was a pale spider that had crawled out from under the bed. Hacker felt bones splinter under his heel and he stamped harder, harder, harder still, cursing, his breath fluting through clenched teeth.

Nora's hand, which in life had been a dove's wing of slender beauty, was, in death, a crushed, cracked, and broken thing.

No longer did Hacker have the strength or inclination to kick the hand back under the bed.

He grabbed a towel from the rail beside the water basin and dropped it over the hand, hiding it from view.

Exhausted, Hacker took the chair by the window. Within moments his sweaty face took on an expression of fear mixed with the darkest dread.

An iron crab reached out for him, clasped his chest in its claws . . . and crushed.

Hacker gasped as pain spiked behind his breastbone as though he'd been run through by a rusty saber.

Like a symphony composed by a sadist, the agony proceeded through its appalling movements, climaxed, and wrenched a stifled scream from Hacker before it slowly ebbed away . . . and left him.

Ranger Hank Cannan woke to the dawn and a steady THUMP . . . THUMP . . . THUMP . . . on the stairs.

It wasn't Roxie or her friend Nancy Scott, since both young women moved with the quiet, rustling grace that Victorian society demanded of the fairer sex.

A man then, heavy and wearing boots.

Cannan drew his Colt from the holster hanging from its belt on the bedpost and, his eyes on the door, waited.

The events of the night had worn on the Ranger, and his habitually gloomy features were gaunt, his great mustache overhanging a mouth that was gradually losing its ability to smile.

The thumping on the stairs ceased, replaced by a soft, *squeak . . . squeak . . . squeak*, accompanied by the footfalls of a man steadily walking in the direction of Cannan's door. The Ranger thumbed back the hammer. Given his physical weakness he was determined to shoot first and apologize later.

Someone rapped on the door and Cannan, surprised at the feebleness of his voice, said, "Identify yourself and state your intentions."

A pause then, "Why it's me, cap'n, Ephraim Slough, beggin' your pardon I'm sure."

"Come in slow with your hands where I can see them."

The door opened and a grinning Slough stepped inside.

"See, cap'n, ol' Ephraim as ever was."

Cannan holstered the Colt.

"What can I do for you, Ephraim? Apart from not shooting you?"

"That ain't the question, cap'n, an' it be all the same to you. The question is, what have I done fer you?"

"All right then, what have you done for me?" Cannan said. He had a splitting headache.

"Lookee!" Slough said, with the air of a magician pulling a rabbit out of a top hat. He stepped back into the hallway and then, to the Ranger's surprise, pushed a contraption through the doorway.

"What the hell is that?" Cannan said.

"It's an invalid chair, cap'n. It will get you around today, an' no mistake. I mean, you feelin' right poorly an' all."

Cannan said, "Do you expect me to sit in that thing and have someone push me around?"

Slough's grin grew wider. "You catch on real quick, cap'n. I already spoke to big Simon Rule the blacksmith and he says he'll push you around an' be right happy to do it as a Christian duty."

Cannan was outraged, but he managed to keep his voice calm. "Ephraim, you've got five seconds to take both you and your invalid chair out of this room."

"But cap'n—"

"Now!"

Slough waved a placating hand. "All right, all right, but if you need it I'll—"

"I won't need it."

Slough angled the Ranger a whipped puppy look and backed the chair out of the room.

Once he had the chair in the hallway, he stuck his

head around the half-shut door and said, "If you change your mind—"

"Ephraim, get the hell away from me!" Cannan yelled.

The door closed and a moment later opened again.

Cannan sat bolt upright in bed. "Ephraim Slough! Step through that door and I'll shoot you!"

"Wait, cap'n, I forgot something," Slough said.

"If it's about the damned invalid damned chair I'll shoot you twice."

A careful man, Slough stayed behind the door but shoved his arm inside and waved the Ranger star.

"Lookee what I found, cap'n," he said. "Beggin' your pardon."

Cannan looked at the star and felt a chill deep in his belly.

"Let me see that, Ephraim," he said.

Slough, with the wary, shifty eyes of a man who was ready to duck, stepped inside and handed over the star. "Found it in an alley between the general store and the Cattleman's Hotel," he said.

"I gave this to young Andy Kilcoyn after I swore him in as an acting Ranger," Cannan said. "How did it come to be there?"

"The boy either dropped it or threw it away, cap'n. But knowing Andy, he wouldn't get rid of a valuable piece of silver."

"Then he must have lost it," Cannan said. "Though what he was doing near the Cattleman's Hotel I can't imagine."

"Seems like the case, cap'n," Slough said. "Boys are a savage breed and they do lose things."

"Well, I'm due to meet my particular savage this morning, so I'll return it to him then."

Cannan felt a twinge of guilt for treating Slough so badly over the chair, an act of kindness he should have appreciated.

"My wife's coming in on the noon stage today," he said.

Alarm showed on the old sailor's face, but he managed to banish it with a smile.

"Glad to hear that, cap'n. I'm sure you're looking forward to seeing the missus again."

"Yes I am Mrs. Cannan is a fine woman."

"And purty, too, I bet," Slough said.

"I think so."

A silence stretched between the two men and both knew what was going unsaid.

Finally Cannan brought it into the open. "Ephraim, if things go badly at the river and I should fall . . ."

"Yes, cap'n?"

The Ranger swallowed hard. "If Sancho Perez and his bandits break us and get into town, you're in command of the reserve regiment and . . ."

"I'll do my duty, cap'n. Neither Mrs. Cannan nor any other woman of this town will be carried off by Mexican bandits. Not alive, they won't."

The Ranger nodded.

"It's a mighty hard thing to talk about, Ephraim. But it's something a man must consider. "

"I reckon homesteaders who lived in Apache country talked about it often enough, both men and womenfolk."

"I don't want to talk about it any more, Ephraim, do you?"

"No, I don't." Slough smiled. "We have Independence

Day to celebrate, and I reckon tonight Mrs. Cannan will be dancing like a bobber on a line."

"If we don't have too many new widows," the Ranger said.

The old mariner's smile faded. "Yes, cap'n," he said. "There's always that."

CHAPTER FORTY-THREE

The tomblike silence of the hotel room and the steady tick of the grandfather clock in the hallway had Abe Hacker teetering on the edge of hysteria.

The sudden attack of chest pain had terrified him. Like fairy gifts, were all his dreams about to fade away?

Hacker sat by the window, his chin sunk on his chest.

How could the delights of his child bride, his future political career, and above all the rest, his son, be held hostage to a weak heart?

A tear trickled down the fat man's cheek. It was so unfair, so damned unmerited.

Hacker stood, sat down again. He did this several times. No pain. Surely that was good?

Perhaps the attack, now it had happened, would take years to happen again? If ever? He had no way of knowing.

Ahead of him in Washington awaited great mental and physical exertions, in the marital bed as well as the political arena.

If he was to become president, his heart must hold up. Be as strong as Chicago steel.

Indian clubs would help, those and freedom from the stress of this latest enterprise, a complicated business from the start. Hacker sighed and brushed away a tear.

The damned street boy and Nora hadn't helped.

Both had heaped a lot of strain on him and brought on the chest pain. Damn them both, they were to blame.

Hacker got to his feet.

He could not remain in this room so close to Nora's body.

He'd shave, get dressed in his best, and take a stroll down the street to the restaurant and partake of beefsteak and eggs for breakfast and then step into a saloon for coffee and brandy. Under the circumstances it was better to be bold, show himself, and, should anyone inquire, Nora was still in bed sleeping off a hangover.

When Perez's onslaught came, he'd retreat to the livery stable and await the arrival of Mickey Pauleen . . . then on to Washington and his golden future.

The water in the basin was red from the boy's blood, so Hacker decided to forgo the shave and immediately get dressed. He stepped to the wardrobe and glanced at the floor.

The towel had been removed from Nora's hand.

Hacker stared, blinked, stared again.

There was no mistake. The towel was gone and the

woman's hand was exposed. It looked like a claw and the index finger still beckoned him. Hacker shrieked.

He yanked clothes out of the wardrobe and hurriedly dressed, as though the wrath of God was about to descend on him.

CHAPTER FORTY-FOUR

Weary . . . that's how Ranger Hank Cannan described himself to Roxie Miller when she brought him breakfast.

"You should be in bed," the woman said. "How many times have I said that to you over the last couple of months?"

"Quite a few, I fancy," Cannan said.

Despite the early hour and her plain gray morning dress, Roxie's vivid beauty stunned Cannan as it always did. Then, almost guiltily, he said, "My wife is coming in today."

"I know, you told me that already," Roxie said. She laid the tray on the table. "You must be very happy."

"I am. But I wish it was any other day than this one."

"Maybe it won't happen. The attack, I mean."

"It will happen, Roxie, depend on it." Cannan opened his mouth, then closed it again.

He couldn't find the words.

But Roxie, well used to tongue-tied men, read his eyes. "You're worried about me, aren't you?"

"You, my wife, all the other women in this town."

Roxie reached into the pocket of her dress and produced a .32 caliber Sharps four-barreled pepperbox, ornately engraved with ivory grips. "Baptiste Dupoix worries about the same thing," he said. "He gave me this and told me when to use it."

The Ranger managed a smile. "I don't think it will come to that, Roxie."

"Well, if it does, I know what to do."

Cannan had shaved and dressed. His gun belt and hat lay on the bed.

"You look very handsome, Ranger," Roxie said. "Your wife will be pleased."

"Dupoix tells me I look like a walrus."

"One of those big seal-y things with tusks?"

The Ranger smiled. "Yeah, one of those. They live up in the Eskimo territory."

Roxie put her forefinger to her chin and stared into Cannan's face. "Well, maybe a little," she said. "Of course, I've never seen one except in a drawing."

Cannan laughed and it felt good. "I guess looking a little like a walrus is better than looking a lot like a walrus."

Roxie smiled. "No matter, Ranger Cannan. You still look very handsome this morning."

"And you are very beautiful."

Roxie smiled and gave a little curtsy. "Why, thank you Mr. Cannan. You are *très galante.*"

After Roxie left, Cannan ate a hurried breakfast then buckled on his gun belt and adjusted the lie of the holstered Colt. Roxie had put a brave face on things, but he'd read fear in the young woman's eyes.

If he was a betting man he'd stake the farm that the eyes of every man and woman in town revealed the same sense of dread.

And then it dawned on him that he was also scared, for his wife, for the people, and for himself.

Dupoix had not returned and Cannan didn't know if he was alive or dead. The gambler was steady, and his presence would have been reassuring, to say nothing of the ranchers and their tough hands.

Now the whole burden of command lay heavy on Cannan's shoulders, and he had no idea if he was man enough to bear it.

Ranger Cannan took the stairs one step at a time, pausing often as the cumulative effect of wounds, a loss of blood he'd not yet restored, and restless sleep that was no sleep at all took their toll.

When he stepped out of the hotel the town hall clock, which never kept the right time, claimed it was ten after eight. In fact it was not yet eight o'clock.

The morning smelled fresh of sagebrush and cedar and a faint whiff of gunpowder as a couple of Chinese children, too young to know what they were celebrating, set off firecrackers in the alley next to the laundry.

Ephraim Slough, his face tingling with anticipation, stood beside the invalid chair and behind it the stocky, stalwart form of Simon Rule the blacksmith.

Studiously ignoring the chair and its eager attendants, Cannan looked up and down the street.

Every storefront made a patriotic show of red, white, and blue bunting, some of it quite frayed and torn, the wear and tear of many Independence Days past.

Outside the Last Mile saloon the Polish brothers,

hammers in hand, had almost assembled a temporary dance floor, and married women and their young daughters were already setting up trestle tables in the street, covering them with spotless white linen.

The street was already crowded with people, but they seemed to move sluggishly and without enthusiasm and there was no movement toward the tapped beer barrels, though children watched with intense interest the whole hogs turning on spits.

The town knew what was about to happen and what Sancho Perez and his bandits would bring. For the first time in their lives, the people of Last Chance took no joy in Independence Day, and it stabbed Cannan to the heart.

He finally said good morning to Slough and the blacksmith. "Ephraim, still no sign of Andy Kilcoyn?" he said.

"Beggin' your pardon, cap'n, neither hide nor hair. His ma says he didn't come home last night and she's beside herself with worry."

Despite his growing concern for the boy, Cannan's priority was still the defense of Last Chance. "Ephraim, I need someone to take Andy's place," he said.

"What would be his duties, cap'n?" Slough said.

The Ranger repeated what he had told the boy about scouting for a dust cloud.

"Hell, cap'n, I'll do it myself," Slough said.

"You can't do it, Ephraim. You're in command of the reserve regiment."

"Well, cap'n, I don't think I'm likely to have a regiment. Once the shooting starts, the boys and the old coots like me will grab their squirrel rifles and head for the sound of the gunfire."

"He's right, Ranger," Rule said. "The boys aren't about to stand in line doing nothing while their pas and older brothers are fighting for their lives. As for the old-timers, they'll do whatever they damn well please anyway."

"You know what we need here, cap'n?" Slough said. "A regiment of U.S. cavalry."

"Well we don't have one of them, Ephraim," Cannan said, irritated.

"Or a battery of cannon," Rule said.

As Slough nodded his approval of the blacksmith's suggestion, the Ranger snapped, "We don't have one of them, either."

Two young matrons carrying parasols stopped and Cannan touched his hat brim. "Ladies."

The one who spoke was a handsome woman with hazel eyes and chestnut hair, swept up and topped by a flowered hat so small it was barely there. "You are the Texas Ranger person?"

"Your obedient servant, ma'am," Cannan said with a little bow.

"Is it true we will soon be under siege by bandits?" the woman said.

The Ranger saw little point in trying to soften the blow.

"I'm afraid that is so, ma'am."

"And where, pray, is our army?"

"I imagine still trying to get the Apaches settled, ma'am."

"Well, it's most inconsiderate of them." The woman turned to her companion. "Is that not so, Rebecca?"

The other woman nodded without opening her tight little mousetrap of a mouth.

"I strongly suggest, ladies, that when you hear gunfire you immediately lock yourselves in your homes," Cannan said.

"Indeed we will not, sir," the woman called Rebecca said. She tossed her head. "Not when our men are exposed to danger. The very idea!" She offered her arm to her companion.

"Come, Susan, let us remain outdoors and explore the festivities further."

The young women walked away with stiff backs, their bustles swaying back and forth in unison.

"Seems like them two ladies don't plan to be in the reserve regiment, either, cap'n," Slough said.

Cannan managed a stiff smile. "I don't know if I want to hug them or take a stick to them."

"One would be quite as unpleasant as the other, Ranger Cannan," the woman called Susan said over her shoulder.

Slough grinned. "Cap'n, anybody ever tell you that you got a voice like a foghorn and that women can hear a mouse squeak from half a league away?"

Cannan nodded. "I knew it, but I'd forgotten."

"Your missus will remind you real soon," Slough said.

Mention of his wife returned Cannan to the present. He told Slough what he'd ordered Andy Kilcoyn to do.

The old sailor knuckled his forehead. "I'll saddle my mare right away," he said.

"No, not yet, Ephraim. But stay close to me."

"As you say, cap'n."

"Now I want to inspect the trenches at the river," Cannan said. "Then I'll come back and gauge the mood of the men and remind them of their orders."

"Your chariot awaits, Ranger," Rule said.

"Get rid of that damned thing," Cannan said.

He took a step, then another, and staggered a little as a wave of weakness washed over him. He sat on the edge of the boardwalk, his head spinning.

Cannan groaned, feeling his wounds. *Dear God, am I ever going to feel strong again?*

Big Simon Rule stepped beside him.

"Man hasn't been born yet who never needed help now and then, Ranger."

Cannan lifted his eyes to the blacksmith. "Bring that infernal contraption over here," he said.

CHAPTER FORTY-FIVE

To Mickey Pauleen the Mexican peons looked like the damned shuffling toward the gates of hell.

Sancho Perez's men drove them on with whips in the direction of the river, and too thirsty, hungry, and sick to resist, the host of men, women, and children staggered onward under a merciless sun.

Bodies, some of them tiny bundles, littered the sand where the peons had last camped, a sight that disturbed Pauleen.

"Damn it, Sancho, did you have to lose so many?" he said, as he and the bandit sat their horses and watched the procession.

"There's enough left, Mickey my fren'," Perez grinned. "We have all we need."

"If more die before we reach the Rio Grande," Pauleen said, "you'll lose money."

"Not too many more will die, I think," Perez said. "They have not far to go."

The bandit stood in the stirrups and yelled a stream of cursing Spanish at one of his men who'd ridden past a woman who sat on the ground.

"I told him to get her to her feet," Perez said to Pauleen. "If one is allowed to sit, they'll all sit."

The bandit was dressed for battle, ammunition bandoliers across his chest, a belt gun and spare tucked into his embroidered pants. He still wore a sombrero, but the poke bonnet hung by its ties from the saddle horn.

Perez produced a bright blue bandana from his sleeve and wiped his sweaty face. "Mickey, my very good fren'," he said. "Sancho longs to be in his cool hacienda, drinking tequila and attended by his women."

"You'll be there soon enough," Pauleen said. "And I'll be with my own woman."

"Ha! Is she pretty, this woman?"

"Real pretty." The little gunman cupped his hands and held them in front of his chest. "And she's got a pair of big ones."

Perez grinned and his teeth flashed. "Sancho would like such a woman."

"She's mine, sorry."

The bandit shrugged. "No matter, the town of Last Chance is full of such women."

Pauleen nodded. "Of course it is. You and your men can take your pick, Sancho." The gunman kneed his horse forward. "We'll be choking in peon dust and stink if we don't move," he said. He and Perez rode until they took the point of the moving human herd.

Whips cracked and now and then someone cried out as braided leather cut into thin, dehydrated flesh. Some cried out for water, but Perez and Pauleen ignored them.

The peons must hit the river thirsty and the town starving.

"Let me tell you something, Mickey," Perez said. "In

my hacienda I have much treasure, gathered together after years of raiding and robbing."

"What you going to do with it all, Sancho?"

"Retire after this raid and no longer ride the desert. I plan to spend the rest of my life in Guadalajara or maybe Mexico City and live like a rich man should." The bandit turned to Pauleen and grinned. "Come work for me, Mickey. I like you, and it is good for a wealthy man to have a famous pistolero by his side."

Pauleen shook his head. "I can't do that, Sancho. The thing you ask I already promised to Abe Hacker."

"Ah, then I will not try to tempt you from such an honorable man. But poor Sancho is ver' sad."

Pauleen turned in the saddle, his snake eyes troubled. "Sancho, when you start shooting up the town, take care you don't hit my woman. You understand me?"

"*Sí*, I do. But how to know one woman from so many others?"

"She'll be in the Cattleman's Hotel. You got that? The Cattleman's Hotel."

"I will take care, but as to my men, who knows?"

"I'll kill any man who lays a finger on her," Pauleen said.

Perez grinned. "She means much to you, this woman, huh?"

Pauleen's gazed into the distance ahead of him. "All my life, I've never owned something beautiful."

"You mean, like a painting or a marble sculpture as I have in my home?"

"Yeah, like that."

"Is she as beautiful as a painting, this woman, Mickey?"

"Enough that I want to own her."

"Then my men won't touch her, my fren'. She is yours."

Pauleen smiled. "One day her loveliness will wane, and she'll change. Her beautiful colors will fade to gray, but until then she'll be my possession. *Mickey Pauleen's property—hands off.*"

Perez laughed and slapped his thigh. Startled, his horse shook its head and the bit chimed.

"You are funny, Mickey. That's why I like you." The bandit knitted his thick eyebrows. "But who owns this woman now?"

"Abe Hacker."

"She is beautiful, yet he gives her away? Sancho does not understand such a thing."

"He has his eyes set on someone much younger he plans to take as his wife."

Perez grinned. "Señor Hacker is . . . how do you say it? . . . a lady-killer."

"That he is," Mickey Pauleen said. "He's a born lady-killer."

CHAPTER FORTY-SIX

Ranger Hank Cannan endured a bumpy, jolting ride to the riverbank, and Simon Rule's lecture on the evils of demon drink added to his misery. To his joy, the trench remained relatively dry, and there was no sign of lifting dust to the south.

"Maybe they ain't comin'," Ephraim Slough said. "Called the whole thing off, maybe so, cap'n."

"They'll come," Cannan said.

He passed Rule his Winchester, then tried to get up from the chair, but the effort overwhelmed him and he quickly sat down again.

Rule smiled. "Don't get uppity, Ranger."

And Slough cackled. "That's a good one, Simon, a real stingeroo."

"Yeah, you boys are just killing me," Cannan said.

He'd sat on his holstered Colt and now he had to stand up again and lift the revolver out of the way, causing more mirth among his companions.

"Ephraim, I want you to stay right here," Cannan said. "When you see the bandit scout leave, get on your horse, cross the river, and watch for dust, then—"

"I know the rest, cap'n, begging your pardon," Slough said. "You done tole me all that maybe sixty times already."

"Then remember it and stay off the whiskey," Cannan said.

"Amen, brother," Rule said.

"The whole town is depending on your courage and your eyesight, Ephraim," Cannan said.

The old sailor knuckled his forehead. "Aye-aye, cap'n. You can depend on me."

"Then let's go, Mr. Rule, and we'll talk to the mayor and anybody else who needs talking to. And keep your eyes open for Andy Kilcoyn. I want to have words with that young man."

"He's a scamp," the blacksmith said.

Cannan said, "I hope he hasn't deserted in the face of the enemy."

"Andy sometimes helps me around the forge," Rule said. "You know how many times he's been burned and never a word of complaint?" Rule answered his own question. "Dozens of times, Ranger. The youngster has sand."

"Then his not showing up for duty is all the more mysterious," Cannan said.

On a normal occasion, a Texas Ranger getting trundled around in an invalid chair by the town blacksmith would have generated a certain amount of questions and suppressed giggles.

But as the reality of the situation took hold the mood in Last Chance had become more somber.

Firecrackers crackled constantly and the trestle tables groaned under the weight of food, the air fragrant with cinnamon from the apple pies and the tang of roasting pork. But there were few smiles.

Mayor Frank Curtis met Cannan in the street. He did not comment on the chair, as though it was an insignificant concern among so many others that were much more pressing. "No sign yet?" Curtis said.

A normally polite man, he did not precede his words with a "good morning"—a measure of his anxiety.

"No, nothing," Cannan said. "Ephraim Slough is down by the river, watching."

"Is that old pirate sober?"

"I reckon he is," Cannan said. "Ephraim knows what's at stake."

A talk between a Ranger and their mayor attracted a crowd, and a score of people stood around listening, their faces solemn.

The saloons, which on a normal Independence Day would have been booming, were unnaturally quiet.

Cannan saw Roxie, wearing a short, bright blue dress, step through the open doors of the Last Mile saloon and stand on the boardwalk. She studied the chair for a few moments and smiled at him.

Cannon touched his hat and looked away.

"Ranger, is there no other way?" Curtis said.

People in the crowd muttered the same question to one another then looked expectantly at Cannan. "Yes, you can surrender and let Sancho Perez and his bandits ride into town," he said.

"Surrender is not an option," Curtis said. "Especially on this Independence Day."

"Then there's no other way," Cannan said.

"My God, how many will we lose?" a woman said.

"I don't know, lady," the Ranger said, his anger flaring. "I don't know when Perez will come. I don't even know if my plan will work. I don't know anything, not a damned thing, so don't ask me."

"It was a fair question, Ranger Cannan," Curtis said mildly.

"I don't care how fair it was, Mayor. I have no answers." Cannan glanced around at the strained faces the surrounded him. He was not a speechifying man, but he tried.

"More than a hundred years ago our Founding Fathers chose liberty over death," he said. "They declared it was better to be free men and die on their feet than be slaves and die on their knees.

"Now you people face the same choice, and only you can decide."

"We've already made our decision," Curtis said. "We'll fight to the last breath, and that's our very own Declaration of Independence."

Now there were cheers and no dissenting voices.

Cannan, much affected by this display, said, "Mayor, I want to swear in every man, woman, and child in this town as deputy Texas Rangers."

"No, Mr. Cannan," Curtis said. "We'll fight this battle as ordinary American citizens, as it should be this Fourth of July." He pointed to the church tower. "Yonder is the bell of freedom. When it rings, we'll answer the call."

Without waiting for a comment from Cannan, they mayor stepped away and walked into the crowd. "Listen up, everybody. I'm tired of seeing all the long faces around me," he said. "Now let's celebrate this memorable day as we've always done in the past."

That last drew cheers, and it seemed as though a good-humored angel had passed through the crowd, slapping backs and shaking hands. At a signal from

Roxie, the piano in the Last Mile started up, and soon others up and down the street joined in, their tinny dueling notes getting hopelessly tangled. It seemed to Cannan that Last Chance had returned to its usual, carefree ways, at least for now.

But the Ranger felt deeply depressed.

He wondered how the townspeople would react when he presented them with the butcher's bill.

CHAPTER FORTY-SEVEN

Roxie Miller hailed Hank Cannan from the boardwalk. She stepped into the street, treading carefully in silk, high-heeled shoes, her vivid blue dress tight across her bust and hips.

"Happy Independence Day, Roxie," Cannan said, touching his hat brim. "I forgot to say it this morning, didn't I?"

The woman didn't answer that. Instead, she said, "Guess who's in the saloon, bold as brass? Abe Hacker."

"What's he doing?"

Roxie smiled. "What any man does in a saloon. He's drinking."

"Is he alone?"

"Yes, he is."

"Where's his . . . where's—"

"Nora? He says she's sleeping off last night's drunk."

"Time for me to read to him from the book," Cannan said. He turned to Simon Rule. "Push me to the boardwalk and I'll take it from there."

The blacksmith did as he was told, but Cannan couldn't step up to the walk without Rule's assistance.

"I swore I'd never again enter a saloon, Ranger," Rule said. "But I'll come in with you if you want."

"Too much temptation for you in there, Simon," Cannan said. "Demon rum is lying in wait in every corner."

"It's pleased I am, Ranger, that I've showed you the righteous path of abstinence," Rule said.

"Amen, brother," Cannan said. He badly needed a drink.

Cannan stepped from the bright street to the cool shade of the saloon, and it took his eyes a while to adjust. When his vision returned he saw Hacker sitting in a corner, his back to the wall.

There were a score of men in the Last Mile, all of them drinking, but none were drunk. "Take it easy now, boys," the Ranger said as he lurched rather than walked to the bar.

"We hear you, Ranger," a man said, nodding.

Cannan ordered a whiskey, then made his way along the bar, not trusting himself to stand without support.

When he was within speaking distance of Hacker, the fat man grinned. "Sorry to see you keeping so poorly, Ranger Cannan. That's who you are, isn't it?

"You know it, Hacker."

The fat man had a pot of coffee and a bottle of Hennessy on the table. "Can I offer you a drink?" Hacker said. "My, my, it looks like you need a brandy, being so weak and sickly and all."

"Where's your boy?" Cannan said.

Hacker pretended puzzlement. "Oh, you mean my associate Mr. Mickey Pauleen? He's out riding or sparking a farm girl, I suppose. He comes and goes."

Hacker was dressed up like a Wall Street banker, but was unshaven. Cannan wondered at that.

"I hope you haven't come to arrest me, Mr. Cannan," the fat man said. Sweat beaded on his forehead. "You'd be making a big mistake." The spout of the coffeepot steamed as Hacker poured some into his cup.

"You're responsible for what's going to happen here today, Hacker," Cannan said.

"Really? Me? The Independence Day celebration? I'm flattered."

"I mean the impending attack on this town by the bandit Sancho Perez and the driving of hundreds of starving Mexicans across the Rio Grande to lay waste to the land."

"And you have proof of this . . . fantasy?" Hacker said. "And a motive?"

"Not yet, but I'll get them. And I'll see you hang."

"Your word is good enough for me, Ranger," a man said. "I say we string him up right now." Cries of agreement from others followed, and angry voices were raised.

The man who'd first spoken, a tall drink of water who wore a store-bought suit and celluloid collar, pointed an accusing finger at Hacker. "His hired gun shot old Marshal Dixon, and I reckon the same man murdered Ed Gillman."

There were calls of "String him up," and "Drag him out of here."

But Hacker put on a remarkable show of calmness. "You're a rabble-rouser, Cannan. I'm a respectable businessman and you won't put the run on me," he said. "Now call off your dogs."

"We'll have no lynching, men," Cannan said. "We won't crawl around in the slime with Hacker and his kind. When you wallow with pigs you can expect to get dirty."

"Eloquent, Ranger," the fat man said, his tight eyes glittering. "Really impressive for an illiterate, dollar-a-day lawman."

Cannan felt someone brush past him, and to his surprise Roxie stepped toward Hacker's table, her heels drumming on the wood floor. Alarmed, Hacker half-rose from his chair and met Roxie's stinging slap across his jowly cheek. "You will not insult Ranger Cannan in my presence," she said, her beautiful face flushed.

For a moment Hacker sat openmouthed in astonishment, then his anger flared into violence. He stumbled to his feet, snarling like an animal, derringer in hand.

"You cheap whore! I'll kill you for that."

No one ever said that Hank Cannan was slow on the draw, just mighty uncertain on the shoot. His Colt slicked out of the holster and he yelled, "Drop it, Hacker or I'll kill you."

The fat man turned, saw both fire and ice in Cannan's eyes, and let the belly gun thud to the table.

"I've had my fill of you, Hacker," the Ranger said. "Get back to your hotel and stay there until I come for you."

The fat man looked at the circle of hostile faces surrounding him and decided not to push it. "You'll regret this," he said. "Every man jack of you."

"Git, Hacker," Cannan said. "Git while you still can."

With as much of his old arrogance as he could muster, Hacker walked toward the door. But the thin man in the celluloid collar blocked his way.

"Know this," the thin man said. "If things come to pass as the Ranger says they will, when the smoke clears you won't be among the living."

"Depend on it," another man said.

* * *

Hacker clove his way through angry, threatening men. His outward demeanor was calm, but inwardly he was in turmoil. No power in heaven or hell could get him back to the hotel room to see again the terrifying specter of Nora's broken claw beckoning to him.

It was time to make another plan.

Hacker passed along the crowded street and saw no one. He was a man alone, an island of seething hatred in a sea of celebrating people.

He avoided the hotel and the alley where he'd dumped the boy's body, and crossed the street and walked into another shady passage between buildings.

He lit a cigar with a trembling hand and considered his options, which were few. Finally he realized that there was really only one course of action open to him.

He must cross the river and fall in with Sancho Perez.

CHAPTER FORTY-EIGHT

Ephraim Slough's eyes smarted from the glare of the sun, and he was dry enough to spit cotton.

He considered it a grave fault in the character of Ranger Cannan that he'd left him out in the broiling heat without a bottle of whiskey to wet his parched lips.

Inconsiderate, that's what it was, no regard for another person's welfare.

It never occurred to Slough that he could sneak into town and buy a bottle. Such an action would be a gross dereliction of duty and it didn't enter into his thinking.

He picked up his telescope and ranged the glass across the desert. He saw nothing.

There was no bandit scout, no dust cloud, only a barren, empty, and sun-scorched landscape of sand, cactus, and brush.

Slough shook his head.

Damn, kicking his heels on the riverbank was a waste of time.

What was it Lord Nelson said before the Battle of Trafalgar?

"Frigates forward, seek out the foe."

Yeah, that was it. Seek out the foe.

Slough's horse, in fact Mrs. Maude Morrison's spotted mare Sophie, stood hipshot and miserable, head and tail lowered, wilting in the heat. "Frigates forward, Sophie," the old sailor said. "We will cross the river and seek out the foe like Nelson done that time." His peg leg a hindrance, Slough clambered into the saddle, then kneed the reluctant mare into the river.

Overjoyed to be taking an active role in the defense of Last Chance instead of waiting passively for the Mexicans to act, Slough threw back his head and burst into song.

> *When the Alabama's keel was laid,*
> *Roll, Alabama, Roll,*
> *'Twas laid in the yard of Jonathan Laird,*
> *O Roll, Alabama, Roll.*

Hate-filled eyes watched Ephraim Slough closely. It looked like the drunken gimp was heading out in search of Sancho Perez.

Abe Hacker smiled to himself.

Well, let him. He'd die all the sooner.

> *'Twas laid in the yard of Jonathan Laird,*
> *Roll, Alabama, Roll,*
> *'Twas laid in the town of Birkenhead,*
> *O Roll, Alabama, Roll.*

Hacker had stripped to his shirt, brocaded vest, shoes, and pants and had dumped the rest in the alley beside the hotel. He stood a ways to the east of the river crossing, hidden from view of the street by a projecting toolshed attached to the rear of the Jenkins Bros. hardware store.

And bided his time.

The riverbank was deserted and as soon as the gimp was out of sight he'd make his move.

> *Down the Mersey way she rolled then,*
> *Roll, Alabama, Roll,*
> *Liverpool fitted her with guns and men,*
> *O Roll, Alabama, Roll . . .*

Slough's raw-edged tenor faded into distance as he was absorbed into the rippling heat haze, and Hacker watched him go.

Hacker was not a swimmer, but judging by the liveryman's horse, the water should only reach as high as his waist. Once into the desert he'd dry quickly.

Sweat beaded his forehead like condensation on an olla, and he had a ferocious headache brought on by stress and fear. As he stepped to the riverbank his earlier feelings were replaced by outrage that a man in his position should be subjected to this indignity. This damned inconvenience.

That he'd killed two people did not enter his mind.

A boy and a whore were nonentities and easily replaceable, but he was not, and that was the crux of the matter.

Abe Hacker, millionaire confidante of presidents, was now running for his life . . . and America should hang its head in shame.

Hacker waded across the Rio Grande without incident but he was exhausted by the time he reached the far bank. Wallowing in the depths of self-pity, he'd noticed Cannan's newly dug trench but its significance didn't register with him. His passing thought was that it was a mantrap and he dismissed it totally as a futile defensive gesture.

Hacker had no canteen, so the immediate need was to tank up with water.

Fearing that he would not be able to rise again if he bellied down to drink, the fat man stooped and used a hand to cup water into his mouth. He drank until he could hold no more, wiped his mouth with his great chubby paw, and began his trek to the south.

He was confident he'd meet up with Perez and the others soon.

And then he would make Last Chance pay . . . and nail the meddling Texas Ranger to a cross hung with red, white, and blue.

Happy Independence Day!

The fat man grinned.

Damn him, Hank Cannan would soon rue the day he was born and curse the two-dollar whore that bore him.

As the hour of the attack on Last Chance grew closer, Mickey Pauleen rode point, a mile ahead of Perez and the Mexicans.

He wanted no unpleasant surprises.

The Texas Ranger might well be a fool, and crippled, but he was a fighting man and such men were hard to kill.

Pauleen's eyes scanned the desert ahead of him. Every square inch sizzled like hog fat in a frying pan and gave off heat that undulated in the distance like a line of dancing cobras. A town animal, Pauleen hated the wasteland with a passion and saw no beauty in it.

Once he spotted a thin dust cloud trail into the air to the west but dismissed it as a stray Mexican making for the river, and gave it no further thought.

A few minutes later Pauleen rode up on what he took to be a large boulder, then realized it was no boulder but a fat man down on all fours.

To his surprise it was Abe Hacker, red-faced, panting like a lizard on a hot rock.

Pauleen drew rein but stayed mounted. "Howdy, Abe," he said. "Fancy meeting you here."

Hacker lifted his head. "Mickey, thank God it's you. I'm dying here."

"Where's Nora?" Pauleen said.

Hacker couldn't see the gunman's eyes in the shade of his hat. "She's safe, Mickey. Real safe."

"Where safe?"

"Back at the hotel getting packed. You know how women are."

"Yeah, I know how women are. Why did you leave her alone?"

Hacker moved his immense bulk and half-lay, half-sat on his side.

"The Ranger was on to me, Mickey. I had to run before they strung me up."

"You're too fat to hang, Abe. Why did you abandon Nora?"

"They've got nothing on Nora, Mickey. She'll be safe at the hotel until we get there."

"I hope for your sake that's the case," Pauleen said. He tossed his canteen to Hacker.

"Drink," he said.

"Thank'ee Mickey," the fat man said. "I knew when you found me you'd take good care of me."

Pauleen let that pass and swung out of the saddle. "Get up on the hoss and I'll take you to Perez," he said. "He's close."

"Mickey, a man with my portly figure can't ride a horse, you know that," Hacker said. His whine sounded like an out-of-tune violin.

Pauleen grinned. "Seems like you have three choices, Abe. Ride the hoss, stay where you're at, or I pull you behind me with a rope."

The fat man's anger flared. "Mickey, a man like you doesn't force Abe Hacker to choose anything. Not a damned thing."

Pauleen's face was ugly. "Abe, never try to corner a man who's a sight meaner than you. Now make your choice."

Hacker read Pauleen's eyes and didn't like what he saw.

"I'll ride the horse," he said.

"Good decision," the gunman said.

"Señor Hacker, I am overjoyed," Sancho Perez said. His face took on a concerned frown. "But what brings you into the desert?"

"They planned on hanging me, Sancho," Hacker said. "I only just escaped with my life."

"Is that so, my fren'? That makes poor Sancho ver' sad. Many will die for such a wicked plan."

Perez had pulled his horse over to one side as his men drove the peons forward with whips. Dead and dying Mexicans littered the churned-up trail behind them, dust sifting over the bodies as though the desert wished to cover up the atrocity.

At Perez's command, three of his men helped Hacker from his horse. Then they stopped one of the donkey wagons bringing up the rear of the column and removed a small tarp and four poles.

"Sancho will give his good fren' shelter from the sun," the bandit said. "Señor Hacker does not look well and Sancho fears he must weep from heartbreak at such a sight." Perez gave Hacker a canteen, a couple of cigars, and a bottle of mescal.

"You are a good and loyal friend, Sancho," Hacker said. He then spoke to the bandit but stared at Pauleen. "Such loyalty will not go unrewarded."

"Alas, Sancho must go now," Perez said. "But when the town is taken I will come back for you and we will return to my hacienda and celebrate with wine and women."

"And afterward, I must return to Washington," Hacker said from the thin shade of his shelter.

"Of course you must return to where your destiny lies, and Sancho will help because you are his very best fren'." The bandit turned his horse and rode after the wailing column.

Pauleen lingered long enough to say, "I hope I find Nora alive and well." The expression on the gunman's face was so malevolent, so dangerous, that Hacker was shocked into silence.

Later, as a hot breeze tugged at his meager canopy, the fat man realized that he was all alone in the middle of the naked desert . . . and very afraid.

CHAPTER FORTY-NINE

Horace Wilcox, the stage depot manager, greeted Hank Cannon with a face even sadder and longer than his own. "Not an auspicious day for your lady wife to arrive, Ranger Cannan," he said. "Oh, I don't mean Independence Day, I mean—"

Cannan nodded. "I know what you mean. Yes, she could have chosen a better one."

Cannan stood on his own feet, the wheelchair parked outside, big Simon Rule keeping close and stern guard lest some unscrupulous thief try to steal it.

"Will the stage arrive on time, you think?" the Ranger said.

"My dear sir, the Butterfield stage always arrives on time, give or take a day or two," Wilcox said. He glanced at the solemn railroad clock on the wall. "It's noon now, Ranger Cannan. I can say with some confidence, but not with certainty, that we will welcome the arrival of your bride in short order."

"How short?" Cannan said.

"That, I cannot say. But short order is short order in the busy world of the Butterfield stage line."

"If I don't see the stage pull in, you'll let me know, huh?" Cannan said.

"Indeed I will, sir. I am your obedient servant."

Cannan touched his hat. "Much obliged," he said.

"And a happy Independence Day to you, Ranger Cannan, if it's in keeping with the doleful circumstances."

"You'll come a-running when the bell rings?" Cannon said.

"Depend on it," Wilcox said. The man nodded to a corner where a Winchester leaned. "I have my rifle and a hundred rounds of ammunition, Ranger. I plan to aim well and do great execution once the battle starts."

Cannan smiled. "Good man. You're true blue." Then he wound it up, "About the stage . . ."

"I won't forget," Wilcox said.

Hank Cannan stepped down from the stage depot into the street. He felt like a ninety-year-old with arthritis.

"Chair?" Simon Rule said.

"Hell, I can't walk."

"Then chair it is," Rule said, his usually dour face cheerful.

Cannan sat and the blacksmith said, "Where to, master?"

"Damn it, Simon, have you been drinking?" Cannan said.

"God forbid."

"Then quit being so all-fired cheerful. It doesn't become you."

"Anything you say, master."

Cannan sighed.

He studied the street, now thronged with people and children. They were doing their best, the Ranger decided. To a casual observer it would seem that the folks of Last Chance were enjoying their Independence Day.

Firecrackers snapped like mousetraps and smoked like fog. Tin-panny pianos jingled in the saloons and men stood in the street and sampled fruit pies that covered their mustaches with crumbs.

But the celebrations lacked spirit. Lacked joy. Lacked life. And Ranger Cannan felt the loss deeply and blamed it on himself.

Cannan swiveled his head and said to Rule, "Think we should go check on Ephraim?"

"No," the blacksmith said.

"How come?"

"We're planning a surprise party, aren't we? We don't want a bunch of folks stomping all over the riverbank and giving the game away."

Cannan thought about that, then said, "Yeah, I guess you're right."

"Ephraim will stick," Rule said.

"If he don't, I'll shoot him."

"If he don't, we'll both shoot him," Rule said.

"Ranger! Ranger! Ranger!"

Half a dozen kids ran toward Cannan, the girls hiking up the skirts of their go-to-Sunday-school dresses.

"Slow down," Rule said, his voice stern. He pointed to a small boy with sandy hair and round glasses. "You, Cad Price, what's going on?"

"It's Andy Kilcoyn," the boy said.

"You found him?" Cannan said.

A pretty, pigtailed girl in a sky blue dress answered. "We . . . we . . ."

"We think he's dead," Cad Price said.

"Where is he?" Cannan said.

"Behind the Cattleman's Hotel among a pile of boxes."

Rule needed no bidding from the Ranger. He immediately pushed the wheelchair in the direction of the hotel, the excited, yelling kids running alongside.

Attracted by the commotion, people tagged along behind, speculating about what was amiss. Cannan and Rule, their faces like stone, said nothing.

But the children, eager for attention, let the cat out of the bag, and the crowd's speculation turned, first to concern, then to wonder.

Little Andy Kilcoyn dead? What on earth happened? Oh, his poor mother.

Rule pushed the chair into the alley and scraped Cannan's elbows along the walls until he pulled them closer to Andy's body.

The kids said they'd been searching for empty pop bottles they could trade for candy sticks, and had dragged away most of the crates and boxes, exposing the boy's body. He'd been stuffed into a tea chest that was labeled CEYLON.

Cannan almost leapt from the wheelchair, an effort that cost him dearly in pain, and kneeled beside acting, unpaid Texas Ranger Andy Kilcoyn. He took the boy from the chest, cradled his head in his arm, and helplessly stared at Rule.

The big blacksmith looked like a man lost.

Andy's face was as white as marble, his eyes wide open in death, a death that had not come easily or without fear. "Bruises all over him, the side of his face smashed from a blow," Cannan said. "And then he was strangled."

"Seems like," Rule said, his voice broken.

"Who?"

Rule said nothing.

Yells of sympathy rose from the people who'd crowded into the alley as Edith Kilcoyn, accompanied by Dr. Krueger, pushed her way through. The woman took in the scene at a glance.

She screamed and ran to her son's body and took him into her arms.

"I'm afraid he's dead, Mrs. Kilcoyn," Cannan said. "I'm real sorry."

Andy's mother said nothing. She hugged Andy close and her tears fell on his shattered face.

Dr. Krueger got as near to the boy as Mrs. Kilcoyn would allow. He spent a few minutes examining the body, at the same time trying to calm the hysterical mother, then rose to his feet.

"He was strangled, Hans," Cannon said.

The doctor shook his head. "No, Ranger Cannan, the boy suffered a terrible blow to his face and was then suffocated."

"Dr. Krueger, you mean by a pillow or something?" Rule said.

"Or something," the physician said.

A couple of women kneeled to comfort Mrs. Kilcoyn, and Krueger said, "I'll take care of things here. You've got other matters that demand your attention, Ranger."

Cannan nodded. "Thanks, Doc." He glanced at the crying women and Mrs. Kilcoyn, who was quiet now, but was in a state of profound shock, numb. "This is a terrible thing," he said.

"Find out who did it," Krueger said.

"The killer was strong enough to cause the boy terrible injuries, and he took the pillow with him," Cannan said. "Are those clues or not?" He turned joyless eyes to the doctor. "Damn it, Hans, I'm not a Pinkerton."

"Speak to the hotel guests," Krueger said. "Maybe somebody heard or saw something."

"I don't have time for that," Cannan said. "You know what we're facing."

"And this heartless murder could be part of it. Who might have had an interest in what happened at the riverbank?" Krueger said. "For some reason did he figure Andy knew?"

Cannan frowned, reaching deep. Then, "Andy wore a Ranger's star I gave him. It was found near the alley."

"The star may have attracted the killer," Krueger said.

"I deputized Andy as an acting, unpaid Texas Ranger," Cannan said. "He may have told his killer that."

"And the man wanted information from him," Krueger said.

"Andy was tough," Rule said. "He wouldn't spill."

"And that's why the man murdered him," Cannan said. He was silent for a while, deep in thought.

Then he threw back his head and yelled, "HAAACKER!"

CHAPTER FIFTY

The door to Abe Hacker's hotel room was locked. "Simon, kick it down," Hank Cannan said.

Rule was horrified. "Ranger, this is private property," he said.

"Kick it down," Cannan said, his face grim.

Rule said, "I hope you know what you're doing."

He raised a great, booted foot and smashed the door at the lock. Timber splintered and the door crashed open.

Gun drawn, Cannan limped inside.

And smelled death.

A woman's slender arm, the hand lying beside a towel, stuck out from under the bed. Cannan pushed the cloth aside and his breath caught in his throat.

The hand had been stamped into a blue-black claw, the index finger bent and beckoning, demanding that the living draw closer to the dead.

"Simon," Cannan said, "get her out from there."

The blacksmith bent and, gently for a man of his size and strength, pulled Nora's body into the middle of the floor. She was wrapped in a man's bloodstained robe.

Her horror at the manner of her death frozen on Nora's face, the woman's slim neck showed the deep bruises of strangulation.

"Hacker murdered her," Rule said.

"Yeah, he did," Cannan said. "And Andy Kilcoyn."

"But why his woman?" Rule said.

"Did she know he'd killed the boy and accused him?" Cannan said. "By the size of it, that's Hacker's robe. There's blood all over it."

"And then he silenced her like he did Andy," Rule said.

"Seems like," Cannan said.

"Where is he?" Rule said.

"I don't know."

"Still in town?"

"Damn it, I told you I don't know." Cannan regretted his snappishness and said, "Simon, go bring Doc Krueger. It's one of the law's traditional death rituals, and we'll observe it."

"Poor lady," Rule said, glancing at Nora's body.

Cannan holstered his gun and leaned against the wall. He looked as exhausted as he felt. "Poor lady. Poor town. Poor Andy. Poor you. Poor me. We're all poor, Simon, every last one of us," Cannan said.

After a while the blacksmith said, "You've got to hold it together, Ranger Cannan. The enemy is at the gates and if you give up, then we're lost."

"Don't worry, I'm not giving up, especially not now," Cannan said. "I'll stand on our ground." He managed a smile. "Now go get the doc. Maybe he has the courage I need in a medicine bottle."

* * *

A search of the town proved fruitless. Hacker had flown the coop.

"He must have crossed the river," Mayor Frank Curtis said.

"And the only spot shallow enough for miles in either direction is guarded by Ephraim Slough," Cannan said.

"Maybe Slough has him," Curtis said. He waited until a string of firecrackers banged to silence. "Ephraim is not a man to desert his post to drag Hacker into town."

"Simon, roll me down to the river," Cannan said. "We'll go talk with Ephraim."

When a man expects to see someone at a certain place and time and that someone isn't there, the empty space seems even emptier. So it was with Ranger Hank Cannan.

It was as though the absence of Ephraim Slough had left a huge hole in the fabric of the day.

"Where is he?" Simon Rule said.

"Not here," Cannan said.

"Hacker?"

The Ranger shook his head. "We heard no gunshots. Hacker wouldn't go up against a tough old coot like Ephraim with his bare hands. It's never wise to pick a fight with an old-timer. He won't fight you, but he'll kill you."

"A club?" Rule said.

"A man the size of Hacker wouldn't get close enough to use a club. Or a knife."

"Well, that means Ephraim was gone when Hacker got here."

"Seems like," Cannan said.

Cannan's eyes reached out across the white-hot inferno that was the Chihuahuan Desert. Nothing moved but a far-off dust devil.

"Any sign of him?" Rule said.

"Not that I can see," Cannan said. "Damn the man. Where the hell did he go?"

There was no answer to the question, and Rule stayed silent.

Finally Cannan said, "We'll stay here, Simon. When we spot a dust cloud in the distance fog it for town and ring the church bell."

"And leave you here alone?"

"Yeah, only I won't exactly be on a high lonesome."

Cannon built himself a cigarette. Then, "Listen up, Simon, as soon as the bell rings I want a half-grown boy with a rifle, a couple of white-haired old-timers, a woman with sand—Polly Curtis the mayor's wife would be ideal—and you. Stash your rifle until the shooting starts. I want you to be armed only with a hammer."

"I'm not catching your drift," Rule said.

Cannan smiled. "You will if my brilliant strategy works," he said. "Just make sure Mrs. Curtis and the rest get here before Sancho Perez attacks."

Rule was a slow-thinking man. But finally he said, "Suppose your brilliant strategy don't work. What then?"

"Then we'll all be dead and it won't matter," Cannan said.

CHAPTER FIFTY-ONE

To Ephraim Slough the dust cloud looked like an approaching fog bank drifting across a yellow and tan sea. He blinked, looked again, but the dust remained, rising thick into the blue denim sky like smoke from a fire.

Slough told himself that he'd never before seen the like, but he had. He'd seen such on the Grand Banks off the Newfoundland coast when the fog rolled in like thunder and chilled many a poor mariner to the marrow of his bones.

Now a similar sight scared Ephraim Slough.

It looked like the whole population of Mexico was on the move, marching on Last Chance and its golden fields and orchards.

He swung his tired mare around and kicked her ribs, urging her into a canter. But all Sophie would do that day was walk, and kicks be damned.

Slough cursed the mare, cursed himself for leaving the Rio Grande, and cursed his lack of whiskey.

His best curses, in several different languages, he reserved for the latter.

* * *

Hank Cannan caught a flash of sunlight on metal. He stared harder, longer, eyes burning.

There it was again.

But not metal. Glass. The dazzling sun blading off the lens of a telescope.

The Ranger said nothing to Rule and waited for the spy to ride closer.

The glass made a man long-sighted and he might well stay far back. But he did not. The horseman came on at a trot, covered several hundred yards, then drew rein again.

"Simon," Cannan said. "Get to the water's edge and gather pretty pebbles."

"Huh?" Rule said.

"Then bring the pebbles over to me and let me examine them one by one."

"Ranger Cannan, have you gone tetched in the head?" Rule said.

"Do it, Simon. Do it now," Cannan said. "There's not a moment to be lost."

"Whatever you say, Ranger, pretty rocks it is. But in my opinion, you sure ain't playing with a full deck." The blacksmith stepped to the water's edge and gathered pebbles, taking little time to see if they were pretty or not.

"Bring them here, Simon," Cannan said. "Show them to me. And grin as wide as a wave in a slop bucket."

Rule's dramatic sigh was worthy of the great Edwin Booth himself.

When the blacksmith returned and revealed the rocks in his hand, Cannan said, "We're under observation—

no, don't look—and we need to appear as harmless as possible."

"Damn it all, Ranger, shouldn't we show our strength?"

"No, Simon. I want to reveal only weakness and lack of preparation." He chose a pebble from Rule's hand and studied it closely. "When the spy reports back to Perez he'll tell him that the rubes are collecting seashells."

"There ain't any seashells in the Rio Grande," Rule said.

"Well, rocks then. Just so long as the bandit thinks we're fiddling while Rome burns."

Rule looked puzzled. "I don't get it."

"So he thinks we're sitting on our asses while Perez gets ready to attack."

"Now I get it," Rule said. "Is he still there?"

Cannan angled his head slightly, gave a sidelong look, and scanned the far side of the river. "I think he's gone," he said. "Seen enough, I reckon."

Rule straightened and did his own looking.

He watched a thin pillar of dust rise above the desert floor and said, "He's on his way back to the bandits to tell them how weak we are."

Cannan smiled. "Then we're going to surprise them, ain't we?"

The last thing Ephraim Slough wanted was to get into a shooting scrape with a Mexican bandit . . . the one he watched in the middle distance.

Slough dismounted, stood beside Sophie's head, and tried to make himself invisible. He saw no future in trading shots with a pistolero. Since the old mariner knew he'd be the one to die, gunplay wasn't even a consideration.

But as it happened, Slough and the little mare were invisible, at least to the casual observer. A layer of yellow, windblown sand covered both horse and rider and made them look like a badly painted child's toy, unseen against the desert floor.

And to Slough's relief, the Mexican rode on. Apparently he'd more important business on hand than to gun an old codger with a wooden leg and a fifty-dollar mare.

"We need to make our report, Sophie," he told the bay. Slough clambered into the saddle and kicked with his good leg. "Sophie, run like the wind," he yelled.

The mare plodded forward and all Slough's kicking and hollering couldn't induce her to walk any faster.

CHAPTER FIFTY-TWO

Mickey Pauleen and Sancho Perez listened as the scout made his report. It was short and to the point.

"The gringos gather things at the riverbank."

"What kinds of things?" Perez said.

"I do not know, *patrón*," the young bandit said. "Little fishes, maybe so."

Perez turned to Pauleen and his eyes asked a question.

The gunman shook his head.

"Damned if I know why. Is it possible they don't expect an attack? Or has the Ranger cooked up some kind of trap?"

"Two men, one of them crippled, are not a trap, Mickey," Perez said.

"I don't know, Sancho, there's something strange about the whole beach business."

He stared hard at the young bandit. "You're sure they were catching fish?"

"Gathering something," the man said. "Fishes, rocks maybe."

"Mickey, my fren', it is simple," Perez said. "The

gringos will throw little stones or little fishes at us. This makes Sancho laugh. It is ver' funny."

Pauleen was silent for a spell, thinking. Then he said, "Sancho, send the peons across the river ahead of your men. Let them take the first fire from any defenders. So we lose a couple of hundred, the rubes will use up most of their ammunition shooting people that don't matter."

Perez asked a question of the young scout, a man with a tough face and coal black eyes. "What do you think of my fren' Mickey's plan, Roberto?"

"*Patrón*, I beg the honor of taking the town of Last Chance. Such glory is for caballeros, not dung-covered peasants."

"And it will be so, Roberto. I will lead the charge myself," Perez said.

The young man grinned. "*Viva Perez!*" he shouted. And those bandits close enough to hear took up the cry.

"*Viva Perez! Viva Perez!*"

The bandit chief smiled and bowed his head, but Pauleen felt sick to his stomach.

The Ranger planned something unpleasant. Of that, he was sure.

"Rider coming," Simon Rule said. "It's the damned spy again."

Hank Cannan's gaze reached out and lingered on the rider for a long while. "No, it's Ephraim Slough," he said finally. "Nobody else but him sits a horse like a ruptured sailor."

"Is he sober?" the blacksmith said.

"He's upright, more or less," Cannan said.

Baptiste Dupoix would have said the Ranger looked as irritated as a stick-poked walrus.

Slough began waving and yelling when he was still a ways off, and Sophie, realizing she was headed for the barn, broke into a shambling trot.

The old sailor urged the mare into the river. Halfway across he yelled, "They're a-comin'."

"How far?" Cannan yelled.

"An hour. Maybe less." Slough rode onto the bank and rolled off the horse, his usual dismount.

"Here," Rule said, "have you been drinking?"

"Not a drop," Slough said. He held out a hand. "Lookee, steady as a rock."

"Did you see one of the bandits? A scout?" Cannan said.

"I surely did."

"Did you engage him?"

"Hell no."

"Good. His report to Perez will do more harm than good."

"We hope," Rule said. Then, "Why did you desert your post, Ephraim?"

"I figgered I'd see better if'n I was closer. Beggin' your pardon, Ranger Cannan."

"No harm done. In fact, you've bought us time," Cannan said.

"That there's a big dust," Slough said. "A lot of people and horses moving."

Rule said, "Should I go ring the church bell?"

"No, not yet," Cannan said. "I don't want the men stuck in the trenches for too long before the action starts. They might start considering stuff."

"Like bullet wounds an' sich," Slough said, looking wise.

"Yeah, and widowed women and orphaned children," Cannan said.

"I catch your drift," Rule said. "All of a sudden I'm studying on the same things my ownself."

CHAPTER FIFTY-THREE

Ranger Hank Cannan first saw the oncoming dust cloud at two forty in the afternoon of Independence Day.

By then, the Butterfield stage was almost two hours late.

And there was no sign of Baptiste Dupoix and the ranchers.

Both these things were uppermost in Cannan's mind as he stared at the rapidly advancing dust like a man mesmerized by a hooded cobra.

"Ring the bell?" Simon Rule said.

Cannan said nothing. He stared into the searing desert.

"Ranger," Ephraim Slough said. "Ring the bell?"

Cannan turned bleak eyes to the man. "It begins, Ephraim, huh?" he said.

"Seems like, Ranger."

"A Texas Ranger never turns his back to the enemy and runs," Cannan said. "That's always been how it is, I reckon."

Slough's voice was quiet. "So I've heard."

Cannan smiled. "Then I'm in a hell of a fix."

"We're all in a hell of a fix, Ranger," Slough said.

"There's only us," Rule said. "I mean the citizens of the town of Last Chance. With or without you, we got it to do."

"Citizens of the United States of America, you mean," Cannan said.

"That goes without saying, Ranger Cannan," Slough said. Then, "You scared?"

"Of course I am."

"Then that makes two of us," Slough said.

"Three of us," Rule said.

"Rangers are not supposed to get scared," Cannan said. "I bet that's written down in a rule book someplace."

"A Ranger can get as scared as any other man," Rule said.

Cannan smiled and his long, sad face brightened. "I guess I'm proof of that." He looked at Rule. "Go ring the bell, Simon, and don't forget what I told you about the old men and boys. Ephraim, get your rifle from the saddle and send the mare back to the barn. I want you here."

Cannan drew his Colt, loaded the empty chamber under the hammer, then laid his Winchester across the arms of the wheelchair.

He was as ready as he was ever going to be.

As the church bell clanged in Last Chance, the Mexican peons across the river smelled water. They smelled food, and they sensed an end to their terrible misery and deprivation. There was no longer any need for Sancho Perez to whip them forward.

Like a great uncoiling snake they broke ranks and staggered in the direction of the river, young, old, babes in arms in headlong flight for the shores of the Promised Land.

Perez waited until the last of the donkey carts passed, then ordered his men forward to take the point.

"Sancho, damn it, man, I'm begging you, let the peons take the first volleys," Pauleen said. "Hell, then you can charge over their dead bodies right into Last Chance."

"Mickey, my fren', Sancho is dressed for war and he will lead the charge. The Madonna of Guadalupe came to me in the night and she smiled at me and said, 'Onward, Sancho, onward to victory.' She is a very powerful Madonna and this makes Sancho ver' glad."

Pauleen, dealing with arrogance and superstition, realized this was an argument he couldn't win.

"Come, Mickey, why so glum?" Perez said. "You will ride at Sancho's side and have your pick of the women, huh?"

"There's only one woman I want," Pauleen said.

"Ah *sí*, the señorita named Nora. Then soon she will be in your arms, my fren'. This is a mighty promise from Sancho." He kneed his horse forward.

"Come, let us join our *compañeros*!"

The desert wind shook Abe Hacker's canopy and drove fine sand over him that sifted into his eyes and every fold of flesh in his huge body, gritty, irritating, maddening.

The Mexicans had vanished to the north, into the distant heat shimmer, and he was alone under the inverted blue bowl of the sky, marooned like a castaway surrounded by a burning sea of sand. Hacker's bottom lip trembled. "Come for me soon, Sancho," he said aloud, talking into a great silence. "Don't leave me in this dreadful place."

CHAPTER FIFTY-FOUR

Forty-seven riflemen filed into the trench dug along the bank of the Rio Grande. Good men as far as Hank Cannan could tell. But silent. Stonily silent.

Whether that was a good thing or bad, the Ranger couldn't tell.

Cannan had Rule push him along the trench, and he repeated constantly, "When they get within seeing distance, down to the bottom of the hole and stay there until I holler, NOW!"

The mayor broke the townsmen's silence.

"We got you, Ranger." Then, "Take care of yourself."

"You too, Frank," Cannan said. "And that goes for all of you."

Solemn faces turned in the Ranger's direction, but the men remained silent. One checked his revolver and another had red rosary beads that looked like drops of blood wrapped around his shooting hand.

Cannan swallowed hard and tried his best to keep his face empty.

My God, when the shooting starts will they stand? Will I stand?

He had no answers, none at all.

* * *

The dust cloud drew closer as the afternoon sun dropped and shadows lengthened. On Cannan's orders, the pianos still played in the saloons and as many people as possible, most of them women, crowded the street.

Roxie Miller, no longer dressed in blue silk, took Daphne Curtis's place on the beach. "Mrs. Curtis has had nursing experience, Ranger Cannan," she said. "She's more valuable where she is." Roxie wore a split canvas riding skirt, a shirt, a man's battered hat, and French perfume. She carried a Winchester.

Cannan wanted to tell her that she was too beautiful to risk her life, but he realized how silly that would sound and kept silent.

Ominous as a twister, the dust was now so close Cannan could see people move within its folds like gray ghosts. He estimated the Mexicans would arrive on the far bank in thirty minutes, maybe less.

Ephraim Slough walked along the trench as confidently as he'd once paced a gun deck. "Easy, lads," he said. "Easy now. Stand to your guns. Easy, lads . . ."

After a few minutes of this, Cannan's heart soared when a man called out, "Ephraim! You say 'Easy, lads' one more time and I'll put a bullet in you."

The Ranger smiled.

That was not the voice of a frightened man.

"Getting close," Simon Rule said.

"Seems like," Cannan said.

"I think I see horseman out front. Do you see that?"

"Yeah, I do," Cannan said. "I'm not a praying man,

CHAPTER FIFTY-FIVE

Sancho Perez stared across the Rio Grande and liked what he saw.

"Look, Mickey, the men have all fled and left their women behind," he said. "This makes Sancho ver' happy."

"It looks like the Texas Ranger in the invalid chair," Pauleen said.

"And a few old men and boys," Perez said.

"I don't like it, Sancho. It could be a trap."

The bandit's grin twisted into a scowl.

"Mickey, are you afraid?" he said.

Pauleen grabbed Perez by this thick bicep. "For pity's sake, send the peons first," he said.

Perez jerked his arm free. "You are a coward, Mickey," he said. "Get away from Sancho." Perez raised a hand and yelled, "Follow me, *muchachos*!"

He swept his hand downward.

Fifty horsemen followed their leader headlong into the river, great fountains of water splashing up around their mounts.

Cannan waited.

Next to him Simon Rule whispered, "Oh, my God."

Ephraim Slough turned his head in the Ranger's direction. "Give the order," he said.

"Not yet," Cannan said.

The bandits were halfway across, a few of them already firing.

A bullet buzzed past Cannan's head and made him flinch.

Unnerved, he roared, "NOW!" And threw the Winchester to his shoulder.

Along the length of the trench works men popped up and stared, stunned, into a nightmare . . .

The bandits, Perez in the lead, were coming on strong. Their faces contorted into war masks, the Mexicans fired as they neared the riverbank, using spurs on their floundering horses.

Cannan fired, missed. Cursed. Fired again.

The townsmen of Last Chance recovered.

A volley, ragged but accurate, tore into the advancing horsemen like grapeshot.

Saddles emptied, horses went down kicking, and men screamed. The charge faltered.

A dozen bodies floated in the river and wide arrowheads of blood streamed in the current.

The bandits swung their horses around and fled for the far bank.

But then Perez was among them. He rallied his men, roared orders, and turned their fear into anger. A quarter of their amigos were dead or dying and now the surviving bandits wanted revenge.

A cheer rose from the trench, and men grinned and waved their hats, thinking the battle was over.

"Get ready," Cannan yelled. "They'll be back." He looked around and what he saw cut him to the bone.

Following his orders, the old men and boys had fled toward town as soon as the Mexican charge started. But Ephraim Slough was down, sprawled on the ground, and Roxie was on one knee, bent over, the front of her shirt red.

"Roxie!" Cannan called out.

The woman turned to his voice, smiled, then fell over onto her side.

Simon Rule was already running. He lifted Roxie in his strong arms, stared at her beautiful face, and gently laid her back on the ground.

When he returned to Cannan's side, he didn't have to say a word.

"They're coming again!" a man in the trench yelled.

And indeed, Perez had re-formed his bandits for another charge.

Unlike the American men in the trench, Sancho Perez had never read accounts of the War Between the States nor had he listened to veterans who'd fought its battles. He didn't know therefore what the generals on both sides had learned from long years of bloody trial and error—that light cavalry should never attack steady, entrenched infantry.

Perez paid for his ignorance.

Withering fire from the trenches again broke his charge.

Then, as the Mexicans wavered, Hank Cannan drew a bead and fired.

Hit hard, Perez shrieked and slumped in the saddle.

Gut shot, he grabbed frantically at his belly, screaming, and then splashed headfirst into the river.

The Ranger had scored a hit, but it made him a prime target.

A bullet hit the receiver of his Winchester, caromed off the steel, and slammed into Cannan's left shoulder. An instant later, as the Ranger's rifle spun away from him, a second round splintered its way across the ribs on the right side of his chest.

He fell forward and Rule, himself bleeding from wounds to his head and right hand, grabbed for him. But his clumsy attempt tipped the wheelchair onto its side and Cannan went with it.

For a moment, it seemed that Perez's men, stung by the death of their leader and half their number, might rally.

But from the direction of town, hooves hammered on hard ground and the strange yodeling wail of the rebel yell pierced the smoke-streaked day.

A dozen hard-riding fighting men, Baptiste Dupoix among them, crashed into the Mexican line, six-guns blazing. Riflemen climbed from their trenches and joined the melee that turned the river shallows red and clogged its flow with dead men and horses.

Their ranks broken, some Mexican banditos fled into the desert to avoid the slaughter, but their numbers were few and those that survived long enough to become old men would recall the *Batalla del Rio Grande* with shuddering horror.

CHAPTER FIFTY-SIX

Mickey Pauleen took no part in the battle.

After he saw the first charge shattered, he rode into the horde of Mexican peons who'd recoiled from the violence at the river and now held back, confused and afraid.

Pauleen used the human shield to loop to the east a hundred yards, and then swung north. He swam his horse across a deep section of the Rio Grande and approached Last Chance from the south.

The street was deserted and he arrived unseen.

It seemed everybody was down at the river and he wondered if Nora was there. If she was, he'd hide in her hotel room until she got back.

Surprise her, like.

Pauleen tethered his horse to a parked freight wagon at the rear of an alley, then drew his gun and angled across the street to the Cattleman's Hotel.

Gunfire rattled in the distance, and Pauleen fervently hoped that Sancho Perez and his rabble were all dead. He had a plan, something he should have thought about before, a plan that would make him rich. But first Perez had to be out of the way.

He smiled, relishing his brilliant scheme. With Nora by his side and a fortune at his back, life would finally be good for Mickey Pauleen. He recalled the quote from the Book of Psalms he'd been taught as a boy:

Surely there is a reward for the righteous. Surely there's a God who judges on earth.

Pauleen had no doubt that those words applied to him.

He stepped into the hotel, ready to kill anyone who stood in his way. But like the town itself, the place was empty, echoing, the only sound the tick of the hallway clock. Pauleen made his way to Nora and Hacker's room. To his surprise, the door hung slightly ajar on a splintered frame. He pushed it open with the muzzle of his Colt.

"Nora?" he said.

There was no answer.

He stepped into the room.

Nora lay on the bed. At first Pauleen thought she was asleep, then he moved closer he realized that she was laid out under a sheet.

A shroud.

The little gunman pulled the sheet off Nora's body. Someone, most probably an undertaker, had crossed her arms over her breasts. Her left hand had been smashed into a blackened claw.

The terrible bruises on Nora's throat, blue, black, and yellow against her gray skin, revealed in gruesome detail the manner of her death.

Pauleen's face tightened into hard, vicious planes.

For years Abe Hacker had used and abused Nora and in the end he'd done for her.

Pauleen didn't love the woman, never had, and never would. But Nora was supposed to be his. He'd even planned that she play a small role in his future life. Now Hacker had stolen her away from him, and that was a thing he could not forget and forgive.

Pauleen replaced the sheet, disturbed by Nora's still, white nakedness, and the loud, unfeeling tick . . . tick . . . tick . . . of the clock.

He left the hotel and retraced his steps to the waiting horse.

A cheer rose from the riverbank, white men's cheers.

So Perez was defeated and most likely dead.

Pauleen figured his plan was working out nicely. Nora's murder was the only fly in the ointment, but in the long run it didn't matter a damn. Money could buy the kind of women he liked.

He swung into the saddle.

Now it was time to settle accounts—with a treacherous fat man.

CHAPTER FIFTY-SEVEN

Mickey Pauleen figured he had a couple of hours of daylight left and that was good. He'd spend the night at Perez's hacienda and even longer, depending on the mood of the bandit's women.

He and his horse ghosted long shadows on the sand when the little gunman saw Hacker's shelter ahead of him, a spindly thing, shaking with every gust of the hot desert wind. Pauleen was close before the fat man caught sight of him.

Abe Hacker rose to his feet and waved. He had stripped to only a shirt.

Pauleen did not wave back.

Hesitancy, concern, showed in the way Hacker stood, his massive belly hanging over his rolling thighs and knock-knees. His little blue eyes were bloodshot; his round nail keg of a head tilted to one side, as though he wondered what Mickey had to tell him. When the gunman was within hailing distance, Hacker cupped a hand to his mouth, "Is Last Chance burning, Mickey?"

Pauleen didn't answer until he was a few feet from the canopy.

He drew rein and said, "Perez is dead. They're all dead."

Shock hit Hacker like a blow and he dropped to a sitting position. "But how . . ."

"The Ranger was too smart for your friend Sancho, I guess," Pauleen said. "You can never trust a greaser, my ol' pappy used to say."

"Then you have to take me away from here, Mickey," Hacker said. "We have to get to Washington."

"To your young bride, huh?"

"Yes, and then the presidency, Mickey. You'll be at my side and along the way I'll make you a rich man."

Pauleen smiled with all the warmth of a Minnesota blizzard. "Why did you kill Nora?" he said.

The fat man's face sagged. "It wasn't me, Mickey. I wouldn't strangle Nora. Never, ever, ever."

"How did you know she was strangled?" Pauleen said.

Hacker knew he'd run out of room on the dance floor. "She was going to tell the law about us, Mickey," he said. "I had to stop her."

"What law? A crippled Texas Ranger?"

"The army. She could've told the army."

"There are no soldiers in Last Chance."

Desperately, Hacker tried a different tack. He grinned and said, "Mickey, come sit in the shade and have a drink and a cigar. We're both men of the world and we shouldn't have a falling-out over a whore."

"She was my woman, Hacker," Pauleen said. "And you took her from me."

"I'll get you another, a dozen others if you want them."

"I wanted Nora. You should've thought about that before you killed her."

"After just a week in Washington you'll forget that Nora ever existed," Hacker said. "Now sit beside me in good fellowship and we'll have a drink."

"On your feet," Pauleen said. He drew his gun. "Now, fat man."

Hacker struggled erect. He trembled and his fat bottom lip quivered. "Mickey, be reasonable. All the money you want . . . power . . ."

"Turn around, then run," Pauleen said.

"My heart, Mickey. My heart . . ."

"Run, you fat, useless pig."

Hacker looked into merciless eyes and felt fear.

"Make it to Perez's hacienda and I'll let you live," Pauleen said.

"I can't run that far, Mickey. And I think I'm having another heart attack."

"Try," Pauleen said.

But Hacker dropped to his knees, then rolled on his back. His blue lips peeled back from his teeth and his face knotted in pain.

"Help me, Mickey," he said, gasping.

Pauleen smiled. "Sure, Abe, sure."

He grabbed a canopy leg and dragged the whole thing with him as he rode away. After a hundred yards, he dropped the canopy and looked back. Hacker rolled back and forth on the sand, his hands convulsively clutching at his chest.

It was, Pauleen decided, a terrible way to die. He raised a hand and smiled.

"Adios, amigo!"

CHAPTER FIFTY-EIGHT

The Mexicans lined the far bank of the Rio Grande that still ran red from the carnage that had taken place.

Dead men and horses bobbed in the current but refused to be swept aside. It would take days to clear the river.

Baptiste Dupoix's body had been dragged onto the bank close to where Hank Cannan slumped in his wheelchair. The gambler had died well, getting his work in even after he'd suffered a mortal wound, and Cannan felt deep sorrow for his loss.

"You've got four ribs broken, and the bullet that hit your shoulder went right through," Dr. Hans Krueger said. He dropped the spent round into the Ranger's hand. "Dug it out of the invalid chair. It looks like it hit bone, so you won't be using your left arm for a while."

The doctor shook his head, and pursed his lips, the sympathetic gesture physicians practice in the mirror, and said, "In fact, you won't be using anything for a while. You'll be in bed."

"All right, Ranger Cannan, back to the hotel," Simon Rule said. A fat bandage swaddled his head.

Cannan was in pain from wounds old and new, and his broken ribs made every breath a torment, but despite feeling half-dead he was reluctant to play the invalid again.

His decision was made for him.

A stocky, tough-looking customer wearing wet range clothes stepped in front of the wheelchair.

"Howdy, Ranger, my name is George Cassidy, I ride for Luke Wright."

"Right glad to make your acquaintance, Mr. Cassidy," Cannan said. "You find me very low, I'm afraid."

Cassidy nodded. "Shot through and through, I reckon."

"Exactly so," Cannan said, needing no reminder of how he shot-up he was.

"Baptiste Dupoix, the gambling man, was a friend of your'n, huh?"

Cannan glanced to where the parson prayed over Dupoix's body. "Yes," he said. "Yes, he was."

"I just want to tell you that he died game," Cassidy said.

"I expected nothing less," Cannan said.

"He was good with a gun, was Baptiste, killed a few before he got shot."

The Ranger nodded, but made no comment.

"A fine man," Cassidy said. "I liked him a lot."

"Thank you, Mr. Cassidy," Cannan said.

"I just thought you should know."

A moment after Cassidy left, his place was taken by Mayor Curtis. He waved a hand to the river where the scared Mexicans were spread out along the far bank. A few had already attempted a crossing but turned back.

"What the hell do we do, Ranger?" Curtis said. "There's hundreds of them, and it will be dark in a couple of hours."

"Fire a couple of volleys over their heads," Rule said. "That will scatter them."

Frank Curtis absorbed that, then said, his voice tinged with doubt, "Fire into them, maybe?"

"You want to kill women and children, Frank?" Cannan said.

"Then what do we do?" Curtis said. "Ranger, you're hurt real bad, and you ain't thinking straight. Smooth it out for me."

"Damn it, Frank, I don't know what to do," Cannan said.

"HENNNRY!"

The woman's yell came from behind Cannan. He laboriously turned his head and saw . . . his wife.

Jane Cannan was a tall, gaunt woman with a slightly pinched face that laid no claim to beauty. Her black hair was scraped back in the severe bun then fashionable among women who aspired to the middle class, and she wore an iron-gray dress, dusty from her travels.

Those who knew her well said her breath was cold.

Jane stepped to the wheelchair and pecked her husband on the cheek.

"How are you, Henry?" she said.

"He's badly wounded, ma'am," Simon Rule said.

"Is your name Henry?" Jane said.

"No, ma'am."

"Then speak when you're spoken to. How are you, Henry?"

"I'm shot up again, Jane." Then, "How did you get here?"

"By stage, of course. What a silly question."

"I mean when did you get in?"

"Half an hour ago. But you know I never interrupt you when you're working." Jane turned. "You there, with the medical bag."

Hans Krueger bowed, "At your service, ma'am."

"My name is Jane Cannan. Are you a fully qualified physician?"

Krueger smiled. "Yes, ma'am. University of Michigan."

"Really? Then I suppose that must do," Jane said. "You will be responsible for my husband's care. I in turn will see to it that he doesn't smoke or drink and is given a liberal dose of prune juice every day. Do you understand me?"

"Perfectly, ma'am," Krueger said.

He gave Cannan a "God help you" look and stepped away.

"Jane, maybe—"

"Do not object, Henry, please," Jane said. "I do resent your little objections to my good sense. Now where is that mayor?"

She looked around, spotted Curtis, and called out, "Yoo-hoo, Mr. Mayor, over here."

When Curtis arrived, Jane said, "I have already organized the ladies, and now it's time to organize the male fraternity."

"To what purpose, ma'am?" Curtis said, after a glance at Cannan's long face.

"Sir, this is Independence Day, and from what I've been told and from the evidence of my own eyes, this town had to fight for independence all over again."

"That is so," Curtis said. "But—"

"Please, don't interrupt," Jane said. "Now, what about those starving people across the river?"

"Ma'am, your husband, I mean Ranger Cannan, is considering a course of action."

"And that is?"

"To shoot into them, ma'am."

"Jane, I didn't—"

"Be silent, Henry. That is a murderous course of action and one we will not tolerate. Now look behind you, Mr. Mayor."

Curtis did and his eyes popped and jaw fell. Every man along the riverbank reacted in much the same way, including the tough ranchers and their hired hands. A line of women, young and old, made their way to the river, all carrying food . . . pies, cakes, bread, meat, and every other edible they could get their hands on.

"Stay to the shallows, ladies," Jane yelled. "And step carefully." Then to Curtis, "Independence Day is a time for sharing, Mayor, and so you will split your men into two divisions. One will carry food, including the roast pigs, tables and, oh yes, lanterns. It will be dark soon."

"Ma'am, Mrs. Cannan, we can't feed that many," Curtis said. "Look at them, there are many hundreds, maybe more than a thousand."

"The Lord will provide," Jane said. "*Then He took the five loaves and the two fishes, and looking up to heaven, He blessed them, and brake, and gave to the disciples to set before the multitude.* Don't you read your Bible, Mayor?"

Curtis opened his mouth to speak, but Jane held up a silencing hand.

"Your second division will immediately clear the river of the deceased Mexicans and remove the bodies of our own suffering dead," she said. Jane looked over the mayor's shoulder. "Reverend, would you be so kind as to come here," she said.

Pastor McRae introduced himself and Jane said, "Reverend, the Mexicans belong to a misguided popish religion, but please see that they're afforded a good Christian burial."

The pastor said he would and attempted to talk further, but Jane had already dismissed him. "Well, Mayor?" she said, "Why are you standing there like a cow in quicksand? Organize your divisions at once."

Jane watched the women, skirts and petticoats billowing, slowly cross the river, food held high above their heads. A few had already reached the Mexicans.

"Wait, Mayor, come back," she said. "Since this is Independence Day and you've won yet another battle for freedom, the saloons may open. After their work is done, just see that your men drink in strict moderation. And for heaven's sake get the pianos playing. Remember, we're celebrating our nation's birth."

Jane turned away and called to a struggling older woman, "Oh, let me help you with those pies. It's time I got my feet wet."

She glared at her husband.

"Shoot into them indeed. I'm surprised and more than a little disappointed in you, Henry."

After Jane left, Curtis shouted, "All right, boys, you heard the lady. Half of you into the river and haul out those dead Mexicans. The others come with me. I want all the food we can spare."

Before he walked away, Curtis stabbed a finger at Hank Cannan. "She's your wife," he said.

"Don't I know it," the Ranger said.

CHAPTER FIFTY-NINE

Mickey Pauleen rode under a bronze sky toward the Perez hacienda. The setting sun tinted its white walls gold, a gleaming El Dorado beckoning the little gunman closer.

Pauleen had no idea how much treasure Perez had stashed, and a safe would present a problem, but he figured there would be jewels and money aplenty lying around for the taking, enough to keep him in grand style for years.

There were no guards at the gate and Pauleen grinned. *All right, so far, so good.*

He swung out of the saddle and led his horse into the echoing courtyard, the clatter and clang of its shod hooves loud on the flagstones. The fountain sang as it played, each drop of water falling like a silver coin into the basin, and to Pauleen this was yet another good omen.

He let the reins drop and looked around. There was no one in sight, and the gunman felt a stab of panic.

Had the place already been looted?

Pauleen took the stairs two at a time and burst into Perez's living quarters.

The ornate room seemed undisturbed, the floor was swept clean, and the furnishings glowed from a recent polish.

Housework suggested the presence of women, and Pauleen decided to take one with him when he left, the prettiest of them.

His spurs ringing on the wood floor, he walked around the room hunting for a safe.

There was none. As he suspected, the damned Mex didn't have enough sense to lock away his valuables. But a massive walnut desk with heavy iron drawer pulls stood near a window and promised much.

Pauleen tried a drawer. Locked. They were all locked.

The gunman gauged the strength of his Barlow and decided its thin blade would not force open such massive drawers. But a bowie would.

When he first entered the room Pauleen noticed a broad-bladed, engraved bowie knife on a deer-antler stand on a top of a dresser. The blade was thick at the base and twelve inches long, ideal for forcing open locked desks.

"Are you looking for these, *señor?*"

Pauleen turned, surprised.

A young woman of considerable beauty, despite a thin knife scar on her left cheek, stood watching him. She had a set of keys in her hand.

The woman wore a peasant blouse, richly embroidered, and a dark red skirt clung to her hips and swept to the floor. Her hair was inky black, falling straight and long over her bare shoulders. A tiny cross on a silver chain hung between her breasts.

Pauleen grinned. Right here was the woman he'd take with him.

"*Gracias, señorita,*" he said.

"*Señora,*" the woman said. "My husband is dead."

"Too bad," Pauleen said. "Give me the keys."

The woman did as she was told.

"Is this where Sancho kept his treasure?" Pauleen said.

"Some of it," the woman said. "There are other hiding places."

"You'll show them to me?"

"Of course."

"And after that pack a bag," Pauleen said, his eyes dwelling on the swell of the señora's breasts. "You're leaving here with me."

"As you wish," the woman said.

After trying several keys Pauleen unlocked the desk's top drawer. Inside was a short-barreled Colt and bundles of money bound by rubber bands, all of it American bills.

Pauleen laid the money on the desktop, ten thousand dollars he reckoned, maybe more.

The bottom drawer was the largest, twice as high as the others.

That's where most of the treasure lay. Had to be. Excited, he bent from the waist and tried a key. Then another.

A moment later he screamed.

Twelve inches of Sheffield steel driven into his back by a hating woman can put a major hurt on a man.

The hilt of the bowie sticking out between his shoulder blades, Pauleen turned, his rodent face twisted by pain, and stared into the flashing black eyes of the Mexican woman.

"My husband was murdered by Sancho Perez only because you needed a horse, remember?" she said.

Pauleen remembered. "Sandoval," he said through the blood that filled his mouth.

"Yes, that was his name. God brought you here to me that I could avenge him."

Pauleen reached for his gun, but it was so heavy he couldn't pull it from the holster. So heavy . . . like an anvil . . .

His eyes flew wide open and he screamed.[1]

Pauleen fell dead at the woman's feet, and she stepped around his body and put the money back in the drawer. She then locked it and left the room.

1. The reason why Mickey Pauleen shrieked in terror at the very instant of his death has never been explained. In her old age the Mexican woman said that he caught his first glimpse of hell, and to this day that remains as plausible an explanation as any.

CHAPTER SIXTY

Jane Cannan sat knitting, stiff-backed and severe in a rattan chair, a ball of dark gray yarn slowly unwinding at her feet.

Ranger Hank Cannan, looking more like a grouchy walrus than ever, contemplated the table beside his bed. It held no whiskey, no makings, just a bottle of prune juice and a spoon. His life, he decided, had taken a decidedly downward turn.

And he was no longer in his comfortable hotel room.

Jane had decided that the hotel was far too expensive and she'd procured a single room in what she'd described as "a respectable, God-fearing home, free of tobacco and strong drink."

That the house had a homicidal cat named Precious who despised Cannan and ambushed him at every turn was neither here nor there to Jane.

Someone tapped on the door and Jane said, "Enter."

Hat in hand, Mayor Curtis stepped inside.

"Good morning, Mayor," Jane said. "And what can we do for you? I see most of the Mexicans have gone."

"Indeed, ma'am," Curtis said. "Word came from the

rurales that there are heavy rains to the south and they've gone home."

"Good news, Mayor. Did you provide adequate provisions?"

"Yes, ma'am. Enough water and food to see them through."

A silence stretched, then Frank Curtis said, "I'm here to see Ranger Cannan."

"His wounds hurt, but Dr. Krueger has supplied laudanum to ease the pain. Apart from that he's feeling as well as expected."

"How long did the doc say you'd be laid up, Ranger Cannan?" Curtis said.

"The doctor says at least another month," Jane said.

"I'm sorry to hear that," Curtis said.

"And so is Mr. Cannan, I assure you."

The mayor reached into his pocket and produced a sheet of paper. "Here are the names of our dead," he said. "It's the decision of the town fathers that we set up a granite memorial on the riverbank to record the sacrifice of those who fought on July fourth for our independence from tyranny and fear."

"Excellent, Mayor," Jane said. "These names will go on the memorial?"

"Yes, ma'am, with Ranger Cannan's approval."

"Then give the list to me, Mayor. I'll take care of it."

"No, you won't!"

Jane and Curtis looked at Cannan in surprise.

"Well, Henry, really," Jane said, her face shocked.

"This is my job, Jane. Leave it alone. Frank, give me the list."

"But—"

"No buts, Jane," Cannan said. "Now mind your own damned business."

Jane dabbed a small lace handkerchief to her eyes. "This is all the thanks I get for my love and devotion," she said, sobbing. "It's too much to bear."

Cannan ignored his distraught wife and took the list from Curtis. After a glance, he said, "Come back later, Frank. I'll write down what I want on the memorial."

"Just too much to bear . . ." Jane sobbed.

"Ranger Cannan, this town owes you its very existence," Curtis said. "We'll inscribe the stone any way you want."

"Half an hour, Frank," Cannan said.

After the mayor left, the Ranger said, "Jane, get me pen and paper."

Her back as stiff as a poker, his wife flounced out of the room. But she returned a little later with pen, ink, and paper, and a small portable writing desk.

"For all the thanks I get . . ."

"Shh, Jane," Cannan said. "Let me write." And this was what Texas Ranger Hank Cannan wrote that day:

ANDY KILCOYN – Texas Ranger. Patriot.
ROXIE MILLER – sporting gal. Patriot.
NORA ANDERSON – sporting gal. Patriot.
BAPTISTE DUPOIX – sporting gent. Patriot.
EPHRAIM SLOUGH – mariner, retd. Patriot.
ANDRZEJ ZELAZNY – Polish man. Patriot.
CLEM HARTE – drover. Patriot.

Hank Cannan laid down his pen and, for the first and only time in his life, allowed himself a tear.

Keep reading for a special excerpt

National Bestselling Authors
WILLIAM W. JOHNSTONE
and J. A. JOHNSTONE

RIDING SHOTGUN
First in the New RED RYAN Series!

*A blazing new series takes you back to the lawless frontier
where every stagecoach was a moving target. Where every
passenger needed protection. And where every hired gun
who rides along better be fast on the draw—
or be dead on arrival . . .*

RIDING SHOTGUN

If anyone knows the road to purgatory, it's Red Ryan.
As a stagecoach guard, he's faced holdups, ambushes,
and all-out attacks from every kill-crazy outlaw,
Indian, and prairie rat. But even Red is a bit reluctant
to take on his next job: riding shotgun with his driver,
Buttons Muldoon, on a stage bound from Fort
Concho, Texas, to Fort Bliss. Word has it the Apaches
are on the warpath. They're being led by a vicious
war chief who means business, as in slaughtering
every Texan from here to El Paso. Thus begins a
nightmare journey into 400 miles of harsh,
unforgiving terrain and blood-drunk killers
who plan to paint the town of El Paso red—
starting with Red's blood . . .

Look for *Riding Shotgun*, on sale now.

CHAPTER ONE

"Ryan! Red Ryan, I'm calling you out! Damn your eyes, fill your hand, and get down here!

"Red, do you hear that?"

"Yeah, I hear that. Ignore him, Dolly, and he'll go away," Ryan said. "Now, where were we?"

The naked woman in the bed smiled. "I was asking if you love me, Red."

"Love you? I sure do, and that's a natural fact."

"Do you tell the other girls that you love them?"

"Nah, Dolly, I just tell it to you."

"Patsy Prentice says that every time you're in town you talk all kinds of pretties to her. You never talk pretties to me."

"Yeah, I do, all the time. Hell, Dolly, you're as pretty as a speckled pup under a wagon. When I first rode into Cassidy Crossing and saw you standing on the balcony with the other ladies that time, I thought, 'Well, Red, she's the only gal for you an' no mistake.'"

"That time? Red, it was only yesterday."

"Times flies when you're having fun, don't it? Now,

come closer and give me some more of that good ol' Texas lovin' . . ."

"Ryan! Are you coming down or do I have to come up there after you?" The man's voice from the street, strident and angry. "I aim to shoot you down like a dog, Ryan, and be damned to ye."

"Go away!" Red called. "At the moment, I'm real busy!"

"Come down here, Ryan!"

"Later!"

"Now!"

"Give me ten minutes, you damned nuisance, whoever you are. You should be hung for disturbing a man."

"Get down here now, damn you!" The bullet that crashed through the bedroom window added the exclamation point to the end of that sentence.

"That's it, I'm out of here!" Dolly said. "Everybody told me you were a crazy man, Red Ryan, and you are."

The girl rolled off the bed, gathered up her frillies, and then stood at the door, staring expectantly at Red. Even when she frowned as she was doing now, he had to admit that she was a real purty little gal. "In my wallet," he said.

Dolly grabbed the wallet from the dresser and took out some bills. "There's only three dollars here."

"And you're most welcome to it, l'il darlin'," Ryan said.

"That's all?" Dolly said. "That's all the money you have?"

"It's all I got, and when three dollars is all a man has, he's giving you his entire fortune."

"You damned cheapskate, Red Ryan," Dolly said. "Who's going to pay for the window?"

"I'll talk to Dark Alley Jim, tell him I'll pay him for the window next time I'm in town." Ryan ducked as a bullet shattered another pane. "Uh-oh, make that two windows."

Now there was a deal of shouting and screaming in the upstairs rooms of the Golden Garter Saloon & Sporting House, and the proprietor, Dark Alley Jim Mortimer, loudly demanded to know who was trying to murder his whores.

Dolly Barnes opened the bedroom door and yelled, "Jim, it's Red Ryan. He's been called out."

"Ryan, you damned troublemaker, git away from here and deal with this afore my place is all shot to pieces," Mortimer hollered. Then the man himself burst through the door, saw Ryan struggling into his long johns, and said, motioning with a Greener 10-gauge for emphasis, "Git out there on the street and don't come back here ever again."

"I thought you were my good friend, Jim," Ryan said.

"I've shot good friends afore," Mortimer said. "And you're not my friend, good or any other kind."

Ryan pulled on his boots, slammed a derby hat on his unruly mane of red hair, and slid his Colt from the holster, leaving his own Greener shotgun in a corner. Scatterguns always meant a killing, and he was hopeful that this situation could be resolved by prudent words rather than buckshot.

Red stepped to the window, flung it open, and yelled, "I'm coming down!" He caught a brief glance of an angry but respectable-looking gent in the street who held a revolver in each hand.

Dressed only in hat, boots, and fire-engine red underwear, Ryan brushed past Mortimer and thumped down the stairs and onto the porch that ran the length of the building.

The respectable-looking gent was obviously not in

the mood for words, prudent or otherwise, and he didn't waste any time in palaver. He cut loose with both six-guns, and Ryan ducked as bullets crashed into the door and the woodwork around it, and one round, better aimed than the others, drilled a neat hole through the crown of his derby.

"Well, the hell with this," Red said.

He thumbed off a shot, and the respectable-looking man clutched his right shoulder, dropped his guns, and howled, "Damn! He's shot me!"

Ryan stepped off the porch into the street, his Colt hanging by his side, and said, "What the hell did you expect me to do? Mister, with all that shooting you did, you could've plugged Dolly Barnes, the best value-for-money whore this side of the Concho River."

"I was trying to kill you, not a lady," the respectable-looking man said. His face was ashen, and he was in obvious pain, grimacing under his mustache.

"Why? I never seen you before in my life," Red said.

"You're Red Ryan, ain't you?" the man said.

A crowd had gathered and looked on Ryan with hostile eyes, seeing a known rowdy who'd just drilled a respectable-looking gent in a frock coat and morning top hat.

"Yup, that's my name," Ryan said.

"You ride shotgun for the Patterson and Son stage?"

"I have that honor, at least some of the time."

"Then you're the one that killed my young brother."

Amid cries of "Shame!" and "Disgraceful" and "String him up," from one half-drunk, banty rooster who'd just stumbled out of the saloon and had no idea what the hell was going on. Ryan said, "When was this, and who was your brother?" And then, voicing his growing irritation, "As of right now, I'm starting to regret not putting another bullet into you, mister."

"There speaks a born killer," a man wearing a store-keeper apron said.

"String him up," the banty rooster said.

"Here comes the doctor," a woman said.

Dr. Miles Davis, short and stocky with gray hair and a melancholy face, helped the wounded man out of his coat and then stared hard at the bloodstained shoulder.

"My brother's name was Lou Richards, and you gunned him five miles east of El Paso, not three weeks ago," the respectable man said. He winced as the doctor worked his arm up and down, testing his shoulder.

"I remember that. Your brother Lou Richards was a road agent," Ryan said. "He tried to hold up my stage, him and Banjo Bob Kidd. I knew Kidd from a couple of years back when he was a younker. He was still carry-ing the buckshot in his ass he got from my Greener when he tried to rob a Butterfield I was guarding. He was lucky that day. I wasn't aiming for his ass."

"It's only a scratch," Dr. Davis said, "Mister . . ."

"Richards, Hugh Richards."

"Well, Mr. Richards, you're burned up some, but no bones broken." He looked at Ryan, not liking what he saw, and then back to the wounded man. "Here, take your coat. Come to my office later, and I'll give you a salve for the bullet burn . . . if you're still aboveground."

"Listen to me, Richards, you damned fool. Yeah, I killed Banjo Bob on that El Paso run three weeks ago," Ryan said. "But I didn't kill Lou."

"For shame," a woman in the crowd said.

"Then who did?" Archie Richards said, grimacing as his wound pained him.

"Dallas Stoudenmire did. That's who," Red said. "Only a halfwit like Lou would try to steal a gold watch from an almighty dangerous gunfighter like Dallas."

"How did it happen?" Richards said. If he was skeptical he didn't let it show.

"How did it happen? I'll tell you how it happened," Ryan said. "As it came down, Stoudenmire was one of my passengers, and after the holdup, Lou said to him, 'Gimme your wallet, watch, and chain.' Dallas said, 'Try and take them and damn you fer a common thief.' Then Lou said, 'Your funeral, Mary Ann' and he brought up his Colt. But quick as greased lightning Dallas drew two revolvers and put four bullets into Lou. Now, Lou was hit hard, but he managed to put one round into our near-side wheeler horse. Buttons Muldoon, my driver, was sure cut up about losing that two-hundred-dollar hoss, and he would have shot Lou all over again if he hadn't already been dead."

"You swear all that on the Bible," Richards said.

"I don't have a Bible, but I give you my word for it," Red said.

"Then considering how it happened, it seems like I owe you an apology, mister," Richards said. He seemed crestfallen and out of sorts from the pain in his shoulder and from shooting at the wrong man.

"You owe me more than an apology," Red Ryan said. "Call it five dollars for the three panes of glass you broke and three for the services of Dolly Barnes that I paid for but didn't get. That's eight dollars, and I'll forget about the ten cents for the bullet you forced me to shoot at you."

Richards's face stiffened. "You're a hard man, Red Ryan."

"No, pardner, not hard, just broke, and I don't

much feel like telling Dark Alley Jim Mortimer that I can't pay for his broken windows. He has a quick temper and a quicker draw to go with it."

Richards reached into his coat pocket and produced his wallet. "There's a ten, Ryan. We'll call it quits."

"Much obliged," Red said. "Now go see Doc Davis and get that shoulder fixed. And pick up your pistol, and don't ever think of throwing down on a man again. Gunfighting sure ain't one of your hidden talents."

"There's no change back, Red," Dark Alley Jim Mortimer said. "You scared the hell out of my whores and ruined this morning's business. Besides that, one of them bullets went through your wall into the next room and burned across Deacon Elijah Dogmersfield's bare ass. Now he says it's a sign from God that he should quit consorting with fallen women and tread the path of righteousness alongside his three-hundred-pound wife."

"Sorry to hear that," Ryan said. "Seems that everybody is getting burned with bullets this morning."

"You're sorry? Think how sorry I'll be if Deacon Dogmersfield spreads the word that a sporting man can get shot at the Golden Garter and I lose the gospel-grinder trade. This is a serious concern to me, Red."

"Sorry about that too, Jim," Red said, trying his best to look penitent.

Mortimer sighed and said, "All right, here's the way I see it, Red. Loss of the services of four scared whores . . . twenty-five dollars. Loss of revenue obtained from champagne sales to the clients of those four whores . . . twenty-five dollars. Add that up and it comes to fifty dollars."

"And I'll pay you the very next time I'm in town," Ryan said, blinking.

"Figured you'd say that, Red." Jim Mortimer's smile was not pleasant. "That's why I'm holding your shotgun, cartridge belt and holster, your fancy buckskin shirt, and your pants hostage until the debt is paid in full."

Red Ryan was shocked. "Now just hold on there, Jim, you can't do that."

"Yes, I can."

"I can't face the world in my underwear."

"Get used to it," Mortimer said.

Sick at heart, Red Ryan sat on the porch step outside the Golden Garter, his head in his hands, wondering how a morning that had begun so full of promise, so full of the fair Dolly Barnes, could have turned to such complete . . . horse dung.

A shadow fell over Ryan, dark as his mood, and he looked up and saw the large form of his driver, Patrick "Buttons" Muldoon.

"Taking in some sun, Red?" Buttons said.

Ryan shook his head. "Ran into some trouble this morning."

"What was it this time? Fist or gun?"

"Gun. Feller by the name of Richards called me out, the brother of the road agent Dallas Stoudenmire gunned that time on the El Paso run."

"Hell, Red, why blame you? You didn't do it. The only feller you shot all day long was Banjo Bob Kidd. Seen that my ownself."

"Well, we got it sorted out in the end," Ryan said.

"You plug the Richards feller?"

"Scratched his shoulder. He's over at Doc Davis's place getting a plaster."

"Where are your duds?"

"Jim Mortimer is holding them hostage, says I owe him fifty dollars because Richards shot up the place, scared his whores, and shot Deacon Dogmersfield up the ass."

"And you don't have fifty dollars."

"What you see, is what I got."

"You're a sorry sight, Red, and no mistake. I'll talk to Dark Alley Jim," Buttons said.

The stage driver stood only five-foot-six, but he was as wide as he was tall, and a lifetime of rasslin' half-broke horse teams had given him tremendously strong arms. And he had a volcanic temper that showed itself now and then. And now was one of those times.

Muldoon stomped into the Golden Garter, and a few moments later Red Ryan heard bottles smash and furniture splinter . . . and a few moments after that, Dark Alley Jim crashed through the front window of the saloon, landed in a heap, groaned, and lay still. Red stood . . . in time to see an almost naked Dolly Barnes sail through the now destroyed window, but her landing was softer because she fell on top of her unconscious boss.

Muldoon, dressed in a blue sailor coat decorated with two rows of silver buttons that gave him his name, reappeared, Ryan's Greener under his arm, gun leather and duds thrown over his shoulder.

"Jim says you don't owe him a damned thing and I got your three dollars back from the whore he said you was with this morning since services were not rendered," he said. "Now get dressed and saddle your hoss. Did you remember we got a stage to pick up in Fort Concho?"

Red Ryan and Buttons Muldoon rode out of town, dodging rocks thrown by four highly irritated whores led by Dolly Barnes who yelled at Red that he was dirty, no-good, low down . . .

Ryan agreed with what the women called him, but the dirty part hurt.

He and Buttons reached Fort Concho three days later.

CHAPTER TWO

Throughout its twenty-two-year history, construction never ended at Fort Concho, and the day Red Ryan and Buttons Muldoon rode in under a black, growling sky, the post consisted of forty buildings on forty acres surrounded by a vast wilderness of flat, treeless prairie. The buffalo soldiers of the 10th Cavalry occupied the fort, commanded by Colonel Benjamin H. Grierson, a stern man who'd never recovered from his grief over the death of his twelve-year-old daughter, who'd died in an upstairs bedroom of one of the houses at the post.

Red and Buttons rode past the sutler's store, the bakery, and the blacksmith's shop to the sandstone headquarters building. A Patterson & Son stage was parked a distance away, brought there by a relief driver a few days before.

Muldoon stopped to inspect the coach and Ryan swung from the saddle and looped his horse to the hitch rail. He looked around at the scouts coming and going across the parade ground, recognizing big Tam McLeod, who'd scouted for Grierson during the colonel's successful 1880 campaign against Victorio that had ended the Apache threat to West Texas.

"Tam!" Red yelled, waving.

The big man stopped, turned, and looked at Ryan and shook his head. "Hell, I heard you was dead!" he hollered. "And buried."

"Not yet," Ryan called back. "I'm still aboveground."

"I see you got a bullet hole in that fancy hat of your'n," McLeod said.

"Long story," Red said.

The scout, looking more Indian than white man in greasy buckskins and feathered hat, walked up to Red and said, "All right, I got two versions of the happy story of your demise. One is that a jealous husband caught you in bed with his wife and shot you through and through with a pepperbox pistol. The second was that you was hung for a hoss thief in El Paso a year ago by Dallas Stoudenmire. Now which one o' them is true?"

"Neither, Tam, since I'm still alive and kicking."

"Well, that's surely a sore disappointment. Ain't it?"

Ryan watched an eight-man patrol commanded by a boy second lieutenant ride out, their accoutrements jingling, a Pima wearing the blue headband of an army scout ahead of them.

"What's going on, Tam?" Red said. He and the scout went back a ways, and his smile showed that he held no ill will in regard to the big man's chagrin that he was still breathing.

"The Apaches are out. The colonel is bringing in the settlers, them that will come anyway."

"I thought Victorio's death had ended all that warpath stuff."

"And you're not alone, so did a lot of people. For the past two months, there's been a heap of coming and going around the Mescalero wickiups and then a couple of weeks ago about twenty young Chiricahua loiterers left the San Carlos and were welcomed by the Mescalero with open arms."

"How many hostiles are we talking about, Tam?"

"Counting both Mescalero and Chiricahua, about fifty, all of them young bucks, and they're already playing hob. So far, they've murdered twenty-seven Americans, settlers, miners, army supply train escorts and the like, and that number is likely to grow before the army catches up with them."

"Who is leading the broncos? Old Nana? Or is Loco still alive?"

"Yeah, Loco is still alive, but him and Nana are in Mexico where the pickings are easy, and they ain't likely to raid north of the Rio Grande again. This present bunch is led by a young war chief who calls himself Ilesh. In Apache that means Lord of the Earth. From what the Pima scouts tell me, Victorio's spirit came to Ilesh in a great dream and promised him that if he led the united Apache tribes in battle they'd drive out the white man and become lords of the earth." McLeod shook his head and then spat a stream of tobacco juice onto the sand. "It's a bad business, Red."

Ryan watched Buttons Muldoon closely inspect a bright yellow stage wheel and then said, "I reckon the Patterson stage isn't going anywhere until this is over."

"Kinda depends on the attitude of the passengers, don't it?" McLeod said.

* * *

"I have two patrols out and in addition the B Company under Captain Taylor scouting the old Butterfield stage route as far as Ketchum Mountain," Colonel Benjamin H. Grierson, tired and looking older than his years, said. "It's a show of force but a token one. The company is understrength, and if the hostiles are in the area I doubt they'll be impressed. Thank God settlers are few and far between in this part of the country, a good reason for the Apaches to avoid Fort Concho. We just aren't important enough."

Red Ryan didn't like what he heard. "Colonel, I've been hired to guard the Patterson stage to Fort Bliss," he said.

"I know, Mr. Ryan. The passengers have already made that clear." Grierson glanced out his office window and said, "Ah, I see Buttons Muldoon heading this way, and he looks none too happy."

"Somebody must have told him about the Apaches," Red said.

A rare smile from Grierson and then, "That would be my guess."

And the colonel was right. Muldoon's round, whiskered face was wrinkled in concern. He took off his leather glove and extended his hand. "Good to see you again, Colonel. It's been a spell."

"Since the Victorio campaign, Buttons," Grierson said. "You're looking well."

"Wish I could say the same about how I feel," Muldoon said. "I've just been told that the Mescaleros are out."

"And about twenty Chiricahua bucks with them. They left the San Carlos two weeks ago," Grierson said.

"Me and Red have been hired to take the Patterson stage to Fort Bliss," Muldoon said.

"Yes, Mr. Ryan has already informed me of that fact," the colonel said. "I can guarantee your safety as far as Ketchum Mountain and perhaps a distance beyond, at Captain Taylor's discretion. I'll give you a note giving him my permission to use his best judgment."

"Colonel, it's four hundred miles of rough country between here and Fort Bliss," Red Ryan said. "That's four or five days on the trail and maybe longer. I doubt the passengers will want to make the trip."

"On the contrary, Mr. Ryan, they seem eager to leave. At least two of them do. I advised them to wait until the hostiles are corralled, but they insist on making the journey, Indian uprising or not."

Ryan shook his head. "Colonel, who are those people? Are they rubes from back east that don't know any better?"

"Two of them are the wives of enlisted men, and they're traveling to Fort Bliss to join their husbands," Grierson said.

"My God, a couple of washerwomen," Muldoon said.

"No doubt, Buttons, no doubt," the colonel said.

"Are those women the two that want to make the trip?" Ryan said.

"No, the stalwarts are Mrs. Stella Morgan, the wife of soon-to-retire Major John Morgan, currently stationed at Fort Bliss, and Mr. Lucian Carter, a San Antonio bank clerk heading farther west in hope of finding a better career situation. To the best of my knowledge the two are traveling companions but are not related in any way."

"I'll talk to them," Ryan said. "Tell them—"

But a commotion outside the door to the colonel's office stopped Red in mid-sentence. The door burst open and a tall young man barged inside, followed by a harried-looking desk sergeant. "Sorry, sir," the soldier said. "I couldn't stop him."

"It's all right, Sergeant," Grierson said. Then, "What can I do for you, Mr. Carter?"

Carter was blond, blue-eyed, and handsome, but he had a sulky, petulant mouth, almost effeminate in its fullness, and a pale skin that would flush easily and burn in the sun. There were bulges under the armpits of his expensive gray sack coat and Ryan pegged him as a two-gun man, rare in the West and probably unique among bank clerks.

"I'll tell you what you can do for me, Grierson," Carter said, his face bright scarlet. "You can guarantee Mrs. Morgan and me a cavalry escort between here and Fort Bliss."

"On the frontier there are no guarantees, Mr. Carter," the colonel said. "My command is already spread thin, and I cannot spare men for escort duty. I suggest you remain here at the fort until the Apaches are rounded up and returned to the reservation."

"No, that won't do," Carter said. "Mrs. Morgan is an army officer's wife and she's anxious to be reunited with her husband because she has some tragic news to impart. She will brook no delay and neither will I. As a gentleman, it is incumbent on me to see her safely to her destination."

"There are two other army wives involved, and they are willing to remain at the fort until the Apache threat is over," Grierson said.

Carter's peevish mouth twisted into a contemptuous

grin. "A couple of fat women married, or so they claim, to corporals," Carter said. "Who cares about such people?"

"I do," Red Ryan said. "If the two ladies in question are passengers of the Patterson and Son Stage and Express Company and they paid the same fare to Fort Bliss as you did. Until they reach the fort they are my responsibility."

"And who the hell are you?" said Carter, a truculent, arrogant man Ryan had disliked on sight.

"Name's Ryan. I ride shotgun for Abe Patterson."

Again, Carter's insolent grin, then, "Yeah, then that makes me feel a whole lot safer."

"You should," Buttons Muldoon said. "Red's the best scattergun guard there is, and I've ridden with a few."

Carter turned to Grierson. "You still insist that I can't have an escort?"

"I'm afraid it's out of the question," the colonel said.

"Then you will take us there, Ryan?" Carter said. "We've paid our fares."

"Listen to the colonel, Carter," Ryan said. "Wait until the Apaches are penned."

"I'll pay you double what Patterson is paying," Carter said.

"No deal," Ryan said.

"Triple."

"I'll be on my way, Colonel," Ryan said. He stepped past Carter, but the man shot out his arm and with considerable strength grabbed Ryan's right bicep and squeezed . . . hard. "Don't you ever walk away from me when I'm talking to you," Carter said.

There were a couple of warning signals Carter should have noticed about Red Ryan, but didn't.

Most obvious was the fact that Red stood six feet and a half-inch tall, and under his buckskin shirt his shoulders and arms bulged with a pugilist's muscle, a holdover from his days as a bare-knuckle booth fighter with Dr. Edwin Drake's Medicine & Curiosities Show. Red had taken on all comers in the ring, had never once failed to come up to scratch, and his quick fists earned him a record of sixty-three wins with only one defeat, and that at the hands of an up-and-coming youngster by the name of Joseph Choynski, the California Terror, who would later in his career fight the likes of James J. Jeffries, James Corbett, and Jack Johnson.

The second fact Carter should already have known . . . that it's never a good idea to muscle a quick-tempered, redheaded man with an arm as hard and big around as an iron stovepipe.

Lucian Carter paid dearly for his oversight.

Ryan twisted a little to his left as he wrenched his arm free and at the same time unleashed a powerful left cross that connected with Carter's chin. The man's legs turned to rubber and he staggered back a few steps before crashing into the office door, splintering the lock. But as Carter slid to the floor, his right hand moved under his coat and emerged with a short-barreled Colt in his fist.

"I wouldn't," Buttons said, his own Remington hammer-back and ready. "Mister, you could be about to make the worst mistake of your life."

Carter thought it over, but he knew the portly stage driver wasn't bluffing, and now wasn't the time to take chances. He holstered his gun and rose to his feet, a trickle of blood running down his chin from the corner of his mouth.

Carter pointed at Red and said, "Damn you, you'll live to regret this."

The man turned on his heel, threw the door wide, and lurched outside.

Buttons looked at Grierson and said, "Colonel, whenever this show hits the road, I've got the feeling it's gonna be a fun trip."

Both Red Ryan and the colonel laughed their agreement.

CHAPTER THREE

Red Ryan and Buttons Muldoon shared a spare room that in the past had been reserved for a couple of infantry sergeants. Apart for a threadbare rug on the stone floor and a couple of chairs, two iron cots, a dresser, and a full-length mirror were its only furnishings. Buttons was cleaning his revolver, and Ryan sat in one of the chairs reading a book he'd found, *Middlemarch* by George Eliot, a morbid, depressing novel that was then unaccountably popular among Western men.

The moon was on the rise and coyotes yipped in the dreary darkness when a soft, hesitant tapping came to the door. Ryan marked his place in the book and rose to answer, allowing inside a young woman who instantly banished the bleak lamplight with her luminous beauty.

Buttons, ever a gentleman when he was around the ladies, especially pretty ones in their early twenties, rose to his feet and joined Ryan as the girl smiled and said, "Ah, which one of you gentlemen is Mr. Ryan?"

"I am," Red said. "And this here is Buttons Muldoon, the best whip in Texas."

"I'm so glad to meet you both. My name is Stella Morgan, originally of the Philadelphia Morgans. I'm booked on the Patterson and Son stage."

"Yes, you are indeed, pleased to meet you, Mrs. Morgan." Red waved to his recently vacated chair. "Would you care to sit?"

Buttons would later accuse Red of "grinning like a possum eating persimmons" when he first beheld the fair Stella, and Red readily agreed that he was smitten by the woman's dazzling loveliness.

"Ma'am, we have whiskey but no glass, if you'd care to make a trial of it," Buttons said.

"No thank you," Stella said. "I've already taken tea with Colonel Grierson."

Red smiled. "What can we do for you, Mrs. Morgan?"

"Please call me Stella. Mrs. Morgan sounds so formal, especially out here in the wilderness." The woman returned Ryan's smile and said, "Red . . . may I call you Red?"

"Please do."

"Red, the colonel told me of the unfortunate unpleasantness between you and Lucian Carter, and it distressed me terribly. I can tell you that Lucian is very upset about it."

"I imagine he is," Red said. He wanted to say that a left cross to the chin with a lot of shoulder behind it would upset just about anybody, but he didn't. Instead he did his best to look sympathetic. "We all let our tempers get the better of us at times."

"Well, please let bygones be bygones," Stella said. "Lucian told me he's most willing to forget the whole unhappy incident. But . . . Red . . . it is imperative that I reach Fort Bliss within the next few days."

"Why the hurry?" Red said.

"I've been living in San Antonio with my husband's mother—"

"Major Morgan's ma?" Buttons said.

"Yes, a dear, sweet lady, but unfortunately she passed away over a week ago. It was all very sudden, I'm afraid. But thank God, she didn't suffer too much."

"Sorry to hear about the lady's death, Stella," Ryan said.

"Well, she was old and very sick and it was her time," the woman said. "But John was very attached to his mama, and I want to be the one to break the sad news to him before someone less caring than myself does. I think you will understand that time is of the essence."

"Ma'am, you know the Apaches are out?" Buttons said.

"Yes, I do. But to spare John further heartbreak I'm willing to take my chances. I must be at my husband's side at this trying time."

Buttons said, "Mrs. Morgan—"

"Stella."

"Stella, do you know what Apaches do to women?"

"Buttons, I'm sure Stella has a pretty good idea," Red said, angling him a look.

"I am not well versed in the ways of the world," Stella said. "But I imagine being a prisoner of the savages would not be pleasant."

"You're so right about that, little lady," Buttons said, but when the woman took out a little handkerchief and dabbed her eyes it banished his smile.

"I must be with John . . . I just . . . must be on hand

to succor my husband," she said. "I know he'll be heartbroken."

A woman's tears are corrosive enough to melt a man's heart, and Red Ryan was not immune.

"I must say that I admire your courage, Stella," he said. "Such fortitude is rare, even among Western women."

"Red, say you'll take me to Fort Bliss," Stella said, sobbing slightly. "Please, please say you will."

"I'll study on it," Ryan said. "You have my promise on that."

"I need more than a promise, Red," Stella said. "If I'm not with John when he learns of his mama's death, I'll never forgive myself. Red, he doted on her, loved her with all his heart and soul. I'm an army wife, and I can't fail my husband now because of some savages. John himself has faced so many dangers on the frontier, can I do any less?"

Red saw more tears budding in the woman's eyes, and he said hastily, "Well, it's a big country and the Apaches are few, it's just possible we can make the trip without encountering any hostiles."

Stella managed a smile. "Red, you are my gallant knight in shining armor. Mr. Muldoon . . . Buttons . . . we can't do it without you."

"No, you can't. That is, unless you can handle a six-horse team over four hundred miles of the worst country this side of perdition," Muldoon said.

"I beg you, Buttons, take me to Fort Bliss," Stella said.

"If Red is willing to make the trip, then I'll go along," Buttons said. "But I think you two are making a big mistake."

"No, everything will be just fine," Stella said. "I just know it will."

The girl leapt up from her chair and kissed Buttons on his whiskery cheek and then Red. "I'm so happy now," she said. "Thank you both, my wonderful . . . frontier heroes."

After Stella left, Red said, grinning, "I've got tears on my mustache. Imagine that."

He sat on his chair again, the room once more in dusky lamplight, and picked up *Middlemarch*, trying to regain his interest in young Dorothea Brooke, who married a husband so old, his head was almost a skull. But after a few minutes he closed the book with a thump and stared at Muldoon and said, "What the hell did we just do?"

Buttons shook his head. "You tell me, Mr. Knight in Shining Armor."

CHAPTER FOUR

Stella Morgan was quartered with the wives of the Fort Bliss corporals, plump, contented matrons who talked all the time as they knitted winter mufflers for their husbands and munched constantly on sugar cookies, of which they seemed to have an inexhaustible supply.

Making the excuse of a headache, Stella said she was going for a walk before she turned in. "Some fresh air may help," she said.

"You be careful, dearie," one of the women said. "It's cold outside. Take your shawl and don't get a chill in the bladder."

"And remember . . . there are bloodthirsty savages about," the other said.

"I'm not going far," Stella said, throwing her shawl around her shoulders.

She stepped into the starless murk and, keeping to the shadows, walked past the troopers' barracks and then angled across the parade ground toward the sutler's store. Colonel Grierson had pickets out, but they were invisible in the darkness, and the woman moved on soundless feet.

Stella passed between the side of the store and the blacksmith's shop and then walked more quickly toward the wood-frame cabin that lay some thirty yards away. She tapped on the cabin door, and it opened immediately. Lucian Carter, stripped to his pants and undershirt, stepped back to allow the woman inside. He stuck his head out of the doorway and looked around. Satisfied, he closed the door again and said, "You spoke to them?"

Stella smiled. "Yes, they'll do it."

"Thank God," Carter said. "The sooner we get away from this godforsaken post and put some distance between us and San Antonio the better."

"Take it easy, Lucian, and content your mind," Stella said. "Remember, the San Antonio police have nothing on us."

"They were suspicious, Stella. I knew that by the way they were sniffing around. One of the detectives said to me that it was surprising that a healthy, active old lady like Martha Morgan should die so unexpectedly of natural causes. He had a big copper's nose and sneaky eyes, the kind that told me he was saying one thing but meant another."

"Yes, perhaps it was all a little surprising," Stella said. "But the police said nothing about murder."

"I know, but that damned nosey little detective . . . was not the word murder on the tip of his tongue?"

"Hardly. Lucian, you left no mark on the miserable old biddy."

"No, I didn't mark her." Carter smiled. "It was a very soft feather pillow."

Stella put her arms around the man's neck, tilted

back her head, and spoke directly into his handsome face. "We've come far, Lucian, you and I, haven't we?"

"And we have farther to go, Stella. The money and jewelry we have is only a start."

"A small start, my darling. There is so much more ahead of us."

"What about that damned redheaded shotgun guard I had the trouble with?"

"What about him?"

"Did he swallow your story?"

Stella placed the back of her hand on her forehead and pretended to swoon. "Oh, I am undone. I must be with my husband when he hears about the death of his dear, dear mama." The woman's smile was hard, triumphant. "The fool fell for it hook, line, and sinker."

"What about the other one, the driver?"

"He's a harmless idiot."

"I plan to kill them both, Stella," Carter said. "I swear to God, I'll shoot those two barbarians in the belly and listen to them scream."

"Time enough for that when we reach Fort Bliss. Let them get us there first."

"Clever girl," Carter said. He ground his groin into the woman. "Stay a while."

Stella stepped back. "No, not here. What if someone saw us? It's too dangerous. We're just traveling companions, remember?"

"Then I'll wait until we get to Fort Bliss," Carter said.

"No, wait until we get to Washington, Lucian. You'll enjoy me all the more."

Carter grinned. "When we're members of the capital's high society, huh?"

"Exactly. Now, I must go. The fat washerwomen will miss me."

"Until tomorrow then," Carter said.

"Yes, until tomorrow, my one, my only love," Stella said.

Since her head was on his shoulder, Lucian Carter couldn't see the woman's eyes, hard as polished diamonds. Just as well . . . because they were amused . . . and calculating.

"How is your headache, dearie?" one of the army wives said.

"Better, much better now," Stella Morgan said, smiling.

Lucian Carter slid the carpetbag from under the cot. It was large, the kind that had a leather flap across the top fastened with a brass padlock. He took the key from his pocket, unlocked the bag, and peered inside. Dishonest himself, the threat of theft preyed on his mind. Yes, the contents were still intact, fifty thousand dollars in large-denomination bills . . . Martha Morgan didn't believe in banks . . . and jewelry, necklaces, rings, and bracelets mostly, worth at least an additional fifty thousand, and probably twice that. Even more precious was Martha's will, folded into a long manila envelope. Its contents were straightforward enough. In the event of her death—Carter smiled at that—she left all her property to her only child, her son John. The properties consisted of her San Antonio house, a Washington, D.C., town house, railroad shares, considerable holdings in a South African diamond mine, and shares in the White Star shipping line, in all, assets worth a few thousand dollars north of half-a-million. When

Major Morgan died, and his impending demise was a guaranteed natural fact, his fortune would of course fall to his grieving widow.

Stella would be rich, and so would Lucian Carter, her next husband.

Carter stood with the bag open, lost in thought.

Did he love Stella? No, he didn't, not really. But he lusted after her lithe body. Would he be sad if she died? Well, a rich man could choose from plenty of willing women. Would he consider . . . making her die? Of course, murder was always an option, because then all the money would be his.

Carter raised his chin and slowly scratched his throat, his manicured fingernails scratching on bristles. He had a lot to think about, but not now. Later, after they were safely ensconced in a Washington town house and Stella wore his wedding ring on her finger. He'd make his decisions then.

Connect with Us

Visit us online at
KensingtonBooks.com
to read more from your favorite authors, see books
by series, view reading group guides, and more.

for sneak peeks, chances to win books and prize packs,
and to share your thoughts with other readers.

facebook.com/kensingtonpublishing
twitter.com/kensingtonbooks

Tell us what you think!

To share your thoughts, submit a review,
or sign up for our eNewsletters, please visit:
KensingtonBooks.com/TellUs.